PENGUIN BOOKS

TOUGH, TOUGH TOYS FOR TOUGH, TOUGH BOYS

ABOUT THE AUTHOR

Will Self's other books include *The Quantity Theory of Insanity*, one of the most highly acclaimed débuts of 1991 and winner of the 1992 Geoffrey Faber Memorial Prize; the highly original novellas *Cock & Bull*; his novel, *My Idea of Fun*; *Grey Area*, a second collection of short stories; *Junk Mail*, a selection of other work; and *Great Apes*, his recent and highly acclaimed novel. All of these are published in Penguin.

TOUGH, TOUGH TOYS FOR TOUGH, TOUGH BOYS

Will Self

PENGUIN BOOKS

PENGUIN BOOKS

Published by the Penguin Group
Penguin Books Ltd, 27 Wrights Lane, London W8 5TZ, England
Penguin Putnam Inc., 375 Hudson Street, New York, New York 10014, USA
Penguin Books Australia Ltd, Ringwood, Victoria, Australia
Penguin Books Canada Ltd, 10 Alcorn Avenue, Toronto, Ontario, Canada M4V 3B2
Penguin Books (NZ) Ltd, Private Bag 102902, NSMC, Auckland, New Zealand

Penguin Books Ltd, Registered Offices: Harmondsworth, Middlesex, England

First published by Bloomsbury 1998
Published in Penguin Books 1999
6

Set in Monotype Imprint
Printed in England by Clays Ltd, St Ives plc

ACKNOWLEDGEMENTS

'The Rock of Crack as Big as the Ritz' was written with the last series of Penguin Sixties in mind, and was published in that format together with 'Flytopia', which was specially commissioned by Tony Lacey at Penguin. 'The Rock of Crack as Big as the Ritz' has appeared in *Spin* magazine in the USA, and under the somewhat teasing title: *Un Roc de Crack Gros Comme le Ritz* in Editions Mille et Une Nuits in France. In the same volume there's an interesting essay by Olivier Cohen which suggests that despite the fact he has met me personally, I still don't exist. 'Flytopia' also appeared in the *New Statesman* courtesy of Laura Cumming.

'A Story for Europe' was commissioned by Liz Calder for the Bloomsbury Quids series, and 'Dave Too' was commissioned by David Goodhart for *Prospect* magazine and also appeared in a MIND anthology. All the other stories were written with this collection in mind.

Thanks as ever to Mary Tomlinson and all at Bloomsbury, and especial thanks to Noel 'Razors' Smith for his help in researching 'The Nonce Prize'.

W.W.S.
Back in dirty old London, February 1998

For Farrah Anwar, my best man
– *and with thanks – as ever – to*
D.J.O.

'Life is a dream that keeps me from sleeping'

– Oscar Wilde

CONTENTS

THE ROCK OF CRACK
AS BIG AS THE RITZ

A *building, solid and imposing. Along its thick base are
tall arches, forming a colonnade let into its hard hide.
At the centre are high, transparent doors flanked by columns.
There's a pediment halfway up the façade, and ranged along
it at twenty-foot intervals are the impassive faces of ancient
gods and goddesses. Rising up above this is row upon row of
windows, each one a luxuriant eye. The whole edifice is dense,
boxy, four-square and white, that milky, translucent white.*

*Over the central doors is a sign, the lettering picked out in
individual white bulbs. The sign reads:* THE RITZ. *Tembe
looks at the luxury hotel, looks at it and then crosses
Piccadilly, dodging the traffic, squealing cabs, hooting
vans, honking buses. He goes up to the entrance. A doorman
stands motionless by his slowly revolving charge. He too is
white, milky, translucent white. His face, white; his hands,
white; his heavy coat falls almost to his feet in petrified folds
of milky, translucent white.*

*Tembe stretches out a black hand. He places its palm
against the column flanking the door. He admires the colour
contrast: the black fading into the yellow finger flanges and
then into the white, the milky, translucent white. He picks at
the column, picks at it the way that a schoolboy distresses a
plaster surface. He picks away a crumb of the wall. The
doorman looks past him with sightless, milky, translucent
eyes.*

1

Tembe takes a glass crack pipe from the pocket of his wind-cheater and fumbles the crumb into the broken end of Pyrex piping that serves as a bowl. Setting the pipe down on the pavement, at the base of the white wall, from his other pocket he removes a blowtorch. He lights the blowtorch with a non-safety match, which he strikes on the leg of his jeans. The blowtorch flares yellow; Tembe tames it to a hissing blue tongue. He picks up the crack pipe and, placing the stem between his dry lips, begins to stroke the bowl with the blue tongue of flame.

The fragments of crack in the pipe deliquesce into a miniature Angel Falls of fluid smoke that drops down into the globular body of the pipe, where it roils and boils. Tembe draws and draws and draws, feeling the rush rise up in him, rise up outside of him, cancelling the distinction. He draws and draws until he is just the drawing, just the action: a windsock with a gale of crack smoke blowing through it.

'I'm smoking it,' he thinks, or perhaps only feels. 'I'm smoking a rock of crack as big as the Ritz.'

When Danny got out of the army after Desert Storm he went back to Harlesden in north-west London. It wasn't so much that he liked the area – who could? – but that his posse was there, the lads he'd grown up with. And also there was his uncle, Darcus; the old man had no one to care for him now Hattie had died.

Danny didn't like to think of himself as being overly responsible for Darcus. He didn't even know if the old man was his uncle, his great-uncle, or even his great-great-uncle. Hattie had never been big on the formal properties of family – precisely what relation adults and children stood in to one another – so much as the practical side, who fed who, who slept with who, who made sure who didn't play truant. For all Danny knew, Darcus might have been his father or no blood relation at all.

Danny's mother, Coral, who he'd never really known, had given him another name, Bantu. Danny was Bantu and his little brother was called Tembe. Coral had told Aunt Hattie that the boys' father was an African, hence the names, but it wasn't something he'd believed for a minute.

'Woss inna name anyways?' said the newly dubbed Danny to Tembe, as they sat on the bench outside Harlesden tube station, drinking Dunn's River and watching the Job Seekers tussle and ponce money for VP or cooking sherry. 'Our 'riginal names are stupid to begin wiv. Bantu! Tembe! Our mother thought they was kind of cool and African, but she knew nothing, man, bugger all. The Bantu were a fucking *tribe*, man, and as for Tembe, thass jus' a style of fucking *music*.'

'I don' care,' Tembe replied. 'I like my name. Now I'm big –' he pushed his chest forward, trying to fill the body of his windcheater '– I tell everyone to call me Tembe, so leastways they ain't dissin' me nor nuffin'.' Tembe was nineteen, a tall, gangly youth, with yellow-black skin and flattish features.

'Tcheu!' Danny sucked the inside of his cheek contemptuously. 'You're a fucking dead-head, Tembe, an' ain't that the fucking troof. Lucky I'm back from doing the man stuff to sort you, innit?'

And the two brothers sat passing the Dunn's River between them. Danny was twenty-five, and Tembe had to confess he looked good. Tough, certainly, no one would doubt that. He'd always been tough, and lairy to boot, running up his mouth whenever, to whoever.

Danny, many years above him, had been something of a hero to Tembe at school. He was hard, but he also did well in class. Trouble was, he wouldn't concentrate or, as the teachers said, apply himself. 'Woss the point?' he used to say to Tembe. 'Get the fucking "O" levels, then the "A" levels, whadjergonna do then, eh? Go down the Job Centre like every other fucking nigger? You know the joke: what d'jew say to a black man wiv a job? "I'll have a Big Mac an' fries . . ." Well, I'm not going to take that guff. Remember what the man Mutabaruka say, it no good to stay inna white man's country too long. And ain't that the troof.'

So Bantu, as he was then, somehow got it together to go back to Jamaica. He claimed it was 'back', but he didn't exactly know, Aunt Hattie being kind of vague about origins, just as she was about blood ties. But he persuaded Stan, who ran the Montego Bay chippie in Manor Park Road, to get him a job with a cousin in Kingston. Rootswise the whole thing was a shot in the dark, but in terms of getting a career Bantu was on course.

In Kingston Stan's cousin turned out to be dead, or missing, or never to have existed. Bantu got all versions before he gave up looking. Some time in the next six months he dropped the 'Bantu' and became 'London', on account of what – as far as the Jamaicans were concerned – was his true provenance. And at about the same time this happened he fetched up in the regular employ of a man called Skank, whose interests included buying powder off the boat and cooking it down for crack to be sold on the streets of Trenchtown.

Skank gave London regular pep talks, work-incentive lectures: 'You tek a man an' he all hardened, y'know. He have no flex-i-bil-ity so he have no poss-i-bil-ity. But you tek de youth, an' dem can learn, dem can 'pre-ci-ate wa' you tell for dem . . . You hearing me, boy?' London thought most of what Skank said was a load of bullshit, but he didn't think the well-oiled M16s under the floorboards of Skank's house were bullshit, and clearly the mean little Glock the big dread kept stuck under his arm was as far from being bullshit as it was possible to be.

London did well in Skank's employ. He cut corners on some things, but by and large he followed his boss's orders to the letter. And in one particular regard he proved himself to be a very serious young man indeed: he never touched the product. Sure, a spliff now and then just to wind down. But no rock, no stones, no *crack* – and not even any powder.

London saw the punters, he also saw his fellow runners and dealers. Saw them all getting wired out of their boxes. Wired so they saw things that weren't there: the filaments of wire protruding from their flesh which proved that the aliens had put transmitters in their brains. And hearing things as well, like non-existent DEA surveillance helicopters buzzing around their bedrooms. So London didn't fuck with the stuff – he didn't even *want* to fuck with it.

A year muscling rock in Trenchtown was about as full an apprenticeship as anyone could serve. This was a business where you moved straight from work experience to retirement, with not much of a career in between. London was getting known, so Skank sent him to Philadelphia, PA, where opportunities were burgeoning, this being the back end of a decade that was big on enterprise.

London just couldn't believe Philly. He couldn't believe what he and his Yardie crew could get away with. Once you were out of the downtown and the white districts you could more or less fire at will. London used to get his crew to wind down the windows on their work wagon and then they would just blast away, peppering the old brown buildings with 9-mm rounds.

But mostly the hardware was just for show. The Yardies had such a bad reputation in Philly that they really didn't have to do anyone much. So, it was like running any retail concern anywhere: stock control, margins, management problems. London got bored and then started to do things he shouldn't. He still didn't touch the product – he knew better than to do that – but he did worse. He started to go against Skank.

When the third key went missing, Skank grew suspicious and sent an enforcer over to speak to his errant boy. But London had headed out already: BIWI to Trinidad, and then BA on to London, to cover his tracks.

Back in London, London dropped the name, which no longer made any sense. For a while he was no-name and no-job. Floating round Harlesden, playing pool with Tembe and the other out-of-work youth. He lived on the proceeds from ripping off Skank and kept his head down way low. There were plenty of work opportunities for a fast boy who could handle a shooter, but he'd seen what happened in Trenchtown and Philly, he knew he wouldn't last. Besides, the Met had a way with black boys who went equipped. They shot them dead. He couldn't have anything to do with the Yardies either. It would get back to Skank, who had a shoot-to-kill policy of his own.

Without quite knowing why, he found himself in the recruitment office on Tottenham Court Road. 'O' levels? Sure – a couple. Experience? Cadet corps and that. He thought this would explain his familiarity with the tools, although when he got to training his RSM knew damn well it wasn't so. Regiment? Something with a reputation, fighting reputation. Infantry and that. Royal Green Jackets? Why not?

'Bantu' looked dead stupid on the form. He grinned at the sergeant: 'Ought to be "Zulu", really.'

'We don't care what you call yourself, my son. You've got a new family now, give yourself a new name if you like.' So that's how he became Danny. This was 1991 and Danny signed on for a two-year tour.

At least he had a home to go to when he got out of the army. He'd been prudent enough to put most of Skank's money into a gaff on Leopold Road. An Edwardian villa that was somewhere for Aunt Hattie, and Darcus, and Tembe, and all the other putative relatives who kept on coming around. Danny was a reluctant *paterfamilias*, he left all the running of the place to Aunt Hattie. But when he came home things were different: Hattie dead, Darcus almost senile, nodding out over his racing form, needing visits from home helps, meals on wheels. It offended Danny to see his uncle so neglected.

The house was decaying as well. If you trod too hard on the floor in the downstairs hall, or stomped on the stairs, little plumes of plaster puffed from the corners of the ceiling. The drains kept backing up and there were damp patches below all the upstairs windows. In the kitchen, lino peeled back from the base of the cooker to reveal more ancient layers of lino below, like diseased skin impacted with fat and filth.

Danny had been changed by the army. He went in a fucked-up, angry, potentially violent, coloured youth; and he came out a frustrated, efficient, angry black man. He looked different too. Gone were the fashion accessories, the chunky gold rings (finger and ear) and the bracelets. Gone too was the extravagant barnet. Instead there were a neat, sculpted flat-top and casual clothes that suggested 'military'. Danny had always been slight, but he had filled out in the army. Darker than Tembe, his features were also sharper, leaner. He now looked altogether squared-off and compact, as if someone had planed away all the excess of him.

'Whadjergonna do then?' asked Tembe, as the two brothers sat spliffing and beering in front of Saturday afternoon racing. Darcus nodded in the corner. On screen a man with mutton-chop whiskers made sheepish forecasts.

'Dunno. Nuffin' criminal tha's for sure. I'm legit from here on in. I seen enough killing now to last me, man.'

'Yeah. Killing.' Tembe pulled himself up by the vinyl arms of the chair, animated. 'Tell me 'bout it, Bantu. Tell me 'bout the killing an' stuff. Woss combat really like?'

'Danny. The name's Danny. Don' forget it, dipstick. Bantu is dead. And another fing, stop axin' me about combat. You wouldn't want to know. If I told you the half, you would shit your whack. So leave it out.'

'But . . . But . . . If you aren't gonna deal, whadjergonna do?'

'Fucking do-it-yourself. That's what I'm gonna *do*, little brother. Look at the state of this place. If you want to stay here much longer with that fat bint of yours, you better do some yersel' as well. Help me get the place sorted.'

The 'fat bint' was Brenda, a girlfriend Tembe had moved in a week after his brother went overseas. Together they slept in a disordered pile upstairs, usually sweating off the effects of drink, or rock, or both.

Danny started in the cellar. 'Damp-coursing, is it?' said Darcus, surfacing from his haze and remembering building work from four decades ago: tote that bale, nigger; Irish laughter; mixing porridge cement; wrist ache. 'Yeah. Thass right, Uncle. I'll rip out that rotten back wall and repoint it.'

'Party wall isn't it?'

'No, no, thass the other side.'

He hired the Kango. Bought gloves, goggles, overall and mask. He sent Tembe down to the builders' merchants to order 2,000 stock bricks, 50 kilo bags of ballast, sand and cement. While he was gone Danny headed down the eroding stairs, snapped on the yellow bulb and made a start.

The drill head bit into the mortar. Danny worked it up and around, so that he could prise out a section of the retaining wall. The dust was fierce, and the noise. Danny kept at it, imagining that the wall was someone he wanted done with, some towel-head in the desert or Skank, his persecutor. He shot the heavy drill head from the hip, like an action man in a boys' comic, and felt the mortar judder, then disintegrate.

A chunk of the wall fell out. Even in the murky light of the cellar Danny could see that there wasn't earth – which he had expected – lying behind it. Instead some kind of milky-white substance. There were fragments of this stuff on the bit of the drill, and twists like coconut swarf on the uneven floor.

Danny pushed up his goggles and pulled down his mask. He squatted and brought a gloveful of the matter up to his face. It was yellowy-white, with a consistency somewhere between wax and chalk. Danny took off his glove and scrunged some of it between his nails. It flaked and crumbled. He dabbed a little bit on his bottom lip and tasted it. It tasted chemical. He looked wonderingly at the four-foot-square patch that he had exposed. The swinging bulb sent streaks of odd luminescence glissading across its uneven surface. It was crack cocaine. Danny had struck crack.

Tembe was put out when he got back and found that Danny had no use for the stock bricks. No use for the ballast, the cement and the sand either. But he did have a use for Tembe.

'You like this shit, that right?' Danny was sitting at the

kitchen table. He held up a rock of crack the size of a pigeon's egg between thumb and forefinger.

'Shee-it!' Tembe sat down heavily. 'Thass a lotta griff, man. Where you get that?'

'You don' need to know. You don' need to know. You leave that to me. I found us a connection. We going into business.' He gestured at the table where a stub of pencil lay on top of a bit of paper covered with calculations. 'I'll handle the gettin', you can do the outin'. Here –' he tossed the crack egg to Tembe '– this is almost an eightf. Do it out in twenties – I want a oncer back. You should clear forty – and maybe a smoke for you.'

Tembe was looking bemusedly at the egg that nestled in his palm. 'Is it OK, this? OK, is it?'

'Top-hole! Live an' direct. Jus' cooked up. It the biz. Go give the bint a pipe, see how she like it. Then go out an' sell some.'

Tembe quit the kitchen. He didn't even clock the brand-new padlock that clamped shut the door to the cellar. He was intent on a pipe. Danny went back to totting up columns of figures.

Danny resumed his career in the crack trade with great circumspection. To begin with he tried to assess the size of his stock. He borrowed a set of plumber's rods and shoved them hard into the exposed crack-face down in the cellar. But however many rods he added and shoved in, he couldn't find an end to the crack in any direction. He hacked away more of the brickwork and even dug up the floor. Every place he excavated there was more crack. Danny concluded that the entire house must be under-pinned by an enormous rock of crack.

'This house is built on a rock,' he mused aloud, 'but it ain't no hard place, that the troof.'

Even if the giant rock was only fractionally larger than the rods indicated, it was still big enough to flood the market for crack in London, perhaps even the whole of Europe. Danny was no fool. Release too much of the rock on to the streets and he would soon receive the attentions of Skank or Skankalikes. And those Yardies had no respect. They were like monkeys just down from the fucking trees — so Danny admonished Tembe — they didn't care about any law, white or black, criminal or straight.

No. And if Danny tried to make some deal with them, somehow imply that he had the wherewithal . . . No. That wouldn't work either. They'd track him down, find him out. Danny had seen what men looked like when they were awakened at dawn. Roused from drugged sleep on thin mattresses, roused with mean little Glocks tucked behind their crushed ears. Roused so that grey patches spread out from underneath brown haunches. No. Not that.

Danny added another hefty padlock to the cellar door and an alarm triggered by an infra-red beam. Through a bent quartermaster at Aldershot who owed him a favour he obtained an antipersonnel mine in exchange for an ounce of the cellar wall. This he buried in the impacted earth of the cellar floor.

At night Danny sat in the yellow wash of light from the streetlamp outside his bedroom. He sucked meditatively on his spliff and calculated his moves. Do it gradual, that was the way. Use Tembe as a runner and build up a client list nice and slow. Move on up from hustling to the black youth in Harlesden, and find some nice rich clients, pukkah clients.

The good thing about rock — which Danny knew only too well — was that demand soon began to outstrip supply. Pick up on some white gourmets who had just developed a taste for the chemical truffles, and then you could depend on their own greed to turn them into gluttons, troughing white pigs. As long as their money held out, that is.

So it was. Tembe hustled around Harlesden with the crack Danny gave him. Soon he was up to outing a quarter, or even a half, a day. Danny took the float back off Tembe with religous zeal. It wouldn't do for little brother to get too screwed up on his profit margin. He also bought Tembe a pager and a mobile. The pager for messages in, the mobile for calls out. Safer that way.

While Tembe bussed and mooched around his manor, from Kensal Green in the south to Willesden Green in the north, Danny headed into town to cultivate a new clientele. He started using some of the cash Tembe generated to rent time in recording studios. He hired session musicians to record covers of the ska numbers he loved as a child. But the covers were percussive rather than melodic, full of the attacking, hard-grinding rhythms of Ragga.

Through recording engineers and musicians Danny met whites with a taste for rock. He nurtured these contacts, sweetening them with bargains, until they introduced him to wealthier whites with a taste for rock, who introduced him to still wealthier whites with a taste for rock. Pulling himself along these sticky filaments of drug-lust, like some crack-dispensing spider, Danny soon found himself in the darkest and tackiest regions of decadence.

But, like the regal operator he was, Danny never made the mistake of carrying the product himself or smoking it. This he left to Tembe. Danny would be sipping a mai tai or a whiskey sour in some louche West End club, swapping badinage with epicene sub-aristos or superannuated models, while his little brother made the rounds, fortified by crack and the wanting of crack.

It didn't take longer than a couple of months – such is

the alacrity with which drug cultures rise and fall – for Danny to hit human gold: a clique of true high-lowlife. Centred on an Iranian called Masud, who apparently had limitless funds, was a gaggle of rich kids whose inverse ratio of money-to-sense was simply staggering. They rained cash down on Danny. A hundred, two hundred, five hundred quid a day. Danny was able to withdraw from Harlesden altogether. He started doling out brown as well as rock; it kept his clients from the heebie-jeebies.

Tembe was allowed to take the occasional cab. Darcus opened an account at the betting shop.

The Iranian was playing with his wing-wang when Tembe arrived. Or at any rate it looked as if he had been playing with it. He was in his bathrobe, cross-legged on the bed, with one hand hidden in the towelling folds. The smell of sex – or something even more sexual than sex – penetrated the room. The Iranian looked at Tembe with his almond eyes from under a narrow, intelligent brow on which the thick, curled hair grew unnaturally low.

Tembe couldn't even begin to think how the Iranian was getting it up – given the amount of rock he was doing. Five, six, seven times a day the pager peeped on Tembe's hip. And when Tembe dialled the number programmed into his mobile, on the other end would be the Iranian, his voice clenched with want, but his accent still that very, very posh kind of foreign.

Supporting the sex explanation there was the girl hanging around. Tembe didn't know her name, but she was always there when he came, smarming her little body around the suite. Her arrival, a month or so ago, had coincided with a massive boost in consumption at the suite. Before, the Iranian had level-pegged at a couple of forties a day and half a gram of brown, but now he was picking up an eighth of each as soon after Tembe picked up himself as he could engineer it.

After that the Iranian would keep on paging and paging for what was left of the day. Now, at least three nights a week, Tembe would be called at one a.m. – although it was strictly against the rules – and have to go and give the two of them a get-down hit, to stop the bother.

Tembe hated coming to the hotel. He would stop at some pub and use the khazi to freshen up before taking a cab up Piccadilly. He didn't imagine that the smarmed-down hair and chauffeured arrival fooled the hotel staff for a second. There weren't that many black youths wearing dungarees, Timberland boots and soiled windcheaters in residence. But they never gave him any hassle, no matter how late or how often he trod across the wastes of red carpet to the concierge and got them to call up to the Iranian's suite.

'My dear Tembe,' Masud, the Iranian, had said to him, 'one purchases discretion along with privacy when one lives in an establishment such as this. Why, if they attempted to restrict the sumptuary or sensual proclivities of their guests, they would soon have vacant possession rather than no vacancies.' Tembe caught the drift below the Iranian's patronising gush. And he didn't mind the dissing anyway – the Iranian had sort of paid for it.

The girl let Tembe in this time. She was in a terry-towelling robe matching the Iranian's. The dun blond hair scraped back off her pale face suggested a recent shower, suggested sex.

How could the Iranian get it up? Tembe didn't doubt that he got the horn. Tembe got the horn himself. Got it bad. But the stiffie was hardly there, just an ice-cream, melting before there was any chance of it getting gobbled. Not that Tembe didn't try it on, far gone as he was. If he had a pipe at Leopold Road he'd make his moves on Brenda – until she shoved him away with lazy contempt. If he was dropping off for one of the brasses who worked out of the house on Sixth Avenue – who he still served without Danny's knowledge – or even the classier ones at the Learmont, either they would ask, or he would offer: rock for fuck.

It was ridiculous how little they'd do it for. The bitch at the Learmont – who, Tembe knew for a fact, regularly turned three-ton tricks – would put out for a single stone. She stepped out of her skirt the way any other woman took off her coat and handed him the rubber from the dispenser in the kitchenette drawer like it was a piece of cutlery.

Usually, by the time they'd piped up together Tembe was almost past the urge. Almost into that realm where all was lust, and lust itself was a grim fulfilment. He'd try and push his dick into the rubber rim, but it would shrink back. And then he'd just get her to un-pop the gusset of her sateen body. Get her to stand there in the kitchenette, one stilettoed foot up on a stool, while he frigged her and she scratched at his limpness with carmine nails.

Tembe tried not to think about this as the Iranian's girl moved about the bedroom, picking up a lacy bra from the radiator, jeans with knickers nesting in them from the floor. The Iranian was taking a smoke of brown from a piece of heavily stained foil a foot square. Tembe watched the stuff bubble, black as tar dripping from a grader. The girl slid between him and the door jamb. Wouldn't have been able to do that a month ago, thass the troof, thought Tembe. She's that fucking gone on it. Posh white girls don't eat any, and when they're on the pipe and the brown they eat even less. Despite that, skinny as she was, and with those plasticky features like a Gerry Andersen puppet, Tembe still wanted to fuck her.

15

The Iranian finished off his chase by waving the lighter around hammily, and said, 'Let's go into the other room.' And Tembe said, 'Sweet,' keen to get out of the bedroom with its useless smell of other people's sex. The Iranian moved on the bed, hitching up his knees, and for a second Tembe saw his brown dick, linked to the sheet by a pool of shadow or maybe a stain.

The main room of the suite featured matching Empire escritoires that had seldom been written on, an assemblage of Empire armchairs and a divan that had seldom been sat on. In front of the divan there was a large, glass-topped coffee-table, poised on gold claw feet. On top of this were a crack pipe, a blowtorch, a mirror with some smears of rock on it, cigarettes, a lighter, keys, a video remote, a couple of wine-smeared glasses and, incongruously, a silver-framed photograph of a handsome middle-aged woman. The woman smiled at Tembe forthrightly over the assembly of crack-smoking tools.

The room also featured heavy bookcases, lined with remaindered hardbacks, which the hotel manager had bought from the publishers by the yard. The carpet was mauve, the walls flock-papered purple with a bird-and-shrubbery motif worked into them. On the far side of the coffee-table from the divan stood an imposing armoire, the doors of which were open, revealing shelves support-ing TV, video and music centre. Scattered around the base of the armoire were videos in and out of their cases, CDs the same.

Somewhere inside the armoire Seal was singing faintly: 'For we're never going to sur-vive/Un-less we go a little cra-azy . . .' 'Ain't it the troof?' said Tembe, and the Iranian replied, 'Sorry?' but not as if he meant it.

'For we're never going to sur-vive/Un-less we go a little cra-azy . . .' Tembe warbled the words, more falsetto than

Seal, but with a fair approximation of the singer's rhythm and phrasing. As he neared the end of the second line he did a little jig, like a boxer's warm-up, and wiggled his outstretched fingers either side of his face, his head chicken-nodding. '. . . You know, man, like cra-azee.'

'Oh, I see. I get you. Yeah, of course, of course . . .' The Iranian's voice trailed away. He'd put himself down in the centre of the divan and was using the flap of a matchbook to scrape up the crack crumbs on the mirror, sweeping them into a little vee-shaped pile, then going over the same surface again, creating a regular series of crack smears.

Tembe looked at the pipe and saw the thick honey sheen inside it. There was plenty of return there, enough for five or six more hits. Tembe wondered why the Iranian had called him back so soon. Surely the return alone would have lasted the pair of them another couple of hours? But now Tembe saw that the Iranian had got down on his hands and knees behind the coffee-table and was methodically combing the strip of carpet between the table and the divan with a clawed hand. The Iranian's starting eyes, hovering six inches above the carpet, were locked on in the hand's wake, crack-seeking radar.

Thass it, Tembe realised. The fucker's so fucking far gone he's carpet-cruising. Tembe had seen it enough times – and done it himself as well. It began when you reached that point – some time after the tenth pipe – where your brain gets sort of fused with crack. Where your brain *is* crack. Then you start to see the stuff everywhere. Every crumb of bread on the carpet or grain of sugar on the kitchen lino looks like a fragment of ecstatic potential. You pick one up after the other, checking them with a touch of wavering flame, never quite believing that it isn't crack until the smell of toast assaults your nose.

The Iranian had turned in his little trench of desperation and was crawling back along it, head down, the
knobbles of his spine poking up from behind the silvery
rim of the coffee-table. He was like some mutant guard
patrolling a perverse check-point. His world had shrunk to
this: tiny presences and gaping, yawning absences. Like all
crackheads, Masud moved slowly and silently, with a
quivering precision that was painful to watch, as if he
were Gulliver, called upon to perform surgery on a
Lilliputian.

The girl wandered back in, tucking the bottom of a
cardigan into the top of her jeans. She fastened the fly
buttons and then hugged herself, palms going to clutch
opposing elbows. Her little tits bulged out.

'Fuck it, Masud,' the girl said, conversationally, 'why
have you got Tembe over if you're just gonna grovel on the
floor?'

'Oh, yeah, right . . .' He slid his thin arse back up on to
the divan. In one hand he held a lighter, in the other some
carpet fluff. He sat and looked at the ball of fluff in his
hand, as if it were really quite difficult to decide whether
or not it might be a bit of crack, and he would have to
employ his lighter to make absolutely certain.

Tembe looked at the blue hollows under the Iranian's
almond eyes. He looked at the misnamed whites of those
eyes as well. Masud looked up at Tembe and saw the same
colour scheme. They both saw yellow for some seconds.
'What . . . ? What you . . . ?' Masud's fingers, quick
curling back from exploded nails, bunched the towelling
at his knee. He couldn't remember anything – clearly.
Tembe helped him. 'I got the eightf anna brown.' He took
his hand from the pocket of his jacket, deftly spat into it
the two marbles of clingfilm concealed in his cheek and
then flipped them on to the table. One rolled to a halt at

the foot of the portrait photograph of the handsome woman, the other fetched up against the video remote.

This little act worked an effect on Masud. If Tembe was a cool black dealer, then he, Masud, was a cool brown customer. He roused himself, reached into the pocket of his bathrobe and pulled out a loose sheaf of purple twenties. He nonchalantly chucked the currency on to the glass pool of the table top, where it floated.

Masud summoned himself further and resumed the business of having his own personality with some verve, as if called upon by some cutting-edge *auteur* to improvise it for the camera. 'Excuse me,' he stood, wavering a little, but firm of purpose. He smiled graciously down at the girl, who was sitting on the floor, and gestured to Tembe, indicating that he should take a seat on the divan. 'I'll just throw some clothes on and then we must all have a big pipe?' He cocked an interrogative eyebrow at the girl, pulled the sides of the bathrobe around his bony body and quit the room.

Tembe looked at the girl and remained, rocking gently from the soles to the heels of his boots. She got up, standing in the way young girls have of gathering their feet beneath them and then vertically surging. Tembe revised his estimate of her age downwards. She sat on the divan and began to sort out the pipe. She took the larger of the two clingfilm marbles and laborious unpicked it, removing layer after layer after layer of tacky nothingness, until the milky-white lode was exposed and tumbled on to the mirror.

She touched a hand to her throat, hooked a strand of hair behind a lobeless ear, looked up and said, 'Why don't you sit here, Tembe? Have a pipe.' He grunted, shuffled, joined her, manoeuvring awkwardly in the gap between the divan and the coffee-table.

Masud came back into the room. He was wearing a shirt patterned with vertical stripes of iridescent green and mustard-yellow, sky-blue slacks in raw silk flapped around his legs, black loafers squeaked on his sockless feet, the froth of a paisley cravat foamed in the pit of his neck. What a dude. 'Right!' Masud clapped his hands, another ham's gesture. Upright and clothed, he might have been some motivator or negotiator freeing up the wheels of commerce, or so he liked to think.

The girl took a pinch of crack and crumbled it into the bowl of the pipe. 'I'm sure,' said the Iranian, his tone hedged and clipped by annoyance, 'that it would be better if you did that over the mirror, so as to be certain not to lose any –'

'I know.' She ignored him. Tembe was right inside the bowl of the pipe now, his boots cushioned by the steely resilience of the gauze. The lumps of crack were raining down on him, like boulders on Indiana Jones.

Tembe mused on what might be coming. Masud had paid for this lot, but could he be angling for credit? It was the only explanation Tembe could hit on for the welcome in, the girl's smiles, the offer of a pipe. He decided that he would give Masud two hundred pounds' credit – if he asked for it. But if he was late, or asked for any more, Tembe would have to refer it to Danny, who would have the last word. Danny always had the last word.

The girl lit the blowtorch with the lighter. It flared yellow and roared. She tamed it to a hissing blue tongue. She passed Tembe the pipe. He took the glass ball of it in the palm of his left hand. She passed him the blowtorch by the handle. 'Careful there . . .' said Masud, needlessly. Tembe took the blowtorch and looked at his host and hostess. They were both staring at him fixedly. Staring at him as if they wouldn't have minded diving down his throat, then swivelling round so they could suck on the pipe with him, suck on it from inside his lips.

Masud hunched forward on the divan. His lips and jaws worked, smacking noises fell from his mouth. Tembe exhaled to one side and placed his pursed lips around the pipe stem. He began to draw on it, while stroking the bowl of the pipe with the tongue of blue flame. Almost instantly the fragments of crack in the pipe deliquesced into a miniature Angel Falls of fluid smoke that dropped down into the globular body of the pipe, where it roiled and boiled.

Tembe continued stroking the pipe bowl with the flame and occasionally flipped a tonguelet of it over the rim, so that it seared down on to the gauzes. But he was doing it unconsciously, with application rather than technique. For the crack was on to him now, surging into his brain like a great crashing breaker of pure want. This is the hit, Tembe realised, concretely, irrefutably, for the first time. The whole hit of rock is to want *more rock*. The buzz of rock is itself the wanting of *more rock*.

The Iranian and the girl were looking at him, devouring him with their eyes, as if it was Tembe that was the crack, their gazes the blowtorch, the whole room the pipe. The hit was a big one, and the rock clean and sweet, there was never any trace of bicarb in the stuff Danny gave Tembe, it was jus' sweet, sweet, sweet. Like a young girl's gash smell sweet, sweet, sweet, when you dive down on it, and she murmurs, 'Sweet, sweet, sweet . . .'

It was the strongest hit off a pipe Tembe could ever remember taking. He felt this as the crack lifted him up and up. The drug seemed to be completing some open circuit in his brain, turning it into a humming, pulsing lattice-work of neurones. And the awareness of this fact, the giant nature of the hit, became part of the hit itself – in just the same way that the realisation that crack was the desire for crack had become part of the hit as well.

Up and up. Inside and outside. Tembe felt his bowels gurgle and loosen, the sweat break out on his forehead and begin to course down his chest, drip from his armpits. And still the rocky high mounted ahead of him. Now he could sense the red-black thrumming thud of his heart, accelerating through its gearbox. The edges of his vision were fuzzing black with deathly, velvet pleasure.

Tembe set the pipe down gently on the surface of the table. He was *all*-powerful. Richer than the Iranian could ever be, more handsome, cooler. He exhaled, blowing out a great tumbling blast of smoke. The girl looked on admiringly.

After a few seconds Masud said, 'Good hit?' and Tembe replied, 'Massive. Fucking massive. Biggest hit I ever had. It was like smoking a rock as big as . . . as big as . . .' His eyes roved around the room, he laboured to complete the metaphor. 'As big as this hotel!' The Iranian cackled with laughter and fell back on the divan, slapping his bony knees.

'Oh, I like that! I like that! That's the funniest thing I've heard in days! Weeks even!' The girl looked on uncomprehendingly. 'Yeah, Tembe, my man, that has a real ring to it: the Rock of Crack as Big as the Ritz! You could make money with an idea like that!' He reached out for the pipe, still guffawing, and Tembe tried hard not to flatten his fucking face.

At home, in Harlesden, in the basement of the house on Leopold Road, Danny kept on chipping, chipping, chipping away. And he never ever touched the product.

FLYTOPIA

'Ending up as I am with animals and alcohol, one of her last friends, when she was losing her faculties, was a fly, which I never saw but which she talked about a great deal and also talked to. With large melancholy yellow eyes and long lashes it inhabited the bathroom; she made a little joke of it but was serious enough to take in crumbs of bread every morning to feed it, scattering them along the wooden rim of the bath as she lay in it, much to the annoyance of Aunt Bunny, who had to clear up after her.'

J. R. ACKERLEY
My Father and Myself

In Inwardleigh, a small, Suffolk town which had been marooned by the vagaries of human geography, left washed up in an oxbow of demography, run aground on the shingle of a failing economy, and land-locked by the shifting dunes of social trends, the landlords in the three desultory pubs on the main street (the Flare Path, the Volunteer and the Bombardier) drew pints for themselves in the cool, brown, afternoon interiors of their establishments. The landlords stretched across the bars, from where they sat – feigning custom – tipped the handles of the pumps down with the heels of their hands, and then brought the glasses to their lips before the yellow foaming had subsided, before head had been separated from heart.

In the Volunteer a lone young lad, who was skiving off from the harvest, played pool against himself. He made risky shots, banging the balls off the cushion, hazarding tight angles. He felt certain he could win.

Jonathan Priestley, an indexer by profession, came bouncing on balled feet, out from the mouth of Hogg Lane and into the small council estate flanking the village. He savoured the anonymous character of the place, the semis' blank, concrete-beamed façades; the pebble-dashed lamp standards; the warmed gobs of blue-black tarmac in the dusty, spore-filled gutters. Savoured it, and thought to himself how it was that while in turning in on themselves some places achieve character, Inwardleigh had been visited only with anonymity.

In the windows of Bella's Unisex, Jonathan observed a young woman. She wore a blue, nylon coverall, elaborately yet randomly brocaded with the abandoned hairs of a sector of the population. She was sitting in one of the battered chairs, head tilted back against the red vinyl headrest, and as Jonathan passed by he saw her reach up to pluck, pull and then deftly snip at a lock of her own. He sighed, shifted the strap of the small rucksack he carried from one arm to the other, tried whistling a few notes through gummy lips, abandoned the attempt, proceeded.

Jonathan tripped on down the main street. His socks had peristalsized themselves down into the ungy, sweaty interior of his boots. He passed flint-knapped houses kneeling behind low walls, with peeling paint on their lintels, window frames and doors. The shutters on the windows of the small parade of shops were mostly rolled down. It was Wednesday, early closing in Inwardleigh. Have to buy everything in Khan's, thought Jonathan.

He passed by the window of Ancient Estates. The photographs which depicted properties for sale or rent were curling up like the eaves of pagodas. Jonathan sighed. Some of the asking prices were ridiculously low, Mars Bar money really. But then no one much wanted to live in Inwardleigh and its environs, where self-abuse was rife and the vet shot up his own horse tranquilliser.

Some way to the north and east of Inwardleigh a vast nuclear power station crouched on a lip of shingle and dune abutting the North Sea. The station hummed both sub- and ultrasonically. Its very size made it paradoxically invisible, as if its presence were quite simply too monumental to be apprehended.

Almost daily Jonathan would drive up there and walk out along the beach below the power station. The thing was so vast as to defy human scale, or even purpose. The reactor hall, a great dome coated in some ceramic material, was scored into so many panels, or cells, like the compound eye of Moloch. It sat on a murkily iridescent plinth. The whole was frequently wreathed in tissuey steam, sea mist, even low-hung cloud. At night the place was orange floodlit, and at all hours it echoed and crackled with amplified announcements. Announcements for whom? And by whom? He never saw any of the workers. Perhaps there weren't any; and the place was talking to itself, soliloquising while the brown waves slapped the shingle, the violet butterflies tumbled on the tips of the dune grasses and the geese honked overhead.

Inwardleigh was outflanked by the two mighty pylon lines which leapt from the power station, marched over the gorse and scrub and passed either side of the town, giving it a wide berth as if anxious to avoid being netted in for a quiz night at the Flare Path, or a cake-bake at the Methodist Hall.

These behemoth lyres, strung with lethal strings, sang the life out of the town and its environs, made them feel scorched, irradiated, scarious and desiccated. And so the working-class trippers and the middle-class weekenders steered clear of Inwardleigh, heading for the twee villages further up the coast.

Yet for Jonathan the pylon lines were part of the district's appeal. They provided what little relief the countryside possessed, for this was an area of low, rolling farm land, studded with dense copses and gouged with gravel pits dug from the sandy soil. It was a landscape of ingress and of repose: a tired body lying down on an old, horsehair mattress.

In Khan's Jonathan moved up and down the aisles putting bits of stuff in his wire basket. Joy had been gone two days and there were two more before she would return. Could he be bothered to cook something proper for himself, or would he go to the pub for fish and chips again that evening? He stood, hand hovering over a small freezer full of eugenic vegetables and macerated, frozen beef, lost in thoughts of the kitchen at the cottage.

If he cooked and didn't vigorously clean afterwards he could be guaranteed an invasion of insect life. Should he bother therefore? But to not cook was to counsel defeat, to acknowledge the unsustainability of life at the cottage. That, or maybe only its unsustainability without Joy.

The cottage was small. The summer heat percolated it entirely, forcing its way through the gaps in the dusty, velveteen curtains. Even if Jonathan kept them drawn throughout the day, it was still hot enough in his study for the sweat dripping from his fingers to gum up the keyboard of the Macintosh. And then there were the flies.

Jonathan didn't think of himself as squeamish or phobic about insects, but this long, hot summer had brought the six-legged kine out in force.

Every room in the cottage had its own, buzzing pavane; which revolved ceaselessly, with unsettling inertia, usually beneath the light fitment. There were other species as well. Daddy-long-legs which fluttered and thirruped in the evenings, skipping up the Artex pinnacles in the bathroom, then abseiling down them, like spindly climbers. Wasps also frequently diverted into the cottage. As he worked, Jonathan would become teased into awareness of them by their doodle-bug droning, which undercut the higher whine of the houseflies. This noise was insistent and somehow predatory in its very essence. He would abandon work on the index, grab whatever magazine or journal was to hand and hunt out the hunters. He would not be satisfied until he had created another pus-like smear, another shattered tangle of broken legs and wings, of mashed thorax, head and abdomen.

When Joy was staying the insects barely bothered Jonathan. She did the annoyance and upset for him. But since she had gone they had begun to irritate him more and more. He tipped back in his chair and contemplated them from under furrowed brows. How to kill? Why to kill? What the killing meant? The insects – and in particular the flies – were becoming an object of study, a platform for obscure games in virtuality.

Jonathan was compiling the index for a scholarly work on ecclesiastical architecture – or meant to be. Normally the whirrings and clickings of the Macintosh soothed him, as he moved from application to application, working in symbiosis with the mechanism. But now he found himself listening the whole time, listening for the other whirrs and clicks of his fellow residents. It occurred to him that perhaps they were learning to imitate the noises of the computer; that through some quantum, phylogenetic leap, the insects were becoming computer-like. An outrageous act of Batesian mimicry, akin to that with which the undistinguished wasp beetle jerkily pretends to the status of its more dangerous namesake.

The heat. The fucking heat. He was broiled in vexation. Mr Khan manifested himself by Jonathan's elbow. A dun pyramid of a man who multiplied his chins to acquiesce with his customers, and divided them to dissent. 'Was there anything else?' he said. Jonathan flailed, he had been lost in the fugue, staring sightlessly at the frozen vegetables. 'Garden peas, French beans?'

'No, no, silly of me . . . I don't – all I can think of that I really need is some of those Vapona thingies. I'm convinced the ones I've got at the moment must be losing their effectiveness.'

'They're meant to last at least a month.' Mr Khan regarded Jonathan quizzically, from out of an eye with a bruised ball.

'That's as may be, but the house is still full of flies.'

'We-ell, that's the summer we've been having, isn't it? And with the harvest on now, you'll be lucky if you don't get a lot of mice and rats coming into your place as well. So how many will it be?'

'Give me another five, Mr Khan, and I'll take a box of fly-papers as well please.'

Inwardleigh was stretching and yawning as Jonathan came back up the main street. A knot of teenagers was gathered outside the public toilets, opposite the defunct Job Centre. They were smoking, hands cupped around fags, bodies cupped around hands. A couple of cars stood by them, doors open so that the techno which blared from their stereos was clearly audible from well down the road.

It was, Jonathan reflected, not exactly music at all; more like a sound effect devised by a radiophonic composer to accompany a film featuring giant, mechanical cockroaches.

The teenagers ignored him. He walked on by, conscious of the weight of the rucksack, parasitic on the small of his back, and the damp partings and clammier marriages of his nether limbs. Reaching the end of the estate, Jonathan dropped back into Hogg Lane. Two gossamer lines wavered some three feet above the track, each one following the line of the rut below. They were comprised of many many thousands of tiny midges, which hovered, tumbling over and over and over. Why would the midges gather in this way? Jonathan thought as he pushed on into the tunnel of greenery, his waist cresting the wave of life-forms. Could it be an attraction to the moisture latent in the rut? Or animal droppings? Or was it some new behaviour? Certainly the summer had been doing things to the insects, gingering them up, pushing the hot air faster through their spiracles, so that they were able to fly faster, feed faster, and reproduce in even greater numbers.

The haunch slathered with infective matter. Bulging from within, the fact of decay possessing and altering it, changing it from organism to environment. Delicately, methodically Mustica Domestica *goes about her business of insertion.*

Almost every week there were irruptions of silverfish or ants into the kitchen. Usually Joy was first up in the morning, so it would be her cry that awoke Jonathan: 'Ayeee!' she would bellow, and the sound would yank him from sweat-impacted sheets, pull him down to where she stood, her nightdress clutched up in folds around her belly by one hand, while the other flapped in the air. Did she imagine they were intent on accessing the pit of her body? 'What! What!' he would cry, angry with her and hating the little kitchen as well, despising its linoleum confines, the ruched, muslin, pseudo-curtain in the tiny window over the sink. She would gesture to one or other of the wooden, Melamine, or stainless steel surfaces, where the invaders were boiling up from crack or join.

Were silverfish insects? Jonathan bent down low to examine them. They flowed as much as crawled, each wriggling driblet of a creature adopting a piscine undulation. Were they recently hatched, or fully mature? On these occasions he sent Joy back up to bed, boiled the kettle, located the break-out point and poured down libations of exterminatory water into the navel of the silverfish world.

Ants didn't bother him as much. It was like a racial prejudice. The ants carried things. Teams of them would move crumbs with an orderly sideways shuffle; or one would roll a nugget of sugar on to another's back. They were like the Japanese: small, efficient, manifesting an unknowable, collective mind.

Back upstairs Jonathan would reassure Joy. Roll her on to her carapace and investigate the damp portions of her thorax and abdomen. Then the two humans adopted peculiar, mating postures, their limbs outlined against the pink, vernal riot of the flower-patterned wallpaper. Jonathan nuzzled her and struggled not to think of the insects nuzzling all about them, the pillowy dust mites labouring below the pillows as they laboured above them, carrying away the dead epidermal portions of Jonathan and Joy.

And in the primal, physical contortions of sex, Jonathan laboured as well not to think of the earwigs. The earwigs bothered him the most of all the insects. These prehistoric beasts, with their excremental bodies both shiny and somehow unclean, made it their business, their *métier* even, to seek out the dampest and most intimate portions of the cottage. Were they parodying Jonathan and Joy's efforts to keep the cottage clean, keep it as a viable, human-supporting environment? Whenever he picked up a dishcloth, a mug, a cake of soap even, one of the earwigs would emerge, moving unsteadily, antennae and forceps waggling, and mooch off across the allegedly clean surface. It was the insouciance that did it. Jonathan would take the offender between thumb and forefinger, crush the life out of it.

Don't think of the earwigs as she lifts my balls. Don't think of them as her pink triangle of a tongue traces the brown crinkles of my perineum. Don't think of them as I palp the gristle between her legs; gristle beneath hairs as insubstantial as frass. Don't think of earwigs emerging from beneath labia or foreskin. Don't think of earwigs, don't think of her. Gone.

So the insects whirled in front of and behind Jonathan's grey eyes; and he walked on unseeing. Beyond the thick hedging bordering the lane, the pylons kept pace with him, their cables thrumming in the late-afternoon heat.

The cottage reposed at the bottom of what passed for a combe in this relaxed landscape. A stream-cum-drainage ditch ran alongside the garden hedge. When there was any rain it burst its confines, flooding lane and field. On all sides of the cottage the fields swept up at a modest angle for some hundreds of yards, on two sides meeting the pylon lines, on the third a liner-shaped copse, and on the fourth the paddock of tumbledown jumps and dried-out pits where his landlord's tinkly-voiced daughters rode their ponies.

Jonathan's cottage pinioned this awning of fieldscape, weighed it down at its centre. He debouched from the lane and walked the hundred yards of his landlord's drive to the cottage gate. Arbuthnot – the landlord – was away. Jonathan could tell this from the pile of black plastic bags set at the end of the drive. As he passed by them, the black bucklers the bags formed palpably radiated heat, and then a cloudlet of scintillating flies, gold and blue, arose from them to dance on the tiny thermals.

Jonathan entered his cottage, went through the breakfast room to the kitchen and unloaded his rucksack on the work surface by the fridge. The fly-paper dangling by the window was full. So full that the gooey corpses of its victims entirely covered it, like an advanced chancre on a tongue. As he watched a fly homed in on the thing, circling, dipping and finally alighting on the back of one of its conspecifies. Jonathan watched, only slightly sickened, as the fly applied its nozzled proboscis to the chink betwixt the head and thorax of the corpse and began to feed.

Then the repulsion did come, and Jonathan found himself moving from room to room, fetching chairs so that he could rear upwards, prise out the drawing-pins in the ceiling and take down the tacky mausoleums. Such was his hurry over this loathsome work that on two occasions the fly-papers came down on top of him, gifting him a head-dress repellent in the extreme. He ran from the house, hunched over, head and arm angled as if he were a Pompeian, about to receive a lava bath; and then ran back in again, mewling; there was no succour abroad. He had to wash his hair before he could resume work on the index.

In the study a gold beam lanced down from a chink in the curtain, to spotlight a patch of wear on the carpet. On the screen of the Macintosh, small pellets ricocheted about like insects in a killing jar. Jonathan sat down in his swivel chair and clicked on the Anglepoise. He flicked the mouse and the screensaver dissolved into a body of text.

Jonathan had reached the term 'nef' before going out to do the shopping. It was an obscure term meaning the nave of a church. He plugged the three letters into the word-search and hit the control key. The computer went about its work, chomping through the text, looking for instances. He felt himself relax into the machine's labour. It made its clicks and whirrs companionably, this clean thing, this ergonomic thing. Jonathan honed his appreciation, concentrated, tried to ignore the deeper zzzing undercutting them . . . the deeper, more organic, more moribund zzzing.

A fly was dying in the lea of his mouse mat. As Jonathan watched it span out from the thin, hard-edged shadow and into the full glare of the Anglepoise. The fly was on its back. Must be propelling itself with its wings, thought Jonathan, as it span to a halt like a minuscule merry-go-round, the wings, the hairs, the compound eyes, returning from blur.

Was the fly a victim of Vapona? Jonathan had erected the little venetian-blind slatted units, one to each room, but done it in the spirit of magic, not really believing that they worked. How could the poison affect the flies – and not me? Or the earwigs for that matter? It started up twirling again, buzzing again. The upside-down fly moved top-like across the desk, batted off the edge of a piece of paper and came to rest among some breadcrumbs. How long, Jonathan wondered, will it take to die?

And this query sent his febrile mind spinning into an orbit of twisted, insect supposition. Why? Why were flies' bodies full of what appeared to be pus? From where Jonathan sat he could see the smear paths of two of his earlier executions. Was it perhaps an adaptive response to parasitising humans? Making sure that the act of killing was an unpleasant, if marginal activity? And why did killing flies need to be unpleasant at all? Why couldn't it be made into some kind of pastime, or sport even. That's it! A solution to the need for blood sports and the need to kill flies. Perhaps miniature needle-guns could be developed, able to achieve the pin-point accuracy necessary for targeting flies?

Jonathan tilted back in his chair, imagining the ramifications of his new idea. A fully functioning hunting field contained within the compass of a single Axminster carpet. Beaters – or rather beetles – moving through the pile, flushing out the grazing flies. The huntsmen sitting motionless at their workstations, needle-guns at the ready. The quarry has broken from behind its cover of lint and fluff. It's in the air! And the guns lead the flies, their muzzles moving sharply up, down, obliquely, tracking the erratic paths. A slight pressure on the trigger and the needle flies fast and true, skewering the droning bluebottle precisely through one wing and its bulbous abdomen. Crunch! It falls to the twistpile, bounces, settles down into death, like a slo-mo film of a wildebeest dropping on the veldt. Small wicker cages are opened by the guns, and specially trained wasps fly out. They bank, right themselves, lose altitude to the carpet, move in to retrieve the quarry.

Outside the summer afternoon droned on. The sun drummed on the hard, cracked earth. The cicadas, crickets and grasshoppers chafed and stridulated, rubbing leg on leg, wing-case on wing-case, or else popping a rigid tegument of their bodies, so as to produce noises like a child's toy. The land pulsed, as a woman's vagina does in the aftershocks of orgasm: holding the hot air to itself, and releasing it; holding the hot air to itself, and releasing it.

Jonathan's head fell back, jerked forward, rolled some, righted itself, fell back. His eyelids fluttered, then fell. He slept. In his dream Joy returned to the cottage. The taxi from Saxmundham station dropped her in the lane. She looked tremendous, her high, pointed shoulders enveloped in clear, veined wings. She had – he was amused and titillated to see – three, dear little pairs of hands. Her hands, so small, he found the thought of their childish grip on his thickening penis insistently erotic, even as he pitched and yawed in sleep, and the computer's screensaver enveloped the recondite text.

'Look,' Joy said, gesturing with three hands towards her lower body, and twitching the drapery of wings to one side, 'I bought it at Harvey Nick's, it's the very latest in abdominal sacking.' 'Darling!' he exclaimed. 'It's tremendous.' And it was. Alternate filleted panels of silk and satin, in two shades of blue, ran from her thorax, down in smooth and sensual slickness, to where a simple tassel hinted at the delights within.

In the bedroom Jonathan stripped nervously, like an adolescent, hunching up to remove his trousers and pants, as if he could somehow hide his ravening erection. She stood by the window to disrobe, and as she removed epidermis after epidermis, the sun streamed through her wings, creating a jalousie pattern on the ceiling. Her six hands moved rapidly, speeded by her own, insistent appetite. Then they were one writhing thing on the sheet. She arched above him, her multifaceted eyes capturing and scattering the light. He groaned – in awe and pleasure. Out of the line of his sight, her modified ovipositor pushed smoothly from the tip of her abdomen, each one of its barbs dripping with Cacharel. She arched still more, bending herself back underneath him. The ovipositor nuzzled his anus; and then the sting oozed up, killing him at the moment of climax.

Jonathan awoke, his mouth full of glutinous, mucal crud. It was ten thirty in the evening, and he was now living in Flytopia.

This he realised on entering the kitchen. Silverfish boiled up from the crack at the back of the sink and spread out over the draining-board. Their myriad bodies formed some comprehensible design. Jonathan leant down to see what it was. It was writing; the silverfish had formed themselves into a slogan: WELCOME TO FLYTOPIA . . . it said, the leader dots being, as it were, the fifty or so stragglers who couldn't make it into the final leg of the 'A'. Jonathan rubbed his eyes and exclaimed, 'Well, this is a turn up. Tell me – if you can act in this fashion presumably you can understand my speech – what does being in Flytopia entail exactly?'

The swarm of silverfish fused into a single pullulating heap and then fissioned back into readable characters, spindlier this time, which ranged across the corrugations of the draining-board, as if they were lines on a sheet of paper:

IN FLYTOPIA HUMANS AND INSECTS LIVE TOGETHER CO-OPERATIVELY. WE HAVE UNDERSTOD YOUR ANXIETY AND REVULSION FROM US, BUT WISH NOW TO LIVE AT PEACE WITH YOU. YOU ASSIST US – WE WILL ASSIST YOU.

'That should be "understood",' said Jonathan, 'not "understod".' The silverfish rearranged themselves to correct the living typo. 'Hmm,' Jonathan continued to speak aloud as he got a beer from the fridge and opened it, 'I suppose you want some kind of quid pro quo then?'

IT WOULD BE KIND IF YOU GOT RID OF THE VAPONAS AND THE FLY-PAPERS – INCIDENTALLY, SINCE YOU WERE WONDERING, THE VAPONAS EMIT A KIND OF NEUROTOXIN THAT PARALYSES US. IT'S NOT A NICE DEATH.

'I'm sure . . . I'm sure . . . but you must appreciate, I don't want to relax my campaign against you until I have more evidence of your goodwill.'

WE UNDERSTAND THAT. IF YOU CONTINUE ABOUT YOUR DAILY EXISTENCE, WE WILL DO OUR BEST TO ACCOMMODATE OURSELVES TO YOUR NEEDS. I THINK YOU WILL FIND THAT WE CAN BE SURPRISINGLY USEFUL. YOU ARE TIRED NOW, WHY NOT GO AND SEE WHAT WE'VE DONE IN THE BEDROOM?

Jonathan went upstairs and snapped on the overhead light in the bedroom. The bed, normally a slough of damp and disordered sheets, was not only neatly made, but peculiarly clean in appearance, clean as if burnished from within. A four-inch-wide rivulet of mites was flowing off the plumped-up pillow, down to the floor, across the intervening strip of carpet, up to the window-sill, and out the window itself. 'What's going on here?' Jonathan asked, taking a slug of his beer. The back end of the stream of tiny insects quivered, detached itself from the larger body of its kine and began to form characters on the pillow. Within seconds a slogan arranged itself:

WE ARE THE DUST MITES WHO HAVE BEEN LIVING IN YOUR BEDROOM. IN THE MATTRESS, THE PILLOWS, AND THE CARPET. AS A GESTURE OF GOODWILL FROM OUR ORDER WE HAVE THOROUGHLY CLEANED YOUR BEDDING AND NOW WE ARE DEPARTING. SWEET DREMS.

'That should be "dreams",' said Jonathan pedantically, but the dust mites, paying no attention, had already reformed their column and were completing their ordered withdrawal.

It was the first night of dreamless and undisturbed sleep that Jonathan could remember having in weeks. But when he awoke the following morning the bedroom was humming with insect life. As he opened his eyes he saw that the ceiling immediately above him was carpeted with flies. DO

NOT BE ALARMED! The flies quickly and quiveringly arranged themselves into the words: WE WISH TO ASSIST YOU WITH YOUR TOILET.

'Fair enough,' said Jonathan, heaving himself blearily up on to his elbows.

A beautiful flight of cabbage white butterflies then came winging into the room, for all the world like a host of angels. Before Jonathan could react they had blanketed his face with soft, faintly damp wings. He felt their tiny mandibles pluck and nibble at the crusted matter on his lips and eyelids. He lay back on the pillow and let the insects give him what amounted to an entire facial. When the butterflies lifted off, regrouped and flew out the open window, he arose, refreshed and ready for the day.

All morning the insects proved as good as their command of words. Whenever Jonathan needed something, a pencil or a computer disk, he had only to point to it for an insect formation to arrange itself in the air, lift the required object, and port it to where he sat, labouring at the Macintosh. Once their task was completed, the flies quit the room, leaving him with blissful quiet. No noise of miniature timpani, as tiny heads butted giant panes.

The sight of a clump of blue-black flies, holding within their midst such quotidian human artefacts, was also, in and of itself, a kind of displacement activity. Jonathan found that with these little breaks in the work to entertain him progress on the index was effortless. He was on to 'rood' before the end of the morning.

At lunch he had a protracted dialogue with the draining-board. 'OK,' he told the silverfish, 'I accept that so far you have acted in good faith. I will throw the Vaponas away!'

HOORAY! wrote the silverfish.

'I will also remove the spiders' webs I have allowed to be established around the cornices and the architrave.'

THANK YOU! THANK YOU! WE WILL CONTINUE TO SERVE YOU.

Jonathan was using the broom to knock out the last of the webs in the spare bedroom when Joy rang. 'Everything all right?' she asked.

'Fine, fine.' For some reason he found the very sound of her voice, vibrating in the receiver, intensely irritating, as if she were somehow trapped there, her nails rap-rap-rapping against the Bakelite.

'Insect life not getting to you then, is it?' She laughed, another tinkly, irritating noise.

'No, no, why should it?'

'Well, it's been bothering you all summer. And frankly I can't tell you what a relief it is to be in London, away from all of that bloody nature . . .' She paused, and Jonathan bit his lip, restraining himself from pointing out that 'bloody nature' could just as well do without her. '. . . Still, I'm sure I'll be longing for it by Friday. I'll be on the three-forty train, would you get a cab to pick me up from Sax?'

Jonathan filed this request away, but as soon as he hung up, Joy vanished from his mind. He was finding Flytopia an exhilarating place to live in. They left him well alone in the study, but whenever he emerged he found orderly teams of insects going about their business of assisting him elsewhere in the house. Neat phalanxes of beetles trundled across the carpets, their mandibles seeking out whatever detritus there was. Similar teams of earwigs were at work in the bathroom, and in the kitchen all signs of his breakfast, right down to the ring of coffee powder he had left by the jar, were eradicated by the industrious ants.

At lunch he took down the remaining fly-papers, and had a more protracted dialogue with the silverfish on the draining-board. AS YOU ARE NO DOUBT AWARE . . . they began, to which Jonathan expostulated: 'I'll thank you not to adopt that high-handed tone with me!' The insects immediately reformed into a demurral:

SORRY! WHAT WE WANTED TO SAY WAS THAT WE DON'T LIVE IN YOUR COTTAGE OUT OF CHOICE. WE COME INSIDE BECAUSE IN THE NORMAL COURSE OF THINGS THERE IS USUALLY SOME CARRION WITHIN WHICH WE CAN DEPOSIT OUR EGGS, SO THAT OUR LARVAE MAY GROW AND BECOME FULLY FUNCTIONING AND WELL-ADJUSTED MEMBERS OF FLYTOPIA.

'I see.'

HOWEVER, IF WE ARE CLEANING EVERYTHING UP FOR YOU, WE'RE RATHER DOING OURSELVES OUT OF A KEY COMPONENT IN OUR OWN ECOSYSTEM.

'I understand that, of course.'

WHAT WE WONDERED WAS WHETHER YOU MIGHT CON-SIDER TURNING THE SPARE BEDROOM OVER TO US EXCLU-SIVELY. IN WHICH CASE WE WOULD BE MORE THAN HAPPY TO ABANDON THE REST OF THE HOUSE TO YOU –

'– But I'm rather pleased by the way you've been helping me –'

– APART THAT IS FOR THE WORK WE NEED TO DO TO HELP YOU.

'I see. Well, I'll give it some thought.'

And he did, but really Jonathan's mind was already made up. The insects were proving such capable little friends. He no longer found them revolting at all, and when he saw them at work on the carpet he would bend down so as to catch whatever expressions might be contained in their alien faces. He also found their assis-tance in his toilet not simply helpful, but peculiarly sensual.

At night the moths tapped at the panes of the bathroom window until he allowed them access, and then they would blanket him with their softly pulsing wings. They tenderly licked away the encrusted sweat and dirt of the day, before drying him off with teasing flutterings of their wings. He didn't bridle when the silverfish on the draining-board suggested that he might like some of the beetles and earwigs to seek out the more intimate portions of his body and give them a thorough scouring as well.

Jonathan wondered if he had ever felt in more harmony with his environment. Not only that, but wondered if the grosser manipulations of human intercourse weren't becoming altogether more alien to his nature than these subtlest of digitations. In the morning he walked into Inwardleigh and bought ten pounds of pork sausages at Khan's. 'Barbecue?' asked Mr Khan, quadra-chinned today. 'Not exactly,' Jonathan replied.

He laid them out in the spare bedroom on the white plastic trays he had taken from the fridge. He left the door open for most of the day, but when evening came the silverfish told him that there was no need for this. So he shut the door and fell asleep in his voluntarily insect-free cottage.

The next morning, when Jonathan peeked inside the spare bedroom he felt a rush of paternal pride to see the bulging, bluing aspect of the rotting sausages, each one stippled with the white nodules that indicated the presence of maggots. Maggots chewing, maggots growing, maggots that he had gifted life to. A group of female flies who had been methodically working their way across the last five pounds or so of sausages, injecting their eggs into the putrefying meat, rose as he entered the room, and executed what looked to Jonathan like a gay curtsey, acknowledging his assistance and his suzerainty.

He worked steadily all morning. One particularly faithful fly proved the most adept of wordfinders, shuffling over the open spread of the *OED* until it found the correct entry, and then squatting there, gently agitating its wings, so as to act as a living cursor.

MORE MEAT? queried the silverfish on the draining-board, when he went in to make a sandwich at lunch. 'I'll think about it,' Jonathan replied, tossing them a sliver of ham to be getting on with. Then he retreated to the study, to phone for a cab to pick Joy up from the station.

Jonathan was so engrossed in the index that he didn't hear the squeal of brakes as Joy's cab pulled up outside the cottage. 'I'm home!' she trilled from the front door, and Jonathan experienced the same revulsion at the sound of her voice as he'd had on the phone. Why must she sound so high-pitched, so mindlessly insistent? She came into the study and they embraced. 'Have you got a fiver for the cab, darling?'

'Um . . . um . . . hold on a sec.' He plumped his pockets abstractedly. 'Sorry, not on me. I think there's a pile of loose change up in the spare bedroom . . .'

Jonathan listened to her feet going up the stairs. He listened to the door of the spare bedroom open, he heard the oppressive, giant, fluttering hum, as she was engulfed, then he rose and went out to pay the cab.

A STORY FOR EUROPE

'*Wir-wir*,' gurgled Humpy, pushing his little fingers into the bowl of spaghetti Miriam had just cooked for him. He lifted his hands up to his face and stared hard at the colloidal web of pasta and cheese. '*Wir müssen expandieren!*' he pronounced solemnly.

'Yes, darling, they *are* like worms, aren't they,' said the toddler's mother.

Humpy pursed his little lips and looked at her with his discomfiting bright blue eyes. Miriam held the gaze for a moment, willing herself to suffuse her own eyes with tenderness and affection. Blobs of melted cheese fell from Humpy's hands, but he seemed unconcerned. '*Masse!*' he crowed after some seconds.

'*Very* messy,' Miriam replied, hating the testiness that infected her tone. She began dabbing at the plastic tray of his high chair, smearing the blobs of cheese and coiling the strayed strands of spaghetti into edible casts.

Humpy continued staring at the toy he'd made out of his tea.

'*Masse*,' he said again.

'Put it down, Humpy. Put it in the dish – *in the dish!*' Miriam felt the clutch on her control slipping.

Humpy's eyes widened still more – a typical prelude to tears. But he didn't cry, he threw the whole mess on the

43

just-cleaned floor, and as he did so shouted, '*Massenfertigung!*' or some such gibberish.

Miriam burst into tears. Humpy calmly licked his fingers and appeared obscurely satisfied.

When Daniel got back from work an hour later, mother and son were still not reconciled. Humpy had struggled and fought and bitten his way through the rituals of pre-bedtime. Every item of clothing that needed to be removed had had to be pulled off his resisting form; he made Miriam drag him protesting every inch of the ascent to the bathroom; and once in the bath he splashed and kicked so much that her blouse and bra were soaked through. Bathtime ended with both of them naked and steaming.

But Daniel saw none of this. He saw only his blue-eyed handsome boy, with his angelic brown curls framing his adorable, chubby face. He put his bag down by the hall table and gathered Humpy up in his arms. 'Have you been a good boy while Daddy was at the office –'

'You don't have an office!' snapped Miriam, who like Humpy was in terry-towelling, but assumed in her case for reasons of necessity rather than comfort.

'Darling, darling . . . what's the matter?' Carrying the giggling Humpy, whose hands were entwined in his hair, Daniel advanced towards his wife.

'*Darlehen, hartes Darlehen,*' gurgled Humpy, seemingly mimicking his father.

'If you knew what a merry dance he's led me today, you wouldn't be *quite* so affectionate to the little bugger.' Miriam shrank away from Daniel's kiss. She was worried that, if she softened, let down her Humpy-guard at all, she might start to cry again.

Daniel sighed. 'It's just his age. *All* children go through a difficult phase at around two and a half; Humpy's no exception –'

'That may be so. But not all children are so aggressive. Honestly, Daniel, I swear you don't get to see the half of it. It's not as if I don't give him every ounce of love that I have to give; and he flings it back in my face, along with a lot of gibberish!' And with this Miriam did begin to cry, racking sobs which wrenched her narrow shoulders.

Daniel pulled Miriam to him and stroked her hair. Even Humpy seemed distressed by this turn of events. '*Mutter*,' he said wonderingly, '*Mutter*,' and squirmed around in his father's arms, so as to share in the family embrace.

'See,' said Daniel, 'of course he loves his mother. Now you open a bottle of that nice Chablis, and I'll put young Master Humpy down for the night.'

Miriam blinked back her tears. 'I suppose you're right. You take him up then.' She bestowed a glancing kiss on the top of Humpy's head. Father and son disappeared up the stairs. The last thing Miriam heard before they rounded the half-landing was more of Humpy's peculiar baby talk. '*Mutter–Mutter–Muttergesellschaft*' was what it sounded like. Miriam tried hard to hear this as some expression of love towards herself. Tried hard – but couldn't manage it.

Daniel laid Humpy down in his cot. 'Who's a very sleepy boy then?' he asked.

Humpy looked up at him; his blue eyes were still bright, untainted with fatigue. '*Wende!*' said Humpy cheerily. '*Wende-Wende-Wende!*' He drew his knees up to his chest and kicked them out.

'Ye-es, that's right.' Daniel pulled the clutch of covers up over the bunched little boy. 'Wendy *will* be here to look after you in the morning, because it's Mummy's day to go to work, isn't it?' He leant down to kiss his son, marvelling

– as ever – at the tight, intense feeling the flesh of his flesh provoked in him. 'Goodnight, little love.' He turned on the nightlight with its slow-moving carousel of leaping bunnies and clicked off the main light. As Daniel went back downstairs he could still hear Humpy gurgling to himself, '*Wende-Wende*,' contentedly.

But there was little content to be had at the Greens' oval scrubbed-pine kitchen table that evening. Miriam Green had stopped crying, but an atmosphere of fraught weepiness prevailed. 'Perhaps I'm too bloody old for this,' she said to Daniel, thumping a steaming casserole down so that flecks of onion, flageolets and juice spilled on to the table.' I nearly hit him today, Daniel, hit him!'

'You musn't be so hard on yourself, Miriam. He is a handful – and you know that it's always the mother who gets the worst of it. Listen, as soon as this job is over I'll take some more time off –'

'Daniel, it isn't that that's the problem.'

And it wasn't, for Miriam Green couldn't complain about Daniel. He did far more childcare than most fathers, and certainly more than any father who was trying to get a landscape-gardening business going in the teeth of a recession. Nor was Miriam cut off from the world of work by her motherhood, the way so many women were, isolated then demeaned by their loss of status. She had insisted on continuing with her career as a journalist after Humphrey was born, although she had accepted a jobshare in order to spend two and a half days a week at home. Wendy, the part-time nanny who covered for Miriam during the rest of the week, was, quite simply, a treasure. Intelligent, efficient and as devoted to Humpy as he was to her.

No, when Miriam Green let fly the remark about being 'too old', her husband knew what it was that was really troubling her. It was the same thing that had troubled her throughout her pregnancy. The first trimester may have been freighted with nausea, the second characterised by a kind of skittish sexiness, and the third swelling to something resembling bulgy beatitude, but throughout it all Miriam Green had felt deeply uneasy. She had emphatically declined the amniocentesis offered by her doctor, although at forty-one the hexagonal chips were not quite stacked in her favour.

'I don't believe in tinkering with destiny,' she had told Daniel, who, although he had not said so, thought the more likely reason was that Miriam felt she had tinkered with destiny too much already, and that this would, in a mysterious way, be weighed in the balance against her. Daniel was sensitive to her feelings, and although they talked around the subject, neither of them ever came right out with it and voiced the awful fear that the baby Miriam was carrying might turn out to be *not quite right*.

In the event the birth was a pure joy – and a revelation. Miriam and Daniel had lingered at home for the first five hours of the labour, mindful of all the premature hospital-dashes their friends had made. When they eventually got to the hospital Miriam's cervix was eight centimetres dilated. It was too late for an epidural, or even pethidine. Humphrey was born exactly fifty-one minutes later, as Miriam squatted, bellowing, on what looked to Daniel suspiciously like a school gym mat.

One moment he was watching the sweating, distending bulk of his wife, her face pushed about by pain; the next he was holding a blue-red ball of howling new vitality. Humphrey was perfect in every way. He scored ten out of ten on the first assessment. His features were no more oriental than those of any other new-born Caucasian baby. Daniel held him tight, and uttered muttered prayers to the idea of a god that might have arranged things so perfectly.

The comfortable Victorian house in Muswell Hill the Greens called home had long since been tricked out with enough baby equipment to cope with sextuplets. The room designated as the young master's had had a mural of a rainforest painted on its walls by an artist friend, complete with myriad examples of biodiversity. The cot was from Heal's, the buggy by Silver Cross. There were no less than three back-up Milton sterilisers.

Daniel had worried that Miriam was becoming obsessive in the weeks preceding the birth, and after they brought Humpy home from the hospital he watched her closely for any signs of creeping depression, but none came. Humphrey thrived, putting on weight like a diminutive boxer preparing for life's title fight. Sometimes Daniel and Miriam worried that they doted on him too much, but mostly they both felt glad that they had waited to become parents, and that their experience and maturity was part of the reason their child seemed so pacific. He hardly ever cried, or was colicky. He even cut his first two teeth without any fuss. He was, Daniel pronounced, tossing Humpy up in the air while they all giggled, 'a mensch'.

Daniel and Miriam delighted in each stage of Humpy's development. Daniel took roll after roll of out-of-focus shots of his blue-eyed boy, and Miriam pasted them into scrapbooks, then drew elaborate decorative borders around them. Humpy's first backwards crawl, frontwards crawl, trembling step, unassisted bowel movement, all had their memento. But then, at around two, their son's smooth and steady path of development appeared to waver.

Humpy's giggles and gurgles had always been expressive. He was an infant ready to smile, and readier still to give voice. But at that time, when from many many readings of the relevant literature his parents knew he should be beginning to form recognisable words, starting to iterate correctly, Humpy changed. He still gave voice, but the 'Da-das' and 'Ma-mas' garbled in his little mouth; and were then augmented with more guttural gibberish.

Their friends didn't really seem to notice. As far as they were concerned it was just a toddler's rambunctious burbling, but both Daniel and Miriam grew worried. Miriam took Humpy to the family doctor, and then at her instigation to a specialist. Was there some hidden cleft in Humpy's palate? No, said the specialist, who examined Humpy thoroughly and soothingly. Everything was all right inside Humpy's mouth and larynx. Mrs Green really shouldn't be too anxious. Children develop in many diverse ways; if anything – and this wasn't the specialist's particular expertise, he was not a child psychologist – Humpy's scrambled take on the business of language acquisition was probably a sign of an exceptional growing intellect.

Still, relations between mother and son did deteriorate. Miriam told Daniel that she felt Humpy was becoming strange to her. She found his tantrums increasingly hard to deal with. She asked Daniel again and again, 'Is it me? Is it that I'm not relating to him properly?' And again and again Daniel reassured her that it was 'just a stage'.

Sometimes, pushing Humpy around the Quadrant, on her way to the shops on Fortis Green Road, Miriam would pause and look out over the suburban sprawl of North London. In her alienation from her own child, the city of her birth was, she felt, becoming a foreign land. The barely buried anxieties about her age, and how this might be a factor in what was happening to Humpy, clawed their way through the sub-soil of her psyche.

Herr Doktor Martin Zweijärig, Deputy Director of the Venture Capital Research Department of Deutsche Bank, stood at the window of his office on the twentieth storey of the Bank's headquarters building looking out over the jumbled horizon of Frankfurt. All about him, the other concrete peaks of 'Mainhattan', the business and banking district, rose up to the lowering sky. Zweijärig's office window flowed around a corner of the Bank's building, and this, together with his elevated perspective, afforded him a view of the city cut up into vertical slices by the surrounding office blocks.

To his left, he could view an oblong of the university, and beyond it the suburb of Bockenheim; to his right the gleaming steel trapezoid of the Citibank building bisected the roof of the main station, and beyond it the old district of Sachsenhausen. Zweijärig couldn't see the River Main – but he knew it was there. And straight in front of him the massive eminence of the Messeturm, the highest office building in Europe, blotted out most of the town centre, including, thankfully, the mangled modernism of the Zweil shopping centre. Zweijärig had once, idly, calculated that, if a straight line were projected from his office window, down past the right-hand flank of the Messeturm at the level of the fifteenth storey, it should meet the earth two thousand and fifty-seven metres further on, right in the middle of the Goethehaus on Hirschgrab Strasse; forming a twanging, invisible chord, connecting past and present, and perhaps future.

'We must expand!' The phrase with its crude message of commercial triumphalism kept running through Zweijärig's mind, exhorting his inner ear. Why did Kleist feel the need to state the obvious in quite so noisy a fashion? And so early in the morning? Zweijärig didn't resent Kleist's elevation above him in the hierarchy of the Venture Capital Division – it made sense. He was, after all, at fifty-five six years Zweijärig's junior; and even though they had both been with the Bank the same number of years, it was Kleist who had the urge, the drive, to push for expansion, to grapple with the elephantine bureaucracy the Treuhand had become and seek out new businesses in the East for the Bank to take an interest in.

But the rescheduling of the directors' meeting for 7.30 a.m., and the trotting-out of such tawdry pabulums! Why, this morning Kleist had even had the temerity to talk of mass marketing as the logical goal of the Division. 'The provision of seed capital, hard loans even, for what – on the surface – may appear to be ossified, redundant concerns, can be approached at a mass level. We need to get the information concerning the services we offer to the widest possible sector of the business community. If this entails a kind of mass marketing then so be it.'

Zweijärig sighed deeply. A dapper man, of medium height, with a dark, sensual face, he was as ever dressed in a formal, sober, three-piece suit. This was one Frau Doktor Zweijärig had bought at the English shop, Barries, on Goethestrasse. Zweijärig liked the cut of English business suits, and also their conservatism. Perhaps it was because he wasn't a native Frankurter, but rather a displaced Sudetenlander, that Zweijärig felt the brashness of his adoptive city so keenly. He sighed again, and pushed his spectacles up on his forehead, so that steel rims became enmeshed in wire-wool hair. With thumb and forefinger he massaged his eyes.

He felt airy today, insubstantial. Normally the detail of his work was so readily graspable that it provided his mind with more than enough traction, adhesion to the world. But for the past few days he had felt his will skittering about like a puck on an ice rink. He couldn't seem to hold on to any given thought for more than a few seconds.

Maybe it was a bug of some kind? His daughter, Astrid, had called the previous evening from Stuttgart and said that she definitely had a viral infection. She'd stayed with them at the weekend – perhaps that was it? Zweijärig couldn't remember feeling quite so unenthusiastic about work on a Tuesday morning. Or was it that Kleist's appointment had irked him more than he realised. Right now he would have rather been in the Kleinmarkthalle, buying sausage or pig's ears from Schreiber's; or else at home with Gertrud, pruning the roses on the lower terrace. He conjured up a vision of their house, its wooden walls and wide glass windows merging with the surrounding woodland. It was only twenty kilometres outside Frankfurt, on the north bank of the river, but a world away.

Zweijärig fondled the heavy fob of his car keys in the pocket of his trousers. He pushed the little nipple that opened the central locking on the Mercedes, imagining the car springing into life, rear lights flashing. He pictured it, under autopilot, backing, filling, then driving up from the underground car-park to sit by the kerb in front of the building, waiting to take him home.

'Childish,' he muttered aloud, 'bloody childish.'

'Herr Doktor?' said Frau Schelling, Zweijärig's secretary, who he hadn't realised had entered the room. 'Did you say something?'

'Nothing – it's nothing, Frau Schelling.' He summoned himself, turned from the window to confront her. 'Are those the files on Unterweig?'

'Yes, Herr Doktor. Would you like to go over them with

me now?' Zweijärig thought he detected a note of exaggerated concern in her voice, caught up in the bucolic folds of her Swabian accent.

'No, no, that's all right. As long as the details of the parent company are there as well – '

'Herr Doktor, I'm sorry to interrupt, but Unterweig has no parent company, if you recall. It was only properly incorporated in May of last year.'

'Incorporated? Oh yes, of course, how foolish of me. Please, Frau Schelling, I'm feeling a little faint. You wouldn't mind terribly getting me a glass of water from the cooler?'

'Of course not, Herr Doktor, of course not.'

She put the folder down on the desk and hustled out of the room. Really, thought Zweijärig, I must pull myself together – such weakness in front of Frau Schelling. He pulled out the heavy leather chair, the one he had inhabited for the past sixteen years, brought with him from the posting in Munich. He allowed the smell and feel of the thing to absorb him. He picked up the folders and tamped them into a neat oblong, then laid them down again, opened the cover of the first and began to read:

Unterweig is a metal-working shop specialising in the manufacture of basic steel structures for children's playground equipment. The main plant is situated on the outskirts of Potsdam, and there is an office complex in the north-central district. As ever in these cases it is difficult to reach an effective calculation of capitalisation or turnover. Since May 1992, the shop has managed to achieve incorporation despite a 78 per cent fall in orders . . .

The words swam in front of Zweijärig's eyes. Why bother, he thought. I've read so many reports like this, considered so many investment opportunities, what can this one possibly have to offer that any of the others didn't? And why is it that we persist in this way with the Easterners? He grimaced, remembering that he himself had once been like the Easterners – no, not like them, worse off than them. There had been no one-to-one conversion rate for the little that the Russians had allowed him to take.

A thirteen-year-old boy carrying a canvas bag with some bread in it, a pair of socks and two books. One, the poems of Hölderlin, the other a textbook on calculus, with most of the pages loose in the binding. He could barely remember the long walk into exile any more. It seemed to belong to someone else's past, it was too lurid, too nasty, too brutal, too sad for the man he'd become. Flies gathering on a dead woman's tongue.

Had the fields really been that beautiful in Bohemia? He seemed to remember them that way. Smaller fields than those in the West, softer, and fringed by cherry trees always in bloom. It can't have been so. The cherry trees could only have blossomed for a couple of weeks each year, and yet that's what had stayed with him: the clutches of petals pushed and then burst by the wind, creating a warm, fragrant snowfall. He couldn't face meeting with Bocklin and Schiele at the Frankfurter Hof. He'd rather have a few glasses of stuff somewhere, loosen this damn tie . . . Zweijärig's hand went to his neck without him noticing, and shaking fingers tugged at the knot.

On her way back from the water-cooler Frau Schelling saw her boss's face half-framed by one of the glass panels siding his office. He looked, she thought, old, very old for a man of sixty-one. And in the past few days he seemed unable to concentrate on anything much. Herr Doktor Zweijärig, who was always the very epitome of correctness, of efficiency. She wondered whether he might have suffered a minor stroke. She had heard of such things happening – and the person concerned not even noticing, not even *being able* to notice; the part of the brain that should be doing such noticing suffused with blood. It would be uncomfortable for Frau Schelling to call Frau Doktor Zweijärig and voice her anxieties – but worse if she did nothing. She entered the office quietly and placed the glass of water by his elbow, then silently footed out.

Miriam placed the feeding cup by Humpy's cot and paused for a moment looking down at him. It was such a cliché to say that children looked angelic when they slept, and in Humpy's case it was metaphoric understatement. Humpy appeared angelic when awake; asleep he was like a cherry blossom lodged in the empyrean, a fragment of the divinity. Miriam sighed heavily and clawed a hank of her dark corkscrew curls back from her brow. She'd brought the feeding cup full of apple juice in to forestall Humpy calling for her immediately on awaking. He could get out of his cot easily enough by himself, but she knew he wouldn't until he'd finished the juice.

Miriam silently footed out of Humpy's room. She just needed five more minutes to herself, to summon herself. It had been an agonised night on Humpy's account. Not that he'd kept Miriam and Daniel up personally – he never did that – but it had been a night of reckoning, of debating and of finally deciding that they should keep the appointment with the child psychologist that Dr Peppard had made for them for the following day.

Daniel had gone off to work just after dawn, giving the half-asleep Miriam a snuffly kiss on the back of her neck. 'I'll meet you at the clinic,' he said.

'You be there,' Miriam grunted in reply.

Dr Peppard had shared their misgivings about consult-

ing the child psychologist, their worries that, even at two
and a half, Humpy might apprehend the institutional
atmosphere of the clinic and feel stigmatised, patholo-
gised, mysteriously different to other toddlers. But more
than that, she worried that the Greens were losing their
grip on reality; she had seldom seen a happier, better-
adjusted child than Humpy. Dr Peppard had great con-
fidence in Philip Weston – he was as good at divining adult
malaises as he was those of children. If anyone could help
the Greens to deal with their overweening affection for
their child – which Dr Peppard thought privately was the
beginning of an extreme, hot-housing tendency – then it
would be Philip Weston.

Miriam now lay, face crushed into pillow, one ear
registering the *Today Programme* – John Humphreys
withering at some junior commissioner in Brussels – the
other cocked for Humpy's awakening, his juice-slurping,
his agglutinative wake-Miriam-up call.

This came soon enough. '*Bemess-bemess-bemess –!*' he
cried, shaking the side of his cot so that it squeaked and
creaked. '*Bemessungsgrundlage,*' he garbled.

'All right, Humpy,' Miriam called out to him. 'All
right, Humpy love, I'm coming!' then buried her head
still further in the pillow. But she couldn't shut it out:
'*Bemess-bemess-bemessungsgrundlage!*' Better to get up and
deal with him.

An hour or so later Miriam was sitting at her dressing
table, which was set in the bay window of the master
bedroom, with Humpy on her lap. It was a beautiful
morning in late spring and the Greens' garden – which
Daniel lavished all of his professional skills on – was an
artfully disordered riot of verdancy. Miriam sighed, pulling the squirming Humpy to her breast. Life could be so
sweet, so good; perhaps Dr Peppard was right and she was

needlessly anxious about Humpy. 'I *do* love you so much, Humpy – you're my favourite boy.' She kissed the soft bunch of curls atop his sweet head.

Humpy struggled in her embrace and reached out to one of the bottles on the dressing table. Miriam picked it up and pressed it into his fat little palm. 'This is kohl, Humpy – can you say that, "kohl"? Try to.'

Humpy looked at the vial of make-up intently; his small frame felt tense in Miriam's arms. '*Kohl*,' he said. '*Kohl!*' he reiterated with more emphasis.

Miriam broke into peals of laughter. 'That's a clever Humpy!' She stood up, feeling the curious coiled heft of the child as she pulled him up with her. She waltzed Humpy a few steps around the room.

'*Kohl!*' he cried out merrily, and mother and son giggled and whirled; and would have gone on giggling and whirling were it not for the sound of the front door bell.

'Bugger!' said Miriam, stopping the dance. 'That'll be the postman, we'd better go and see what he wants.'

The change in Humpy was instantaneous – almost frighteningly so. '*Pohl!*' he squealed. '*Pohl-Pohl-Pohl!*' and then all his limbs flew out, his foot catching Miriam in her lower abdomen.

She nearly dropped him. The moment before, the moment of apparently mutual comprehension was gone, and in its place was a grizzling gulf. 'Oh Humpy – please, Humpy!' Miriam struggled to control his flailing arms. 'It's OK, it's OK,' she soothed him, but really it was she who needed the soothing.

Philip Weston entered the waiting room of the Gruton Child Guidance Clinic moving silently on the balls of his feet. He was a large, adipose man, who wore baggy corduroy trousers to disguise his thick legs and bulky arse. Like many very big men he had an air of stillness and poise about him. His moon face was cratered with jolly dimples, and his bright-orange hair stood up in a cartoon flammable ruff. He was an extremely competent clinician, with an ability to build a rapport with even the most disturbed children.

The scene that met his forensically attuned eyes was pacific. The Green family were relaxed in the bright sunny waiting room. Miriam sat leafing through a magazine, Daniel sat by her, working away at the occupational dirt beneath his nails, using the marlinespike on his clasp knife. At their feet was Humpy. Humpy had, with Daniel's assistance, in the fifteen minutes since they'd arrived at the clinic, managed to build a fairly extensive network of Brio toy-train tracks, incorporating a swing bridge and a level crossing. Of his own accord he had also connected up a train, some fifteen cars long, and this he was pushing along with great finesse, making the appropriate 'Woo-woo' noises.

'I'm Philip Weston,' said the child psychologist. 'You must be Miriam and Daniel, and this is –?'

'Humpy – I mean Humphrey.' Miriam Green lurched to her feet, edgy at once.

'Please.' Philip damped her down, and knelt down himself by the little boy. 'Hello, Humpy, how are you today?'

Humpy left off mass-transportation activities and looked quizzically at the clownish man, his sharp blue eyes meeting Philip's waterier gaze. '*Besser*,' he said at length.

'Better?' queried Philip, mystified.

'*Besser*,' Humpy said again, with solemn emphasis. '*Besserwessi!*' and as if this gobbledygook settled the matter, he turned back to the Brio.

Philip Weston regained the foundation of his big legs. 'Shall we go in,' he said to the Greens, and indicated the open door of his consulting room.

Neither Miriam nor Daniel had had any idea of what to expect from this encounter, but in the event they were utterly charmed by Philip Weston. His consulting room was more in the manner of a bright, jolly nursery, a logical extension of the waiting room outside. While Humpy toddled about, picking up toys from plastic crates, or pulling down picture books from the shelves, the child psychologist chatted with his parents. So engaging and informal was his manner that neither Miriam nor Daniel felt they were being interviewed or assessed in any way – although that was, in fact, what was happening.

Philip Weston chatted their worries out of them. His manner was so relaxed, his demeanour so unjudgmental, that they both felt able to voice their most chilling fears. Was Humpy perhaps autistic? Or brain-damaged? Was Miriam's age in some way responsible for his learning difficulty? To all of these Philip Weston was able to provide instant and total refutation. 'You can certainly set yourselves at rest as far as any autism is concerned,' he told them. 'Humpy engages emotionally and sympathetically with the external world; as you can see now, he's using that stuffed toy to effect a personation. No autistic child ever engages in such role-playing activity.'

Nor, according to Philip, was Humpy in any way retarded: 'He's using two or more coloured pencils in that drawing, and he's already forming recognisable shapes. I think I can tell you with some authority that, if anything, this represents advanced, rather than retarded, ability for a child of his age. If there is a real problem here, Mr and Mrs Green, I suspect it may be to do with a gift rather than a deficiency.'

After twenty minutes or so of chatting and quietly observing Humpy, who continued to make use of Philip Weston's superb collection of toys and diversions, the child psychologist turned his attention directly to him. He picked up a small tray full of outsized marbles from his desk and called to the toddler, 'Humpy, come and look at these.' Humpy came jogging across the room, smiling broadly. In his cute, Osh-Kosh bib 'n' braces, his brown curls framing his chubby face, he looked a picture of health and radiance.

Philip Weston selected one of the marbles and gave it to Humpy. 'Now, Humpy,' he said, 'if I give you two of these marbles' – he rattled the tray – 'will you give me that marble back?' Without even needing to give this exchange any thought Humpy thrust the first marble in the child psychologist's face. Philip took it, put it in the tray, selected two other shiny marbles and gave them to him. Humpy grinned broadly. Philip turned to Miriam and Daniel saying, 'This is really quite exceptional comprehension for a child Humpy's age –' He turned back to Humpy.

'Now, Humpy, if I give you two of these remaining marbles, will you give me those two marbles back?'

Humpy stared at Philip for some seconds, while storm clouds gathered in his blue, blue eyes. The little boy's brow furrowed, and his fist closed tightly around his two marbles. '*Besserwessi!*' he spat at Philip, and then, '*Grundgesetz!*'

It was to Philip's credit, and a fantastic exemplar of his clinical skills, that he didn't react at all adversely to these bits of high-pitched nonsense, but merely put the question again: 'These two marbles, Humpy, for your two, what do you say?'

Humpy opened his hand and looked at the two blue

marbles he had in his possession. Philip selected two equally shiny blue marbles from the tray and proffered them. There was silence for some moments while the two parties eyed one another's merchandise. Then Humpy summoned himself. He put one marble very carefully in the side pocket of his overalls, and the other in the bib pocket. This accomplished, he said to Philip with great seriousness, '*Finanzausgleichgesetz*,' turned neatly on his heels, and went back to the scribbling he'd been doing before the child psychologist called him over.

Daniel Green sighed heavily, and passed a hand through his hair. 'Well, now you've seen it, Philip − that's the Humpy we deal with most of the time. He talks this . . . this . . . I know I shouldn't say it, but it's gibberish, isn't it?'

'Hmmm . . .' Philip was clearly giving the matter some thought before replying. 'We-ell, I agree, it doesn't sound like anything recognisably meaningful, but there is definitely something going on here, Humpy is communicating *something*, something that he thinks we might comprehend. There's great deliberation in what he's saying . . . I don't know, I don't know . . .' He shook his head.

'What?' Miriam was sitting forward on the edge of her chair; she was trying to remain calm, but her troubled expression betrayed her. 'What do you think? Please, don't hold anything back from us.'

'It could be pure speculation. It's something I've never seen before. I tell you, if I didn't know any better I'd be prepared to hazard the idea that young Humpy was originating some kind of idiolect, you know, a private language. His cognitive skills are, as I said, quite remarkably developed for his age. If you don't mind, I'd like to get a second opinion here.'

'What would that entail?' asked Miriam. She was clearly

appalled by this turn of events, but Daniel, by contrast, was leaning forward, engaged, intrigued.

'Well, it just so happens that we have a Dr Grauerholtz visiting us here at the Gruton at the moment. This is a marvellous opportunity. He's a former director of the clinic, now based at the Bettelheim Institute in Chicago, *and* he's without doubt the foremost expert on human-language acquisition in either Europe or the USA. If he's available I'd like him to pop in right away and have a chat with Humpy as well. See if we can get to the bottom of this young man's verbal antics. What do you say?'

'What is the basis of assessment?'

'The same as it's always been.'

'Meaning . . .?'

'Meaning that they did have an open order book, that they did have a capital fund – of some sort. Meaning that both have been subject to the one-on-one conversion rate, and those monies remain in escrow. Meaning that precisely, Herr Doktor.'

'Yes, yes, of course, I know all of that. I know all of that.'

It was late in the morning and Zweijärig was feeling no better – perhaps worse. He'd groped his way through the Unterweig file and now was attempting to discuss its contents with Hassell, his capitalisation expert. At least he'd taken the leap and got Frau Schelling to cancel the meeting with Bocklin and Schiele. 'The unheard-of must be spoken.'

'I'm sorry, Herr Doktor?' Hassell was looking curiously at his boss. Zweijärig noted, inconsequentially, how pink Hassell's forehead was. Pink fading to white at the hairline, just like a slice of ham.

'Ah, um, well . . .' I spoke aloud? Zweijärig fumbled the

ball of thought. What is this — am I really losing my marbles? 'I mean to say, the conversion rate, Hassell, it remains as stupid today as when Kohl proposed it. It's wrecked our chances of building the economy the way we might wish to. It doesn't reflect the constitution – such as it was; and it doesn't accord with the law governing redistribution of fiscal apportionments to the Länder.'

Hassell was staring hard at Zweijärig during this speech. It was about the closest he could remember his boss getting to discussing politics directly in the four years they'd worked together. He normally skated around such topics, avoiding them with something approaching flippancy. Hassell steepled his plump fingers on the edge of the desk, pursed his plump lips, and ventured a query. 'So, Herr Doktor, would you have favoured Pohl's proposal? Do you think things would have gone that much smoother?'

'Pohl-Kohl. Kohl-Pohl. It hardly matters which bloody joker we have sitting on top of the Reichstag. We're a nation of displaced people, Herr Hassell. We're displaced from our past, we're displaced from our land, we're displaced from each other. That's the European ideal for you, eh – we're closer to people in Marseilles or Manchester than we are to those in Magdeburg. It's an ideal of mass society rather than homeland, ach!'

Zweijärig was, Hassell noted, breathing heavily, panting almost. His tie was loosened, the top button of his shirt undone. Hassell didn't wish to be intrusive, but he ought really to enquire. 'Are you feeling all right, Herr Doktor?'

'All right, yes, yes, Herr Hassell, I feel all right. I feel like the smart-aleck Westerner I've become, eh? Wouldn't you say?'

'It's not my position, Herr Doktor –'

'No, no, of course not, of course not. It's not your

position. I'm sorry, Herr Hassell, I'm not myself today, I'm like Job on his dungheap – you know that one, d'you? It's in the Stadel, you should go and look at it. *Job on his Dungheap*. Except in *our* case the dungheap is built of glass and steel, hmm?'

'Dungheap, Herr Doktor?' said Hassell, trying to look unobtrusively over his shoulder, trying to see whether Frau Schelling was in the outer office.

'Playing with shit, Herr Hassell, playing with shit. Have you ever heard the expression that money *is* shit, Herr Hassell?'

'Herr Doktor?'

'Money *is* shit. No, well, I suppose not. Y'know, there are ghosts here in Frankfurt, Herr Hassell, you can see them if you squint. You can see them walking about – the ghosts of the past. This city is built on money, so they say. Perhaps it's built on shit too, hmm?'

And with this gnomic – if not crazy – remark, Herr Doktor Martin Zweijärig stood up, passed a sweaty hand across his brow, and made for the door of his office, calling over his shoulder, 'I'm going for a glass of stuff, Herr Hassell. If you would be so good, please tell Frau Schelling I'll be back in a couple of hours.' Then he was gone.

Hassell sighed heavily. The old man was unwell, disturbed even. He was clearly disoriented; perhaps Hassell should stop him leaving the bank building? Ethics and propriety did battle in the arid processes of Hassell's mind for some seconds, until ethics won – narrowly.

Hassell got up and quit the office at a near-jog, the bunches of fat above his broad hips jigging like panniers on a donkey. But when he reached the lifts Zweijärig had gone. He turned back to the office and met Frau Schelling. 'The Deputy Direktor, Frau Schelling, do you think –?'

'I think he's ill, Herr Hassell – he's behaving very oddly.

I called Frau Doktor Zweijärig just now. I hated going behind his back like that, but –'

'You did the right thing, Frau Schelling. What did Frau Doktor Zweijärig say?'

'Oh, she's noticed it as well. She's driving into town right now. She says she'll be here within the hour. But where has he gone?'

'He said something about getting a glass of stuff. Do you think he's gone to Sachsenhausen?'

'I doubt it, he can't stand the GIs there. No, there's a tavern near the station he often goes to. I'll bet he's gone there now.' Frau Schelling shook her head sorrowfully. 'Poor man, I do hope he's all right.'

'Miriam and Daniel Green, this is Dr Grauerholtz . . . and this is Humpy.' Philip Weston stood in the middle of his consulting room making the introductions. Dr Grauerholtz was a tiny little egg of a man, bald, bifocaled, and wearing a quite electric suit. The contrast between the two psychologists was straightforwardly comic, and despite the seriousness of the situation, Daniel and Miriam exchanged surreptitious grins and jointly raised their eyebrows.

'Hello,' said Dr Grauerholtz warmly. He had a thick but not unpleasant German accent. 'Philip tells me that we have a most unusual young fellow with us today – you must be very proud of him.'

'Proud?' Miriam Green was becoming agitated again. Dr Grauerholtz and Philip Weston exchanged meaningful glances. Dr Grauerholtz indicated that they should all sit down. Then, with rapid, jerky movements he stripped off his funny jacket, threw it over a chair, reversed the chair, and sat down on it facing them with his elbows crossed on the back.

'I don't think I will be in any way upsetting you, Mr and Mrs Green, if I tell you that my colleague has managed to do a rudimentary Stanford-Binet test on Master Humpy –'

'Stanford-Binet?' Miriam was becoming querulous.

'I'm sorry, so-called intelligence test. Obviously such things are very speculative with such a young child, but we suspect that Humpy's IQ may be well up in the hundred and sixties. He is, we believe, an exceptionally bright young fellow. Now, if you don't mind . . .'

Dr Grauerholtz dropped backwards off the chair on to his knees and then crawled towards Humpy across the expanse of carpet. Humpy, who had paid no attention to Dr Grauerholtz's arrival, was playing with some building blocks in the corner of the room. He had managed to construct a sort of pyramid, or ziggurat, the top of which was level with the first shelf of a bookcase, and now he was running toy cars up the side of this edifice and parking them neatly by the spines of the books.

'That's a good castle you've got there, Humpy,' said Dr Grauerholtz. 'Do you like castles?'

Humpy stopped what he was doing and regarded the semi-recumbent world authority on human-language acquisition with an expression that would have been called contemptuous in an older individual. '*Grundausbildung!*' he piped, scooting one of the toy cars along the shelf. Dr Grauerholtz appeared rather taken aback, and sat back on his heels. Daniel and Miriam gave each other weary looks.

'*Grundausbildung?*' Dr Grauerholtz repeated the gibberish with an interrogative-sounding swoop at the end. Humpy stopped what he was doing, tensed, and turned to give the doctor his full attention. '*Ja,*' he said after a few moments, '*grundausbildung.*'

'*Grundausbildung für . . .?*' gargled the doctor.

'*Für bankkreise,*' Humpy replied, and smiled broadly.

The doctor scratched the few remaining hairs on his head, before saying, 'Humpy, *verstehen sie Deutsch?*'

'*Ja,*' Humpy came back, and giggled. '*Geschäft Deutsch.*' Then he resumed playing with the toy car, as if none of this bizarre exchange were of any account.

Dr Grauerholtz stood up and came back to where the adults were sitting. They were all staring at him with frank astonishment, none more so than Miriam Green. To look at her you might have thought she was in the presence of some prophet, or messiah. 'Doc-Doctor Grau-Grauerholtz,' she stuttered, 'c-can you understand what Humpy is saying?'

'Oh yes,' the Doctor replied. He was now grinning as widely as Humpy. 'Quite well, I think. You see, your son is speaking . . . How can I put it? He's speaking what you would call "business German".'

' "Business German"?' queried Philip Weston. 'Isn't that a bit unusual for an English child of two and a half?'

Dr Grauerholtz had taken his bifocals off and was cleaning them with a small soft cloth that he'd taken from his trouser pocket. He looked at the three faces that gawped at him with watery, myopic eyes, and then said, 'Yes, yes, I suppose a bit unusual, but hardly a handicap.' He smiled, a small wry smile. 'Some people might say it was a great asset – especially in today's European situation, yes?'

Humpy chose that moment to push over the pyramid of building blocks he'd made. They fell with a delightful local crash; and Humpy began to laugh. It was the happy, secure laugh of a well-loved child – if a tad on the guttural side.

They found Herr Doktor Martin Zweijärig sitting on the pavement outside the station. His suit was scuffed-about and dirty, his face was sweaty and contorted. All around him the human flotsam streamed: Turkish guest workers, junkies, asylum-seekers and tourists. There was hardly an ethnic German to be found in this seedy quarter of the European financial capital. Zweijärig was conscious, but barely so. The stroke had robbed him of his strength – he was as weak as a two-year-old child; and quite naturally – he was talking gibberish.

DAVE TOO

'Perhaps . . .' Dr Klagfarten leaves this word dangling for a while – he likes to do that. 'Perhaps the blackbird is the real object of your sympathy. After all, it cannot leave the room, whereas you can.'

'Perhaps.' I don't leave the word dangling. I leave it crashing, falling to the floor between us, like a bull at a corrida, and collapsing in undulations of muscle and dust, crumpling on to the hard, deathly ground.

Dr Klagfarten tries another tack. 'I'd like to see you again this afternoon, about another matter – you recall, I mentioned it yesterday?' How typical of the man, that 'recall'.

'Yes, yes, of course.' I'm struggling to my feet. I sit facing Dr Klagfarten for these sessions, inhabiting a low armchair of fifties ilk, wooden arms, cushioned base underslung with rubber straps.

Dr Klagfarten sits some way off, behind a white wooden table which does service as his desk. He's a thin man, quite bald, with an expressive, sensitive face. His lips are alarmingly sensual for a middle-aged psychiatrist. He twists them constantly this way and that in a moue of intense, emotive contemplation. He's doing it now. Doing it as he says, rising from behind the table, 'Well, see you at three this afternoon then.'

And I sort of hunch up, half turn on my way to the door and go 'Y'mf' by way of assent.

What does Dr Klagfarten want, in the midst of his carpeted enclave? That's what his consulting room is like – a carpeted enclave. A modern room, cream of wall, thick of pile. And that pile, after a session of curdling monologue, seems in danger of creeping up the walls, providing further insulation, further deadening. What does he want of me? To slide my hand beneath the curiously thick and defined lapel of his jacket? To caress the front of his shirt; unbutton it, bend, slide tongue and lips in; seek out a depressed, sweaty nipple? Is that what Dr Klagfarten wants?

I woke this morning with the radio burbling in my ear. If I'm alone – which I am more and more nowadays – I always sleep with it on, so that the World Service mixes with my dreams. So that I dream of a riot of headscarved Dr Klagfartens, stoning Israeli soldiers in the Gaza Strip. As I came to consciousness a politician was being interviewed. 'We have to make some terms for the long-term,' he said, and then later he also said, 'I'm going to sit down and think about it – I think.' There's something about these broadcast contexts that does it to people, makes them repeat themselves. It's as if, halfway through their sentence, they lose some sense of what it is to be themselves, they flounder in the very moment of articulation, asking, 'Who am I? Who the fuck am I?' And the only answer that comes back is that they are the person who has just said 'actually' or 'term' or 'policy' or 'whatever', so they have to say it again. Are compelled to say it again.

Dr Klagfarten's consulting room is in the old administration building. It's a blocky thing of weeping concrete and square, green-tinted windows, which project out, as if the interior of the structure were swelling, slowly exploding. As I cross the car-park I look over my shoulder, once. Dr Klagfarten stares down at me from his window. He lifts a hand and carefully swivels it at the wrist, suggesting the possibility of valediction. And as he does this a great gout of chemical smell, like air-freshener, comes into the back of my throat. I gag, turn, walk on.

Dave is waiting for me in the café – as he said he would. He's a very tall, very jolly man, and I think of him as my closest friend. 'Howdy!' he cries as I come in through the door. The café is a long, tunnel-shaped room. Near the back a counter is set on the right, and on the very edge of this a Gaggia huffles and burbles, sending out little local weather systems. Dave is under one of these clouds. 'Howdy!' he cries again. Maybe he thinks I haven't seen him, or maybe he's just reminding himself that he's Dave.

I can't blame him for that. It's such a common name, Dave. There are two other Daves who are usually in the café at this time of the morning. Dave and I call them, respectively, Fat Dave and Old Dave, by way of differentiating them both from him and each other. Fat Dave, who's the owner's rather dim-witted brother, mans the Gaggia. He's a barrel of a being with a bucket for a head. He wraps an apron around his abdomen, ties it with a cord as tight as a ligature, and leaves his big white arms bare. These are constantly in motion, scooping, twisting and pulling at the Gaggia. It looks as if he is deftly, but without much feeling, making love to the coffee machine.

Old Dave is an altogether grimmer figure. He sits, face down to his racing paper, a roll-up made from three strands of tobacco stuck on his lower lip. He never says anything. We only know his name, because from time to time Fat Dave will refer to him in passing, thus: 'Yairs, Dave there used to . . .' or, 'Y'know Dave over there, he could tell you a thing or two about . . .' It seems that this is the fate of these two particular Daves. To be caught, their sembled identities bookending the café, leaning into one another's being.

My Dave is eating a full English breakfast. The eggs have been turned so that a small skin of white has coagulated over the yoke. It has the aspect of a cast over an eye. Dave looks up at me as I sit down opposite him, smiles, then looks down, spears the yoke with his fork, spears a bit of bacon with same, tucks the whole, gnarled mass into his mouth. 'Yungf',' he says, and then, 'Have you seen her?' I sigh. 'No, yungf'-yungf', tell me, have you?'

I shrug, inexpressively, 'Oh yeah. Oh yeah, I have.'

'And?' He's sawing at the fried bread.

'She understands . . . sort of. She, she accepts that maybe I have to . . .' I can't bear to say this, it's so *trite*. 'Have to . . . find out who I really am. I feel so . . . well, you know, we've talked about it. I feel so amorphous, so shapeless, so *incoherent*. I don't feel as if I know myself any more. Especially after a morning like this, when I'm up early and talking to Dr Klagfarten before I'm awake, before I've had an opportunity to, sort of, boot up my identity, become who I really am –'

'Yes, yes, of course, I know what you mean entirely.' Dave has set his knife and fork down, he's kneading one hand with the other, he's completely engaged in the matter, abandoning himself to the discourse – perhaps that's why I like him so much. 'I sometimes feel the same way myself, exiguous, wavering, fundamentally peripheral – '

'And full of fancy words, ha!' We both laugh, our shared laugh, my wheezing giving a windy accompaniment to his percussive ho-ho-hos. And in the moment of this laugh I'm at one with Dave, I feel a real kinship with him. I feel he and I are essentially similar, that no matter what differences may arise between us, of belief, of intent, we will share the same basic character. It's only with Dave that I feel comfortable discussing Dr Klagfarten – or rather, discussing what Dr Klagfarten and I discuss.

It's odd, because I'm sensitive about the therapy, and sensitive about my relationship with Dr Klagfarten, who far from being a distant or impersonal presence in my life, is actually well known in some of the circles I move in. But predictably, it was Dave who ran into him socially. He was at a party in Davyhulme given by some zoologists. According to Dave, Dr Klagfarten was very jolly, drank deep, and sang revolutionary songs in a fine, warm baritone, much to everyone's enjoyment. I find this clip of Dr Klagfarten at play difficult to reconcile with the benign severity he always evinces towards me. I even find it hard to imagine Dr Klagfarten as being anything but a shrink. How could anybody whisper lovers' endearments to him? What could they call him? Klaggy? Farty? The mind boggles.

Lovers' endearments. *Her* endearments. I don't feel I deserve them. Or perhaps worse – I don't quite believe they're directed at me. When Velma looks at me with what are meant to be loving eyes, I see too much comprehension, too much calculation. It's as if she were looking at my face in a spirit of having to do something with it, make it work.

I sign to Fat Dave that I want a double espresso, and turn back to Dave.

'I am going to see her – this afternoon.'

'I thought as much.' Dave bends back down to his breakfast, I am gifted a top view of his head, the island of grey-blond hair marooned on the apex of his skull, like a negative image of a monk's tonsure. 'I couldn't believe that you'd just let it ride, let her go out of your life.'

'No, it's true, but y'know, Dave, the same applies –'

'The same applies?'

'To her, to Velma. Even when I'm with her, and we've made love . . . Well, no, *especially* when we've made love, especially at that moment when I roll away from her, see her face blanched, emptied by orgasm, wrung out. Then I don't know who she is –'

'You don't know who you are –'

'That goes without saying, but I don't know who she is either. She . . . she could be *you* for all I know.'

'Double espresso?' says Fat Dave, putting the cup down in front of me. Out of the corner of my eye I can see Old Dave light his roll-up with a lighter so buried in his calloused, chipped, yellowing fingers, that the flame seems to issue directly from flesh. 'Double espresso?'

'Whassat?'

'Double espresso?' Fat Dave is still standing over me. Has he forgotten that it was I who placed the order, from this very seat, not three minutes ago? I scrutinise his face for traces of irony. I know that Fat Dave feels less fondness for me than he does for his namesake. But Fat Dave doesn't have the contrast control necessary to express irony – he's only looking *at* me.

'Yeah – that's mine.'

Dave observes all this with a wry smile puckering up his long, equine face. His visage is really a series of crescent shapes: long, droopy earlobes; large droopy eyes; cheeks nearing jowl; and straight lines, in the form of fine wrinkles, that experience, twiddling his knobs, has Etch-A-Sketched alongside the crescents. Dave's countenance, I realise for the first time with an access of minor dread, is composed entirely of Ds, letter Ds, Ds for 'Dave'. Dave is, in fact, initialled all over. Like some ambulatory stick of rock, he carries his ascription written on his body. Written *through* his body, for, I feel certain that were I to excavate, dig into one of these fleshly Ds, I would find that it was bred in the bone.

My Dave is, I like to think, a kind of Ur-Dave, a primary Dave. His Daveness, his Davidity, his Davitude, is unquestionable. In a world with so many Daves, Daves running, Daves walking, and Daves standing, desolate, crumpled betting slips at their feet, it's infinitely reassuring to feel that within my grasp is some part of the essential Dave.

But that essential Dave is now talking, wheedling his way back into my thoughts. I tune to this very Dave frequency:

'. . . went back with her. She went into the bedroom. To be frank I was a bit pissed. She called me after about five minutes. I'd poured myself a generous snifter. She keeps a bottle of calvados in her desk . . .' He always speaks in these short sentences. A Moog speech synthesiser – with the 'Hemingway' button permanently on. '. . . on the bed. She's wearing a red rubber dress. The video is on. A Californian pol of some kind is giving a press conference. She was writhing. He was saying something impassioned –'

'Dave –'

'She said, "Come here." But I was watching the pol, who had pulled out a gun. It was quite clear that this was real. All shot by a live-action news camera. He put the gun in his mouth. Big fucker – long-barelled Colt –'

'Dave you –'

'I look from the screen to the bed. She's got her hand up under the rubber dress. She's playing with herself. On screen the pol just does it. Blows –'

'Dave, *you told me this yesterday!* –'

'His brains out.'

Silence in the café. I realise I've shouted. A hiss of steam from the Gaggia, a small cloud floats over me, sends shadows racing across the sward of Dave's face. I look up to where a peg board is affixed to the pine cladding. A peg board with plastic letters, detailing the café's fare. I scan the lettering, picking out As, Vs, Es, and of course, Ds.

Why did he do that? Repeat himself like that. It undermines my whole sense of him. The fact that he could repeat himself so comprehensively, sentence for sentence. It must mean that he didn't register who he was talking to. He didn't know that he was talking to me. He does, after all, have a lot of friends, Dave. And it's often remarked upon how sympathetic he is, how warm, how caring. But it's also true that this quality has to be spread about a bit; a margarine of feeling.

'I have to go now.'

'But —'

'No, really. Velma. I'm going to see her. I told you.'

'Are you sure about . . . I mean that it's a good idea?' He's half rising. Bobbing slightly in the awkward, rigid gap between banquette and bolted table. With his horsy head, painted-on hair and simian arms, he looks puppet-like to me. He isn't in any sense a real Dave, this Dave. How could I be so fooled? His very posture suggests thick, yet invisible, threads running up, through the ceiling tiles, to the spatulate fingers of a giant Dave, who squats above the café, trying to coax dummy Dave into a semblance of humanity. 'Are you seeing Dr Klagfarten again today?' His brow is corrugated with ersatz angst.

'What's it to you?' I'm plunking a handful of change down on the table, rising to leave.

'Oh come on . . . I'm only concerned for you . . .'

He's concerned. Hell, *I'm* concerned. We're all fucking

concerned. We're united in concern, wouldn't you say? United like so many Stickle-bricks, pressed together to form a model society. From the door of the café I turn. All three Daves are in the same positions, frozen. Fat Dave, his hand on the big knob of the Gaggia's handle; Old Dave nodded out over the *Sporting Life*; dummy Dave still deanimate, dangling. I raise an arm, and in imitation of Dr Klagfarten swivel a palm.

I walk swiftly, listening to the arguments of my conscience: pro-Dave and anti-Dave. I know I've been stressed recently. Dr Klagfarten says I shouldn't look to any one of the several therapies we are applying for succour. Rather, I should try and apprehend them as a manifold entity, that cushions and constrains me. But even so – there just is an objective creepiness, a not-quite-rightness about Dave at the moment. Far from finding his very Daveness reassuring this morning, it has instead gravely unsettled me. I can't stand duplication. It *is* replication.

I'm heading back past the old administration building. It's not the most direct route to Velma's house, but I have a kind of urge to make contact again with Dr Klagfarten, if only in the most glancing way. Looking up, I see that a drape or curtain has been pulled across the window of his office. It reminds me of Dave's egg. If a fork like a prop for a Magritte painting were to be plunged through the window of Dr Klagfarten's office, a gush of yellow neurosis would undoubtedly ooze out.

My route to Velma's takes me across the park. As I enter, between cast-iron gates, the sun at last begins to seep through the clouds. I keep my speed up, concentrating on the internal dispositions of muscle, flesh and bone; feeling my shoes as flexible, overall calluses, attached at heel and toe.

By the brackish, oily carp pond, in the very centre of the park, a small wooden bridge is marooned on the impacted earth. Squirrels flow about, grey rivulets of rodent. The hacked and husbanded woodland here is filtering the lax sun, making for bad dappling. At a fence of waist-high, wooden palisades, two young men stand, feeding pigeons and crows.

If not foreign – they ought to be. They both wear expensive overcoats, of lamb's-wool, or cashmere. Their hair is too glossy, too dark, too curly. Even from some fifty yards away I can see the sideburns that snake down from hairlines to jawlines. They are both wearing gloves. I don't like birds at the best of times, and the pigeons and crows in this town are getting quite obese. We don't need types like these coming into our park and feeding them expensive peanuts.

The pigeons and crows rear up so. And they're so big. Today, their bipedalism makes them humanoid to me. In their greasy, feather capes of grey and black, they might be avine impersonators, hustling a sexual practice founded on fluttering and paid for in peanuts.

As I draw level with the two men, one turns away from the fence, scattering peanuts and pigeons from his gloved hands, 'See you, Dave,' says his companion, but not with any real feeling. Dave glances at me, once, but with an unexpected acuity, as if reading me. He strides away in front, kicking up small sprays of old leaves, mould and twigs. It's clear that he is uncomfortable, that he wishes to put some distance between us. I quicken my pace.

I caught him by the octagonal, wooden gazebo, used by the park staff as a place to brew up teas, and stash their tools. He was unexpectedly heavy-set, his body fluent like a waterfall beneath his soft overcoat. There was a nasty, ungainly struggle, which reflected badly on both of us. There was no symmetry, no choreography to our bestial growls and spasmodic cuffs. He went down to his knees, hard and fast, an enthusiastic convert to nonconsciousness.

There was mush on the mattock. I hefted it. It felt so light, so buoyant. I resisted an urge to hurl it up, into the bluing sky, to watch it rise to the heavens, rotating slowly on its own axis, like the transmogrified tool in 2001.

His wallet was made from slightly furry-feeling leather. Possibly pigskin. Credit cards, business cards, driving licence, kidney-donor card, all were in the name of Jonathan D. Sczm. I wondered about the D. Did it stand for David, or was Dave merely Sczm's nickname? Did it matter now?

Velma answers the door looking very grey, very drawn. She only opens the door a fraction, just far enough for me to appreciate how very grey, how very drawn she is. 'You look rather rough,' she says, 'and your jacket's all torn.'

'What's this?' I reply, gesturing, taking in the crack, the vee, of Velma. 'I'm not hawking anything here, Velma, you can take the chain off.'

'I'm – I'm not sure I can do that, I don't think I want you to come in. Dave called me from the café – he said you were in a bit of a state.'

'Oh, for fuck's sake!' I lean against the brickwork, and awkwardly kidney-punch the intervening air. I'm doing my best to affect a manner of complete naturalness – but I have the idea it isn't working.

'Dave said you had an appointment with Dr Klagfarten for three this afternoon.'

'Yeah.'

'After Dave rang, I called Dr Klagfarten, he says it would be fine if you wanted to go back there now, have a word now. He said –'

'What? What did he say?'

'He said you might be a bit upset – upset about me . . .'

'You, Velma?' I'm looking at her now, and I can see the tears swelling in her eyes. 'You? Velma?' She shakes her head.

'Not Velma, not any more, not Velma, not –' And she's sobbing now, the sobs slotting into a cycle, an hysterical cycle which she breaks, crying, 'D-Davina! Davina! That's my name! Davina!'

I'm quite taken aback by my own sang-froid. I straighten up, adopt a conciliatory but vaguely imposing demeanour. Davina is still sobbing, but subsiding. 'When you say your name is Davina now, do you mean that you've changed it by deed-poll?'

'I've applied, yes.' She's composing herself.

'How long will it take?'

'About six weeks.'

'And until then?'

'Well, you encourage the people who know you to address you as you would prefer to be addressed.' She's regained her composure altogether. 'In a sense that's what it is to have a name at all. A name is, after all, simply a certain common ascription.'

'Which in your case is –?'

'Dave.'

'Dave?'

'That's right.'

Dr Klagfarten stands with his back to me, looking out over the rooftops. The yellow-tinted glass imparts a slight, bilious whine to his voice, as he says, 'You are finding this business of the ubiquity of the name Dave unsettling, hmm?'

'Not exactly, no.' I am, for the first time since I left Dr Klagfarten's office two hours ago, at ease. He turns from

the window and retreats behind his desk. He smiles at me
and gives the endearing, lip-twisting moue.

'How would you feel if I told you that the blackbird
which flew down your chimney last week was called
Dave?'

'Both incredulous – and curious.'

'So, this Dave thing isn't entirely awful –'

'I just don't see why it has to be Dave.'

'Well, Colin Klagfarten would be patently risible, like
Ronald MacDonald. Dave Klagfarten has both resonance
and assonance.'

I take some time out to consider this proposition. Dave
goes on smiling benignly. He likes silences, he thinks that
you find yourself in the context of silence, that whether or
not silence is experienced as an absence or a presence gives
you a litmus test for your own identity.

'You aren't telling me,' I say eventually, 'that it all
begins with you?'

'No, no, of course not. This is a non-causal singularity –
of that much I'm certain, although it jibes unpleasantly
with your particular brand of alienation, of depersonalisa-
tion.

'Still, the fact that the biblical David was the individual
who most completely realised the theocratic ideal of the
Israelites, and that the yearning for his return became a
matter of almost messianic fervour . . .' A shrug, another
moue. '. . . Well, it doesn't seem to stretch the analogy
that far to suggest that this new pattern of emergent Daves
represents something similar, a secular ultramontanism
perhaps?'

'But it is *Daves*, not David.' I know I'm nit-picking, but
I can't help it.

'Oh come on, what's in an id. Look, I think you'd feel a
lot better, I think we could consider easing off on the

Parstelin, I think it might be a breakthrough. You know, we could even collaborate on a paper –'

'If I was –'

'If you were –' He's nodding, smiling, every fibre of his body exhorting me to say it, which I do:

'Dave too.'

CARING, SHARING

When Travis came out of the side door of the Gramercy Park Hotel – avoiding the guy who ran the concession stall, because earlier on he'd been embarrassed by his failure deftly to marshal the correct change – he felt pretty hollow. Brion was right behind him, and although Travis thought he really shouldn't need to, he couldn't help reaching back and clutching the emoto's forty-inch thigh.

Brion's response was immediate; he stooped down and grasping Travis by the generous scruff of his tweed suit, lifted him right up, drew him into his arms, and planted a series of wet kisses on Travis's face, while all the time patting his back and muttering soothing endearments.

Travis felt all the knotted tension in his neck and shoulders begin to ebb away. It was a palpable sensation, just as if the emoto had been rubbing some balm into his exposed skin. Travis sighed deeply and snuggled further into the warm-smelling gap between the brushed cotton collar of Brion's shirt and the prickly tweed of his suit collar. Travis always dressed his emoto the same as himself. He knew that some people found it intolerably gauche, like putting twins in matching sailor suits, but he loved Brion so much – the emoto wasn't *just* an emoto, more an aspect of Travis himself.

And Brion smelt good. He smelt of Imperial Leather

soap and Ralph Lauren aftershave. He smelt of sweat and cocktail fish. He smelt of flannel and cigarette smoke. He smelt – in short – very much like Travis himself. Even Brion's kisses smelt good; Travis could feel a slick patch of the emoto's saliva on his upper lip, but he had no urge – as he might with any other individual's secretions – to wipe it off. Instead, he gently scented the enzymic odours, while idly considering whether or not emotos had the same chemicals in their bodies as other humans. They couldn't be exactly the same, because emotos couldn't drink alcohol – or smoke for that matter; and that implied some different oils, boiling in the pullulating refineries of their massive bodies.

Travis didn't like thinking about the inside of Brion's body – it made him distinctly queasy. So he cancelled the observation and snuggled still deeper into the sheltering arms. The emoto's vast hands smarmed over Travis's back, over his shoulders, smoothed down his hair, so gentle, yet so firm. Travis heard Brion's voice rumble in his chest before the words reached his muffled ears, 'Are you worried about the date tonight, Travis?'

Travis stiffened. The word 'date' – how he hated it. It put him in mind of the fruit, not two adults enjoying each other's company. 'You don't even like the word, do you?' The comforting hand almost completely encapsulated Travis's head, as if it were a helmet of flesh and tendon and bone. The voice was beautifully modulated, sonorous even. The emoto's words seemed to come zinging straight to Travis's heart, each one with a top spin of sympathy.

'It makes me think of the fruit . . .' he muttered. Brion chuckled in a rumbly sort of way and hugged him still harder. Hugged Travis and lifted him high up in the early evening air, twisting the grown-up's body as he did so, gifting Travis a few seconds of Gramercy Park upside-down. Travis noted an old douche bag, clanking with jewellery, walking her miniature Schnauzer on the roof of the world. Then Brion deftly lowered him, and bestowing one, final drooly kiss on Travis's forehead, set him back neatly on his feet.

'You shouldn't worry so much,' Brion admonished Travis. 'I'm sure Karin is just as anxious about the whole thing as you are. She probably thinks of the fruit too. Now come on, we better get going if we've got to head uptown.' Brion's armchair hand descended once more and cupping Travis's back, the emoto pushed his grown-up gently in the direction of Madison Avenue. As they walked under a canopy tethering a townhouse to the sidewalk, Brion had to duck down, but then he straightened up, and the two tweed-suited figures, one about six feet tall, the other closer to fourteen, ambled away and were presently engulfed by the croaking roar of Manhattan.

Three miles to the north, in the West Seventies, Travis's date for the evening, Karin, *was* feeling just as uneasy. She was even on the verge of cancelling altogether. Karin had met Travis a couple of weeks ago at a wine tasting arranged by her friend Ariadne. The event was a pure snob thing – Ariadne wanted to show off her wine cellar and her new SoHo loft apartment-cum-studio; which was big enough – Karin had reflected – to enable Auguste Rodin, Henry Moore and Damien Hirst to work alongside one another, with little danger of them muddling up tools, or materials. Really, an exorbitant waste of space when you considered the further fact that Ariadne herself was a miniaturist.

Ariadne's friends were mostly the usual *faux* bohos who congregated in the environs of SoHo, Greenwich Village and Tribeca; affecting the style of penniless, fifties, *rive gauche* students; while living on the income from vast tranches of AT & T stock. These types were always on the verge of exhibiting, publishing, constructing, filming or presenting *something*, but never actually managed it. At one of Ariadne's soirées, a young man with pigtails had even deliriously informed Karin that he was about to present a presentation. 'What do you mean?' Karin politely queried. 'Y'know, make a pitch for a pitch, I guess . . .'

'And if you get the pitch?'

'Aw, hell, I dunno . . . I dunno if I want to follow through that far.'

Karin wandered away from this absurd reductivism. Later, she was pleased to see that the pigtailed pitcher had had to be carried out by his emoto, dead drunk, more incoherency falling along with the drool from his slack mouth.

But on the night of the wine tasting nobody much got drunk – and Karin met Travis. Travis, who seemed initially a little creepy in his immaculately cut English-retro tweed suit. Travis, who smoked, which meant he had to stand out on the fire escape, engaging her in flirtatious conversation through the window. Karin couldn't really approve of the smoking, but nor could she condemn it. In fact, she found something faintly racy and daring about Travis on that first encounter, certainly in comparison to the posing *rentiers*, who were swirling their wine glasses around in the studio as if to the château born.

Travis, it transpired, knew a great deal about wine; or 'fine wine' as he invariably referred to it. He could tell a Chareau-Carré Muscadet from a white Bordeaux by bouquet alone. He knew the names of all the varieties of phylloxera, their life cycles and their effects. He had once rafted down the Rhône, stopping for a bottle of wine in every vineyard he passed. But there was nothing overbearing or self-satisfied in the way he retailed all of this knowledge and experience. Rather, it seemed to be an essential mannerism of the man to be tirelessly self-effacing, albeit with such an ironic inflection to his voice, that it was clear he had a perfectly healthy opinion of his own wit and talents.

'I'm basically a wealthy dilettante –' He paused, his long upper lip twitching with self-deprecation. 'And not a very good one at that.'

'How d'you figure that?' Karin thought she sounded like some whiny co-ed – his diction was so studied.

'Because I can't really settle to anything, the way you have. I just flit from one hobby to the next. But I enjoy my enthusiasms – if that isn't something of a contradiction in terms.'

Karin had told Travis all about the small dress-making business she ran. How she had turned her two-room apartment in the twenties into a miniature atelier, staffed by six deft Filipino seamstresses. How she had made a considerable name for herself selling near-couture to wealthy Manhattanites. And how she had now been offered, by an enormous fashion business, a *prêt-à-porter* range of her own.

Travis listened to all of this intently, nodding and gifting polite noises of encouragement in the correct places. When Karin finally faltered he asked exactly the right question: 'D'you also make clothes for emotos?'

'Oh sure, actually I'm really best known for my fashion wear for emotos. Some people, y'know, some people find it easier to do a bias cut using a bigger expanse of cloth –'

'I guess that's to do with the weight and tensility of the fabric,' Travis replied, in his rather tense, weighty fashion. Karin couldn't believe it – a presentable, youngish man in Manhattan who knew what a bias cut was.

'Is your emoto here?' Travis asked after a short while.

'Yeah, Jane, she's the one with the long blonde hair, over there.' She pointed to the section of the loft that had been set aside for the emotos. Suitably enough this was in the highest section, where a trapezoid skylight formed a twenty-foot-high roof space. A table had been set up for the emotos – a table that was to their scale, about six feet high – and on it were five litre jugs full of Kool-Aid and root beer and cherry cola, the kind of sweet, sickly drinks that emotos preferred. The emotos were supping these and engaging in the slightly infantile banter that passed for conversation among them.

There were about ten emotos, and they were of all types: black, white, old, young. But Travis's and Karin's were easy to spot, for, naturally, they were both dressed identically to their grown-ups. Travis laughed. He turned first to Karin and then to Jane. He compared the trim, thirtyish blonde in front of him to the lissom, twelve-foot emoto at the far end of the loft. Both wore the same well-cut jackets that flared from the hip; and the same velveteen leggings tucked into snakeskin ankle boots. Both had their straight blonde hair cut into bangs, and Travis was even more amused to note that Karin had equipped her emoto with a heavy, scalloped silver choker necklace, the same as her own. This must have cost a great deal of money.

'And that's . . . ?' Karin pointed at the chunky, fourteen-foot emoto in the immaculately cut, English-retro tweed suit.

'Brion – yeah, that's my emoto. We've been together a long, long time. In fact, he's the same emoto that I had when I left group home –'

'Snap!' Karin cried. 'I've been with Jane since I was sixteen too.'

At this point the emotos concerned came over to give their grown-ups a much needed cuddle. Jane, coming up behind Karin, leant down and draped her flawless white hands over the grown-up's shoulders. Then she pulled Karin backwards, so as to nuzzle the grown-up's entire body against her crotch and lower belly. Brion did pretty much the same thing to Travis; so that the two grown-ups continued their conversation from within the grottoes of these massive embraces.

Perhaps it was the security of Jane's arms around her, or that Travis was – in his own eccentric fashion – almost alluring, which made the idea of them meeting again, perhaps enjoying a meal, a movie or a gallery visit together, seem a good one. Jane took Karin's organiser out of her shoulder bag – which for reasons of convenience also held her grown-up's shoulder bag – and Karin exchanged numbers with Travis. Brion had an outsize, Smythe's of Bond Street, leather-bound address book, in which he noted down Karin's numbers with an outsize, gold propelling pencil. 'Wow!' Karin exclaimed. 'Can your emoto *write*?'

Brion laughed. 'No-no, Karin, I don't need to write – Travis does that for me – but I like to make the shapes of numbers!' Both the grown-ups laughed at this typical display of emoto naivety – and that too cemented their acquaintance.

They had both left the wine tasting shortly after this; and the last Karin had seen of her new friend was Travis's face, blooming, like some tall, orchidaceous buttonhole, above the solid tweed ridge of his emoto's shoulder, as Brion bore him off in the direction of Riverside Drive.

That had been a fortnight ago. Travis called Karin a week after the wine tasting and with commendable dispatch suggested they have dinner together. 'What? You mean like a date?' She couldn't keep the incredulity out of her voice.

'Erm . . . yuh . . . well . . .' It was oddly reassuring to hear how discomfited he was. 'I guess it would be a date, sort of.'

'Travis, I haven't been on a date for four years –'

'Snap!' He almost shouted down the phone, and that bonded them with laughter once more. 'I haven't been on a date for four years; and I'll tell you something else, I can't stand the very word – it makes me think of fruit –'

'Fruit?'

'Y'know – dates . . .'

This last little revelation hadn't struck such a chord with Karin, but she still agreed to meet Travis on the evening of the 29th April at the Royalton Hotel. 'You're in the seventies,' he'd said. 'I'm in the twenties – we'll split the difference. Then if things are going well we can head downtown for dinner.' He sounded a great deal surer on the phone than he felt. It was true, Travis hadn't been on a date for four years, and he hadn't slept over with anyone for nearing a decade.

Karen had had a sleepover more recently. About two years ago she'd met a man called Emil at a weekend beach party out on Long Island.

Emil was small, dark, Austrian, in his forties. He'd been living in New York for eight years, and had had an emoto – Dave – for the last five. Emil admitted, frankly, that he'd been a procro in Salzburg, where he'd run a fashionable restaurant before deciding to emigrate. Karin took this in her stride. Emil was very charming, seemed absolutely sincere, and his relationship with Dave was unimpeachable – the big black emoto cradled his little grown-up with obvious affection. Lots of grown-ups had started out as procros and then decided that the whole messy business of sexual and emotional entanglement wasn't for them – there was no shame, or obloquy in that. And just as many procros had found, after getting on in life a bit, that what they wanted more than anything else in the world was the absolute reassurance that an emoto would provide them with. If these procros were lucky the awakening would coincide with children growing up, leaving home, and they could slide without too much disruption from their procro-union to a proper, grown-up relationship with an emoto.

Emil led Karin to understand that this had been the case with him: 'My ex-wife and I met and married when we were very young, you know. We both came from poor families, the kind of background where there were very few grown-ups, very few emotos. I suppose we were happy in a way – we knew no better. But slowly, over the years, the relentlessness of being with someone the whole time . . . someone who you touch intimately' – his voice dropped lower – 'touch sexually . . . Well, you know the terrible things that can happen.' He shuddered, snuggled deeper into his emoto's firehose-thick arms. 'Eventually, after our daughter had gone – at her own request, I must say – to a group home, we were both able to become grown-ups. We're still good friends though, and I see her whenever Dave and I go back to Salzburg – which is a lot. Dave and I even have four-way sleepovers with Mitzi and her emoto, Gudrun.'

They had spent most of that day chatting, both of them cuddled by their emotos; the childlike giants standing waist deep in the ocean swell, cradling their respective grown-ups in their arms. 'There is nothing more sensuous,' Karin had said to Emil in an unguarded moment, 'than the smell of wet emoto skin, wet emoto hair, and the great wet ocean.' Emil gave her a peculiar sideways look.

But Jane had taken to Dave, and encouraged Karin to see Emil. Jane had dinner with Emil twice; and he'd taken her once to the Met, to see *Don Giovanni*. On all three occasions he was charm itself, courtly and leisured; as if, Karin had thought, the Habsburgs were the patrons of taste, rather than Texaco. If later, Karin felt awful for not paying proper attention to the subtext of Emil's charms, it was because she blamed herself. Blamed herself for not paying attention and for putting her trust in Jane's emoto intuition. After all, emotos weren't meant to protect you from others – only from yourself.

On their fourth date Emil suggested that Karen and Jane might like to sleep over at his apartment. Dave nodded his great cropped head vigorously. 'It'll be great!' he said to Jane – and the rest of them. 'We can play together in the morning!' The grown-ups laughed, but it was really Jane who sealed the deal, crying out, 'Yes! With pillows too!'

'Isn't that typical of an emoto!' Emil exclaimed when he and Karin were at last alone together. 'They really can be just like kids –'

'But they aren't.'

'I'm sorry?' Emil was momentarily querulous, shocked by the intensity of her reaction.

'They aren't children. They don't grow – they're big already. They don't make demands on you – you make demands on them. They don't have to be dressed, fed, wiped or groomed in any other way. They have good intuitions – and good dress sense if you trouble to develop it . . .' Karin tailed off, realising that she was beginning to sound oddly impassioned. She was, also, already missing Jane, although the two emotos had only left their grown-ups a few minutes before.

Emil's apartment was on the Upper East Side, and the last thing Karin had seen before going to bed that fateful night were the soaring piles of the Van Eyck Expressway legging over the river's rumpled pewter, so solid, so supportive, so emotolike.

Karin was sleeping in the main bedroom, Emil in the spare. The emotos were closeted in the old water tank on top of the block, which Emil had tastefully converted – like many other financially clever Manhattanite grown-ups – for emoto use. But during the night, despite the friendly locks on the door of the bedroom (friendly because they were bolts), Emil managed to get into the room. Presumably he had a secret passage, or some even stranger means of entry . . .

These thoughts were thumping with awful inconsequence through Karin's mussed mind as she stared at the dapper little man who was sitting beside her, on the edge of the bed, entirely self-possessed, wearing black silk pyjamas, and with his dumpy, manicured hands arranged neatly in his lap. At least he never actually touched her – that was something. But the violation of his presence was enough. To have him, at night, alone, this close to her, this *able* to touch her was – terrifying. Karin didn't so much know that she wanted Jane – as scream it. The scream was the knowledge. Karin screamed and screamed and screamed; at the same time she groped for the emotopager she had slung to one side of the bed a couple of hours before. The first scream chopped off what Emil had been trying to say to her: 'All I want's a little cud –' For ever afterwards Karin wondered what exactly it was that he'd wanted, 'a little cud', it was strangely enigmatic, unlike the man himself, who had been revealed as no grown-up – but a potential rapist.

There was that odd, shadowing memory of the sexual

assault, and there was another discrepancy which Karin kept stuffed to the back of her mind, lest it rock too much the frail boat of her own sanity. Karin knew that Jane and Dave had to have been asleep – that's what emotos did at night, just like other humans. What's more, the emotos were sleeping three storeys up, on top of the building – so it couldn't have been Karin's screams that had woken them; and at the time, even through the fog of fear, she had, with bizarre clarity, appreciated that it might take Jane many minutes to reach her. But in fact Jane was there in seconds. There, and cradling Karin to her massive breast. There, and palming off Emil. There and admonishing Emil in that peculiarly affecting way that emotos – creatures devoid of any vestige of aggression-promoting sexuality – have: 'You've scared, Karin, why did you do it? Oh Emil – this ruins everything. Oh Emil! If you touched her we shall have to call the police –' In the corner Dave cowered, unsure of whether it was safe for him to go and comfort his own emoto. Emil looked inscrutable – altogether beyond cuddling. Dave was naked – another anomaly Karin filed in a bottle.

'It's OK,' Karin nearly shouted, she was so relieved to be able to respond, to react, not to be just a *thing* under the Austrian's bland brown eyes. 'He didn't touch me.'

Jane gave her a searching look and adjudging that this was the truth, scooped up Karin, her clothes, her bag, and before her grown-up had had a chance to respond in any other way, she found herself being borne north towards the corner of the park: 'We can get a taxivan there,' said the willowy emoto, still holding Karin tightly to her. Jane never said anything more about the assault – and nor did Karin.

Not until tonight, that is. Karin sighed again. It was too late to call it off now – Travis would be on his way; and he didn't look like the kind of man who carried a phone with him, more the type to use a liveried servant, porting a missive on a salver. Thinking of this aspect of Travis, his unforced anachronism, made Karen smile. With such an innately gallant man, surely nothing could go wrong? There was this sense of security and there was the tangible security of Jane's arms. As ever, the emoto had sensed her mood perfectly, sashayed across the room and taken the grown-up in her arms. Karen marvelled anew at the grace of the giantess, and her physical perfection. Some emotos were so gross: the genetic effect of pumping the human frame up to two or three times its normal size could have bizarre consequences. Some emotos had hair as thick as wire on their bodies; and if they got bad acne it was truly something to behold, like the Grand Canyon at sunset.

But Jane was perfection. Her skin a delicate honey shade; the down that covered it universally white-blonde; and soft, so soft. Karin relaxed back into the down, allowed herself to be enfolded by the honey. She felt the lower belly and pubic mound of the emoto nuzzle between her shoulder blades. Funny how an emoto's touch was so intimate, so comforting, and yet so utterly devoid of sexuality – let alone eroticism. The idea of Jane's vast vagina being employed in the nonsensical, animal jerkings of copulation was unthinkable, like imagining Botticelli's Venus squeezing a blackhead, or a chimpan-zee addressing both houses of Congress.

Karin relaxed. Jane went on squeezing her in just the right way, swaying gently the while. New effusions of greenery on the trees lining the block below struck Karin's eye with a fresh intensity. It was a beautiful spring evening, she was young, she was secure, perhaps she was even ready for some experimentation, for some fun.

Karin broke from the embrace and turned to face Jane, her arms outstretched. 'Carry?' she asked.

The evening went far, far better than either grown-up could have hoped for – and as for the emotos? Well, they rubbed along pretty well, much as they always do.

Travis hadn't only seized on the Royalton for reasons of mutual convenience – it also made a good talking point. Well past its fashionable sell-by date, the hotel's décor retailed a series of dazzlingly crass decadences, which Travis knew provided salience for his own sepia image. To go anywhere more established, or timeless in its own right, would only set his own fuzzy grasp on contemporaneity off to lesser effect. But in the large, modernist lobby bar of the Royalton, with its primary curves and aerodynamically sound light fitments, he would be thrown into sharp relief, and he would be able to entertain Karin with his pointed remarks about the waxing and waning of status, of money, of beauty, of all things human.

Brion and Travis arrived about twenty minutes early. The emoto ducked down to enter, and then gratefully stretched when they entered the airier purlieus of the bar. 'D'you want to join me, Brion?' Travis asked him as the emoto set him gently down, Church's brogues meeting deep pile with the merest of kisses.

Brion seemed to think for a moment, and a shadow of near-reasoning crossed his ample, freckled brow. 'No, that's all right, Travis, I'll set myself down here.' He gestured to the emotos' portion of the bar. 'You get yourself a dry martini – you deserve it for getting this close to the fruit.'

Was there a trace of irony in Brion's remark? Travis wondered as he walked to the other end of the bar, where he waited to be seated. That was impossible; emotos might have highly developed emotional intelligences – that's what made them so good at caring, at sharing; but irony demanded an ability to realise dramatically situations that was far beyond their mental age, hovering as it did at around seven. Some grown-ups – Travis knew one or two – had emotos with higher mental ages, but they were regarded askance by the majority, almost as if they were engaging in a peculiar form of abuse.

All this weighed heavily on Travis while he waited to be seated. He didn't want to be thinking about emotos in this way, at this time, he had to concentrate on the fruit. However, once he'd been deposited by the graceful waiter in the elegant chair, and had a dry vodkatini the size of a vase deposited with him, Travis began to unwind. He was amused to see a new piece of status style-slavery at the Royalton. The bar seats for grown-ups had always been colour coded, so as to reflect the relative importance of their tenants. High rollers were placed in the purple thronelets, less important ones in the red, and so on, all the way down to the gawking hicks in from the boonies, who were stacked unceremoniously in a distant gulag of far smaller, white-covered chairs. Now the management had taken it upon themselves to do the same with the chairs in the emoto portion of the bar. However, as there were fewer of these, and they were much larger, it was impossible to create proper sections. Instead, the waiters in this area had to wait and see where the emoto's respective grown-up was sitting, then seat them accord-ingly – if possible.

Travis was pleased that Brion had got the purple, and he was just thinking how he might frame this latest bit of Manhattan lunacy as an anecdote for Karin, when she was there in front of him. Travis leapt up, seated her, and without preliminary small talk, launched straight into his Royalton riffs. Karin, far from being discomfited, roared with laughter as he deconstructed the trappings of the luxury hotel. Travis was getting ready to vouchsafe a genuine indiscretion, concerning a certain film star and her football team-sized posse of emotos, when he caught himself. 'But I'm rambling on, I haven't let you get a word in edgeways, and worst of all I haven't told you how radiantly beautiful you're both looking tonight.'

The effect was as instantaneous as it was desired. Karin blushed and tilted her head in a disarming, almost girlish way, turning in the process so that she was angled in the direction of Jane. Although the female emoto was over fifty feet away, and deep in chatter with Brion, she looked up and smiled as well. Clearly, Travis thought, they have a high level of tele-empathy, a good sign. Of course, Travis's compliment hadn't been paid out of any other account but that of The Truth. He wasn't a shameless flatterer, and anyway, Karin just *was* looking fantastic. She was wearing a black silk sheath dress, cut in an interesting, asymmetrical way across the bodice; her thick blonde hair was up, and her sole accessory was the heavy silver necklace, which Travis remembered from the wine tasting in SoHo. Turning to Jane, he observed how well the same dress hung on her far larger frame. He turned to Karin once more. 'Tell me, was this pattern originally cut for Jane or you?' and was rewarded with another peal of joyful laughter.

If things went well at the Royalton, once they got in the taxivan and headed downtown, they began to go – as Travis himself might have said – swimmingly. There was something about these situations that was almost instinctively memorable, something that both grown-ups and emotos intuitively understood: the two grown-ups, intelligent, rational, foresighted; and their two emoto charges, who might be physically larger, warmer and more responsive, more caring; but who wouldn't last for five minutes alone on the scabrous city streets.

The four discovered such ease in each other's company, that within minutes they were developing the syntax and grammar of a cliquey argot. Brion, staring as he always did, out of the back window as the darkened streets and lit blocks strobed past, had spotted a rollerblader coursing through the cars on the far side of the avenue. 'Wow!' he exclaimed – as he always did. 'Those high heels sure let that man go zippy!' Both Karen and Jane laughed, and the emotos high-fived, which is all the physical contact they ever seemed to have with one another. From then on in 'Go zippy!' was one of their gathering number of catch phrases, to be rolled around and then expelled with gusto, as if it were an assayed sip of one of Travis's 'fine wines'.

The restaurant Travis had initially chosen for the evening, Chez-Chez, with its heavy Lyonnaise cuisine, didn't really suit the fruit he was engaged on; so after laboriously rethinking the whole nature of the event, running over his slender stock of Karin intelligence, and even going so far as to ring up Ariadne and ask some circumspect questions, he opted instead for the twin pillars of idiocy: the Royalton and the Bowery Brasserie. He wouldn't be able to smoke there – which might make him a bit nervous, but that there would be plenty to joke about and lots of noise and colour would compensate.

They quit the taxivan. The night was clear, stars wheeling over the jagged cityscape, its stanchions and aerials, fire stairs and emoto-housing converted water tanks. The Bowery Brasserie, like many of the more fashionable Manhattan eateries, had its own sub-restaurant specifically catering to emotos. This was simply called 'The Emoto Hole'. Brion grinned hugely when he realised where they were – like most emotos he had hardly any capacity for effective orientation – and turning to his rangy companion said laughingly, 'You'll love this place, Jane, they've even got root beer on tap!' Once again the grown-ups joined in the effervescent, conspiratorial merriment that the mature traditionally share with the immature.

When they had got their emotos settled next door, Travis and Karin entered the Brasserie and were shown to their table. Travis ordered a bottle of Montrachet and asked Karin, 'D'you mind being apart from your emoto? Because personally I'd rather eat with Brion all the time.'

He was delighted when she replied, 'I feel pretty much the same way,' and then amazed as she told him why.

Karin had made the commitment to tell Travis about what had happened with Emil, when she made the final decision not to stand him up at the Royalton. What was the point, she reasoned, in even going on a date if she wasn't – at least in principle – prepared to consider the possibility of a sleepover? And if Travis couldn't handle it? Well, Jane made the point that he couldn't be worth a great deal.

Travis sat rapt while she told the awful story, nodding and muttering the occasional 'Omigod' in the right places. When she had finished he said very simply, 'Karin, that is hellish, you're a very brave woman,' then went on to amaze her still more than she had amazed him, by fully identifying. Moreover, it wasn't only that the same thing had happened to Travis, but that it had been far far worse. The woman who invited him home for an innocuous sleepover actually *touched* Travis, and intimately, before Brion had managed to come to his rescue. Travis played it down, but Karin could tell that he was massively relieved to get the whole thing off his chest, for he had, naturally, told no one about it.

Which explained his diffidence, and also the very close relationship with his emoto. It also helped to explain his dilettantism; for Travis revealed, *en passant*, that at that time he was assaulted he had been a vastly successful antique dealer, and the abuser one of his clients. Karin understood perfectly that after such an experience he had had to retire.

But while the confessions had been risky on both sides, and the chasms of intimacy they had opened up would've appeared impossible to traverse with the slender bridge of conversation alone, Travis and Karin were after all grown-ups, and so they passed on to other subjects. By the time the entrée had been and gone, the date had swum its way into becoming a veritable whale of a time.

There was no awareness on either side as to who had suggested the idea of coffee and brandy at Travis's house, but both understood what would happen when Karin agreed. Travis said, 'To be frank I'm really gasping for a Havana; and things being still as they are . . .' He shrugged. 'But anyway,' he continued, paradoxically in a breezier fashion, 'if we need either Jane or Brion we can always page them!' and with a flourish he showed her his miniature emotopager, which was concealed beneath the boss of his signet. In return Karin mutely displayed her purpose-built necklace emotopager. They both understood that this was a profound event.

It was a pleasant night, on the cusp of being balmy, so the foursome walked uptown from the Bowery. The grown-ups took the lead, while the emotos followed on behind in their shambling fashion. Glancing back at them Karin remarked, 'It's funny, isn't it, Travis, how when it comes to giving a grown-up a cuddle, or carrying us, or kissing us, emotos are so graceful and deft, but any activity outside of that seems to give them such difficulty.'

'That's why they're emotos,' he replied with finality.

Karin knew plenty of wealthy people, but had never had a friend who actually owned an entire brownstone; let alone one in Gramercy Park. The house was beautiful from the outside, the delicate wrought-iron balconies just beginning to froth with the wisteria that would enmesh them as the summer progressed. Inside the house was furnished in such a way as to suggest both opulence and austerity. Travis hadn't cluttered the rooms, but in each there were a couple of extremely good pieces culled from his antique-dealing days. He showed Karin around the place from top to bottom. 'It's amazing how big these houses are . . . Oh! Gee! Is that what I *think* it is?'

'Hepplewhite, yeah; and that's a Frank Lloyd Wright chair, Chicago 1907.'

He showed her the master bedroom, which had its own emoto room *en suite*. 'That's neat,' said Karin, who was now so relaxed she was content to mouth banalities.

Travis smiled gently. 'I'll show you what's neater.' They continued on up the switchback staircase. On the next floor there was another grown-up-emoto suite, and there was the same on the storey above. 'I guess it's something I thought of after the . . . y'know . . . I thought really I'd rather Brion were on hand during the night, should I need a bit of reassurance, a cuddle, whatever. I know a lot of people prefer to have their emotos closeted up on the roof for the night, but . . . well . . .'

'I understand,' Karin said – and she really did.

They drank a brandy that had been distilled in the year of the Wall Street crash. Travis puffed a Patargas Perfecto. On an antique Victrola Chaliapin creaked and groaned his way through 'The Song of the Volga Boatmen'. They sat facing one another in matching art-deco armchairs, which had semicircular backs inlaid with tortoiseshell. In the shadowy periphery of the room the emotos slouched on a scaled-up divan, drinking Slush Puppies and exchanging the shy glances of overgrown youngsters.

Karin wished the evening could go on for ever. As it was she drank three brandies – and that on top of the two bottles of wine they had shared at the restaurant, *and* the paddling pool of vodkatini she'd supped at the Royalton. Yet she didn't feel drunk – if anything the reverse. It was as if, having cracked the whole hideous problem of dating again, she was liberated, set free into a new kind of intimacy. Karin thought that, as long as she always had Jane with her, always there to care for her, she could cope even with the intimacy of a sleepover.

'You look tired,' said Travis after Chaliapin had creaked and groaned up and down the Volga several times, and Ma Rainey had ululated 'Titantic Man Blues' at least three. 'Would you like Brion to show you and Jane up?'

Karin gathered herself together, Jane came over louring – after all she couldn't help it. Their combined bags were dangling from the emoto's – proportionately – slim wrist. 'No, it's OK, I think we can find our own way.' Karin stood and looked down levelly at Travis, noticing for the first time what a very sky shade of blue his twinkling eyes were. 'Travis.' Her voice dipped into sincerity. 'I just want to thank you for everything, the drinks, the meal, your lovely house . . . It really has been . . . peachy!' They all laughed at this – the fruit gag was well on its way to being iconic.

For a long time after Karin and Jane had left the room Travis sat, silently sipping his brandy and drawing on his Perfecto. Eventually he cleared his throat to summon

Brion, and when the big Celtic emoto was beside him, he reached up his arms and uttered the command that ended all of their days: 'Carry!'

Brion gently lifted Travis up, one massive arm behind his back and the other tucked neatly under the grown-up's legs; and porting him thus like some giant baby, he smoothly exited the room, climbed the angled stair and entered the master suite. Setting Travis down, upright, next to the Second Empire bed, with its curved footboard, and extravagant, overarching pediment, Brion started to undress him, efficiently stripping off the lineaments of Travis's anachronism to reveal first Calvin Klein under-wear, and then latterly the robust, healthy body of a fit man in his middle thirties. 'Pjs?' the emoto queried, and his grown-up nodded acquiescence.

At last Brion had Travis settled in bed. The grown-up lay, arms outside the covers, pyjama top neatly buttoned, looking like some old-fashioned illustration; to complete the engraving the pocket Gargantua sat by him, one atlas hand ever so softly smoothing Travis's sand-blond hair. Travis sighed, 'Night-night, Brion.'

'Night-night, Travis,' the emoto sighed back at him. And in due course the grown-up was asleep.

As was Karin in the suite of rooms upstairs. Jane looked down into her already flickering eyelids with an expression that changed, as she realised her grown-up was definitively unconscious, from cloying compassion to decided relief. She rose from the bedside and shook herself down, as some great mastiff or indeed any other fine, healthy, unneurotic creature might shake itself down after a dousing.

Jane strode to the window, her six feet-long legs divinely scissoring apart the hip-length slash in her dully scintillating silk dress, and picked up her bag. She drew out a five-litre catering bottle of Stolichnaya vodka, sheathed in a coolant sleeve, and holding it to the light from the window, sighed appreciatively to see that the bottle was still frosted. The emoto reached into the bag again and drew out a pack of twenty regular Marlboro and a disposable plastic lighter. These items might have appeared queer in such large hands had they been actual size – but they weren't; they too were scaled up for the use of the emoto, the Marlboro pack the size of a paperback, the lighter as long as a pencil. Holding the long lighter aloft, like a cheap beacon, Jane made her way with ginger grace to the door, opened it, ducked down and withdrew her mighty trunk and endless limbs from the room.

Jane encountered Brion on the half-landing a floor below. The male emoto was backing out of his grown-up's bedroom in much the same way as Jane had: retracting his body in a series of phased movements as he squeezed under the dwarfish lintel. He straightened up to his full, magnificent height. Even in the wan light of the stairwell – provided by two unusual baroque electroliers Travis had snapped up in Venice – Jane could see the shadows of intelligence and amusement pass across Brion's handsome countenance. Jane held the long lighter to one side of her face and the frozen Stoli to the other. 'Party?' she mouthed. Brion grinned hugely and indicated with a series of significant head jerks that they should go downstairs.

Back in the main sitting room of the house, the antique Victrola was curled on the floor, casting its analogous, auricular shadow. The light – orange street stuff – cast itself in splashes on the rich patterning of the Persian rug, working up a beautiful palette. Jane went to the window, while Brion carefully shut the double doors leading to the stairs. She undid the cap of the bottle of vodka and took a long, shuddering pull on it. The great female's throat pulsed and in four large gulps she had managed to decimate the contents. She set the bottle down on the windowsill, and taking out one of the mutant Marlboros, lit it with a flourish of the long lighter. Jane expelled the smoke in a series of hisses and pops: the Morse code of satiation.

Brion had finished securing the door. He hit the lights and the golden oldie tones of the room sprang back up. 'So,' Brion said, 'despite her terrible experiences, and her terrible nerves, she managed to fall asleep in someone else's house for the first time in years?' His voice wasn't just freighted with irony – it was sinking under the weight of it.

'Yup, that's about it – of course that Tylenol/Nytol/ Valium combo helps no end.' The babyish lilt was excised from Jane's voice; and in its place were the definite tones of a woman of the world.

'Poor old Travis.' Brion shook his big, Roman senatorial head. 'He adds Prozac to that downbeat cocktail, sad fucker. I don't think he knows whether he can sleep naturally or not any more, he's been necking them for such a long time.'

'So there's no chance of him waking?'

'None at all – and Karin?'

'Nix. The only thing that could wake the beauty up would be what? A kiss? She'd die!'

'Which leaves us.'

'Indeed. Us. Drink?'

Brion accepted the vodka tank and drained a further tenth of it. He then took a pituitary-case Marlboro from the proffered pack and lit it by pressing its dead end against her live tip. For a few moments the two emotos experienced ignition, then he broke. 'My God!' he guffawed. 'What a nerd – "I do hope you wouldn't mind joining me . . . If it's not too much . . . That would be lovely . . ."

Never saying what he fucking means – never meaning what he fucking said.' The male emoto's voice was below basso; it had ultrasonic undertones which caused the glass of the window they were standing by to vibrate. But now there was no irony in that voice, nor sarcasm, but a genuine – if hideously patronising – concern.

Jane took another hefty draught of vodka before answering – between them they'd now dealt with a quarter of the five litres; then she drawled through a hedge of blue curlicues, '*Fucking* would hardly be the operative word, now would it?'

He snorted, 'No, I guess not, the poor little etiolated mice –'

'Which leaves you – and me.'

'Indeed.' Jane studied Brion a bit more, he really was the most astonishingly handsome male, and freed of the soppy expression he adopted to deal with his grown-up's puling anxiety, he had a countenance of nobility and gravity, tempered by a wild humorousness. Jane found herself saying – rather than said, 'Brion, would you show me your body – please?'

He stripped the foulard tie from his neck with one swipe; he shrugged his shoulders and his suit jacket fell like a theatre curtain; the shirt ballooned away from him; the trousers unsheathed; the underpants were kicked; and finally the socks – and attendant garters – were shot by Brion into the corners of the room, like kids fire off elastic bands. They were both laughing, but she was marvelling, marvelling at the great slab-sided length of him; marvelling at the marbled skin with its endearing rash of brown moles; marvelling at the flames of hair that burned in his crotch; marvelling at his beautiful, two-foot cock. It was curved up prominently; symbol and reality priapically nailed together.

Karen bent down so that her long hair swept the floor. She grasped the hem of her dress with crossed hands and, with a movement not unlike a nursery-school pupil impersonating the growth of a tree, she shed her silken foliage. Then she too was resplendent in the night light and it was Brion's turn to marvel. But before long they were locked in passionate, needful, delirious and athletic congress. The emotos were so large that they could simultaneously brace themselves against either wall, so as to achieve exciting contortions. It would have been fearful – this orgiastic clash of the Titans – were it not for the fact that they were both so beautiful, and so clearly in love with the moment.

When at last they were spent, and lay wrapped demurely in the Persian rug which had been yanked from the floor by their thrashings, Brion lit a Meta-Marlboro with the lanky lighter and turning to Jane, cupped her big face in his big hand. 'Just remember,' he winked at her, 'don't say a word to the grown-ups.'

TOUGH, TOUGH TOYS FOR TOUGH, TOUGH BOYS

B ill saw him about five miles after he had powered past the Dornoch turning. The hitchhiker was walking with one foot in the newly minted road, and one on the just-born verge. He was wearing some kind of cheap plastic poncho, which didn't really cover the confused pack on his back. There were no road markings, as yet, on this fresh stretch. Two hundred metres before he saw the hitchhiker, Bill had passed one of the road workers holding a lollipop sign with GO written on it in white-out-of-green capitals. The traffic was thick – solid files moving at twenty miles an hour in both directions. The cars were kicking up spray, and from out of the sharp blue sky, big, widely spaced drops of rain descended.

The hitchhiker was trying simultaneously to turn and give the car drivers a come-hither grin, keep his footing on the uneven surface, and shelter himself under his plastic poncho. It was, Bill thought, a pathetic sight. There was that, and also an indefinable something about the hitchhiker's bearing – Bill thought later, and then thought that he had thought so at the time, in the precise moment foot slipped from accelerator to brake – which he recognised as being not that of a tourist, but someone going somewhere with a purpose, not unlike Bill himself.

Bill had spent the night at Mrs McRae's bed and

breakfast, at Bighouse on the northern coast of Caithness. In the blustery evening, after a poorly microwaved pie – there was a chilly nugget in its doughy heart – he had stumped to the public phone, the half-bottle of Grouse in his jacket pocket banging against his hip, and called Betty. Once his fingertips had been digitised and resolved into connection the line sounded dead in Bill's ear. He could recognise the tone of Betty's phone – he knew it that well; but the phone was at the bottom of a galvanised metal dustbin. Then Betty was in the dustbin as well, and he was calling down to her: 'Betty? It's me, Bill.'

'Bill, where are you?' She sounded interested.

'Bighouse, I'm at Mrs McRae's –'

'Bill – why are you there, why did you backtrack?'

'I could only get the four o'clock ferry from Stromness, and I wanted to stay between Wick and Tongue . . .' This was an old joke, and Betty didn't laugh. Anyway he was lying – and she knew it.

'What's it like then between Tongue and Wick?' She owed it to the history of the old joke to sustain the repartee – a little.

'Oh, you know, furry, an odd bit of lint here and there, some sweat, a smear of soap, perhaps later some semen –' He broke off – preposterously there was banging on the door of the phone box.

A white face bloomed out of wind and darkness: 'Will you be all night? The wind's bitter.'

'I've only just got through.' He held the receiver out towards the old woman's scarf-wrapped face. She looked at it. Bill thought of Betty on the other end of the line, listening to the gale, participating in this non-conference call.

'The wind's bitter,' the old woman reiterated – she would say nothing more.

Bill jammed himself back inside the phone box, but didn't allow the heavy door to close completely. Pinioned thus, he called down into the dustbin, 'Betty, there's an elderly lady here who needs the phone – I'll call back later.' He heard her faint valediction and hung up. He hadn't called back later.

In the morning the storm that had hung over Caithness and Orkney for the past week had cleared. The sun was chucking its rays down so hard that they exploded off all glass and metal. Looking out from the window of the kitchen, where he sat at Formica dabbling rind in yoke, Bill saw that the aluminium trim around the windows of his car was incandescent. He paid Mrs McRae with wadded Bank of Scotland pound notes – eleven of them. 'Will you be back soon, Dr Bywater?' she asked.

'Y'know, Mrs McRae,' he replied, 'when I'm next up to Orkney.'

'And any idea of when that'll be?'

He shrugged his shoulders and held his hands out, palms uppermost, so as to indicate the maximum possible mixture of doubts and commitments.

Bill threw his bag in the boot of the car and picked up the CD interchanger. He inserted the restocked cartridge of CDs into the rectangular aluminium mouth, and listened with satisfaction as the servomotors swallowed it up. He set the interchanger back in its housing and slammed the boot. He walked round to the front of the car and undid the bonnet. He checked the oil, the water and the windscreen reservoir. He checked the turbo cooling unit pipe that had burst while he was in Orkney, and which he'd welded himself. He did this all quickly and deftly, his blunt fingers feeling the car with unabashed sensuality. Bill was proud of his hands – and his skill with them.

Inside the car he wiped the hands on a rag. He started

the engine of the car and listened carefully to the note of the engine. He stashed the rag and inserted the CD-control panel into its dash mounting. He dickered with the servos that automatically adjusted the driver's seat. He gave the windscreen a few sweeps of soapy water. He programmed the CD to play randomly. Finally, he lit one of the joints that he'd rolled while he was shitting after breakfast. Exhaling the first blast of smoke made the interior of the car seem like a fantastical van de Graaff generator, the lights on the fascia sparking through the haze.

Bill reached behind him, pulled up the bottle of Campbelltown twelve-year-old from under the stack of professional journals he kept on the back floor. He glanced about at the roadway, but there was nothing, only the slate roof of Mrs McRae's, with a bank of grass swaying in front of it. Bill took a generous pull on the whisky, capped the 'car bottle' as he jocularly styled it – to himself – and re-stashed it. He checked his rearview, then planted his foot on the accelerator. The big car shook itself once before plunging along the road. The inertia pressed Bill into the worn leather of the seat, releasing tiny molecules of good smell. He heard the turbo-charger kick in with its pleasing whine. John Coltrane's sax burst from the four seventy-watt speakers, the long flat sheets of sound spooling out like algorithms of emotion.

Bill managed the twenty miles into Thurso in about half an hour, ridiculously good going for this twisting stretch of road, the camber of which constantly surprised with its adversity. But the rain was gone and the visibility good. Bill kept his foot down, feeling the weight of the big saloon slice through the fresh air. The car was so long that if he drove with one arm cradling the headrest of the passenger seat – which he often did – in his peripheral view he could see the back of the car turning, gifting him a peculiar sense of being a human fulcrum.

As he drove Bill looked at the sky and the land. He didn't love Caithness the way he did Orkney. Orkney was like Avalon, a mystical place where beyond the rampart cliffs of Hoy a shoal of green, whale-like islands basked in the azure sea. But this northern coast of Britain was composed of ill-fitting elements: a bit of cliff here, a green field there, a stretch of sand and dunes over there; and over there the golf-ball reactor hall of Dounreay, the nuclear power station, waiting for some malevolent god to tee it off into the Pentland Firth. Caithness was infiltrated with a palpable sense of being underimagined. This was somewhere that nobody much had troubled to conceive of, and the terrain bore the consequences in its unfinished aspect.

It was one of the things Bill loved most about the far north. Professional, middle-class friends down south would have no sense of the geography of these regions. When he told them that he had a cottage in Orkney, they would insistently confuse the islands with the Hebrides. It allowed Bill to feel that, in a very important way, once the *St Ola* ferry pulled out of Scrabster harbour, he was sailing off the face of the earth.

Thurso. A grey, dour place. The council housing hunched, constrained, barrack-like; and pushing its closed face into the light of day, as if only too aware that this sunshine was the end of things, and that soon the long, long, windy nights would be back. Bill stopped at the garage, on the rise from where he had the best possible view of Orkney, sixteen miles away to the north. The day was so clear he could make out the crooked finger of the Old Man of Hoy, where it stood proud of the great sea cliffs. There was a light coping of snow on top of the island, which flared in the sunlight. With a wrench in his heart Bill pulled off the forecourt, and wheeled right.

Once he had left Thurso, and was accelerating up the long gradient out of the town, Bill settled down to think about the drive. Into this mental act came the awareness that he hadn't, as yet, really relaxed into it. The Bighouse to Thurso stretch had required the wrong kind of concentration; Bill needed to sink into the driving more. He liked to trance out when he was driving, until eventually his proprioception melded with the instrumentation of the car, until he *was* the car. Bill conceived of the car at these times as being properly animate: its engine a heart, its sump a liver, its automated braking system a primitive – but engaging – sentience.

The car supported Bill's body in its skin-coated settee, while he watched the movie of the road.

Bill thought about the drive and began to make wildly optimistic estimates of the time each stage would take him: two hours to Inverness, an hour and a half on through the Highlands to Perth, then another hour to Glasgow. Maybe even make it in time for lunch. Then on in the late afternoon, down the M72 to Carlisle. Then the M6 – which felt as if it were a river, coursing downhill all the way to Birmingham. He might be in time to stop off in Mosely for a balti. Penultimately the M40 in the dead of the night, ghostly tentacles of mist shrouding the road as the big car thrummed through the Midlands towards London. And then finally the raddled city itself; the burble of the exhaust reverberating from the glass façades of the car showrooms and office-equipment suppliers along the Western Avenue.

Placing himself in London at 1 a.m. after seven hundred miles of high-pitched driving, Bill could anticipate with precision the jangled condition of his body, the fraying of his over-concentrated mind. He might – he thought – let himself into Betty's flat, then her bed, then her. Or not. Go to the spieler instead. Get properly canned. Ditch the car. Reel home.

The car was lodged behind a glowering seven-ton dump truck. Mud bulged above its grooved sides, the occasional clod toppled off. They were on the long straight that heads down to Roadside, where the A882 pares off towards Wick. There had been rain more recently here and long puddles streaked the road; in the sunlight they were like mirror shards, smashed from the brilliant sky. Without thinking, Bill checked the rearview mirror, the side mirror, flicked on the indicator and rammed his foot to the floor. The car yanked forward, the turbo-charger cutting in with an audible 'G'nunngg!'. Bill felt the wheels slide and skitter as they fought for purchase on the water, mud and scree strewn about the surface. He was two hundred metres past the truck and travelling at close to ninety, before he throttled back and pulled over to the left once more.

The first pass, was, Bill reflected, the hardest. It represented an existential leap into the unknown. If car and man survived they had made their compact for the journey. There were only two ways to do this mammoth run: slowly and philosophically, or *driving*. Bill had opted for the latter. He celebrated by lighting the second of the joints he had rolled at stool. The Upsetter came on the CD, awesome bass noise transforming the doors into pulsing wobble boards, the whole car into a mobile speaker cabinet. Bill grinned to himself and hunkered down still further in his seat.

The car bucketed through the uneven terrain. The landscape was still failing to distinguish itself. From the road a coping of peat bog oozed away into the heart of

Caithness, a caky mush of grasses and black earth. In the distance a single peak raised its white-capped head. It was, Bill considered, a terrain in which a few triceratops and pterodactyl wouldn't have looked altogether out of place. He'd once had an analysand who had a phobia about dinosaurs – not so much their size, or possible rapacity, he could handle that – but the notion of those vast wartinesses of lizard hide. Bill had cured the phobia, sort of. He grinned at himself in the rearview mirror at the memory; he hoped ruefully. But the herpetophobe became correspondingly more erratic in almost every other area of his life. Eventually, psychotic, he ended up being sectioned after ripping the heads off hundreds of model dinosaurs in a spree through South London toy shops.

Bill didn't psychoanalyse anybody any more. He could no longer see the virtue in it – or so he told himself. In truth, he found it easier to sign on with agencies and do various psychiatric locums. He could pick and choose his shifts, and he got a variable case load. Bill had a peculiar affinity for talking down the real crazies; people who might become fork-wielding dervishes. The cops called him a lot nowadays, when they had a berserker in the station and didn't want to get body fluids on their uniforms. Bill wouldn't have said he fully entered into the crazies' mad mad world – that kind of Laingian stuff had gone the way of non-congenital schizophrenia – but he could fully empathise with these extruded psyches, whose points of view were so vertiginous: one minute on the ceiling, the next on the floor.

Bill also liked to live a little dangerously. To swing. He used to seduce women – but tired of it, or so he thought. In truth he had simply tired. He still drove fast and hard. Up and down to Orkney five or six times a year. At the croft on

Papa Westray he mended walls and fences, even built new outbuildings. He had five longhorns – really as pets. And of course there was drinking. He had Betty, sort of. A relationship based on sex on his part, and sex and anticipation on hers. Bill didn't think about his ex-wife. Not that he couldn't bear to acknowledge the truths surrounding her – insight was, after all, his profession – but because he really didn't feel that he needed to harp on it any longer. It was the past.

Bill had a thick leather car coat. Bill had a turbo-charged three-litre saloon. He liked single malts and skunk. He liked boats; he had an Orkney long liner skiff on Papa. He was a blunt-featured man with rough-cropped blond hair. Women used to stroke his freckled skin admiringly. He liked to climb mountains – very fast. He'd often done three Munros in a day. He wasn't garrulous, unless very drunk. He liked to elicit information. He was forty this year.

At Latheron, where the North Sea reared up out of the land, and the low cliffs collapsed into its silver-blue beauty, Bill checked his wrist-watch – a classic chronometer. It was just shy of eleven. The dash clock said five past, the LCD on the CD control panel winked 11 dead on, and as he looked back from the road, winked 11.01. The Portland Arms at Lybster would be opening; after such a tough morning's driving there was a good case for a pint – and a short. Bill lazily circled the steering wheel to the left and headed north up the A9.

In the wood-panelled bar lounge Bill was the only customer. The barking of his leather jacket against the vinyl of a banquette summoned an elaborately courteous man in the Highland toff's – or wannabe toff's – uniform of tweed jacket, waistcoat with horn buttons, flannel trousers, brogues. His Viyella shirt absorbed his tartan tie into its own slight patterning. He sported in addition a ridiculously flamboyant ginger handlebar moustache, which cancelled out his weak-featured face as surely as a red bar annuls smoking. Bill didn't recognise the man, and thought that he must be the winter manager; new to Caithness and perhaps not yet aware of how bleak his allotted four months of erratic pint-pulling would prove.

'Good morning sir,' said the absurdity, 'and it is a fine morning, isn't it?'

'It is.' Bill replied curtly – and then, feeling he had been too curt, 'I've had a clear run all the way from Bighouse; not so much as a shower.'

'Well, they say the gales will be up again tonight . . .' He picked up a half-pint glass from the draining board beneath the bar and began, idly, yet with skill, to wipe it. Bill walked to the bar, and the absurdity took his cue: 'What'll you be having then?' Up close Bill saw brown crap on the man's teeth, and lines of burst blood vessels, like purple crow's feet around his eyes.

Bill sighed – no need to account for his choices with this one: 'Is that a Campbelltown there?' He stabbed a finger towards the bottles of malt brooding on the shelves.

The absurdity got the bottle down without further ado. 'This is the fifteen-year-old?' His tone indicated that this was a request.

'A double,' said Bill.

Bill had brought yesterday's paper with him from the car, but he didn't bother to open it. He knocked back the whisky, and then chased it with a bottle of Orkney Dark Island. The whisky gouged more warmth into his belly, and the ale filled his head with peat and heather. Really, Bill thought, the two together summed up the far north. He was sitting back on the banquette, his feet propped on a low stool. His back and shoulders were grasped by the thick leather of his jacket. It was an old leather jacket, of forties cut. Bill had had it for years. It reminded him of a jacket he'd once seen Jack Kerouac wearing in a photo-graph. He liked the red quilted lining; and he especially liked the label on the inside of the collar that proclaimed: 'Genuine Leather, Made from a Quarter of a Horse'. Bill used to show this to young women, who found it amusing . . . seductive. Bill used to rub saddle soap into the thing, but recently had found he couldn't really be bothered, even though the leather was cracking around the elbows.

While Bill had been drinking, the absurdity was potter-ing around the vicinity of the bar, but now the pint glass was empty, and plonked back on the bar mat, he was nowhere to be seen. Bill pictured him, padding along the chilly corridors of the old granite hotel, like a cut-rate, pocket-sized laird. Impatiently, he rang a small bell – and the ginger moustache appeared instantly, directly in front of him, hoisted by its owner through the cellar hatch, like some hairy standard of rebellion.

'Sir?' came from behind the whiskers.

'The damage?' Bill countered.

'That'll be . . .' He turned to the cash register and played a chord. '. . . Four pounds and seventy-eight pence.' While Bill fought with his jeans for the cash, the absurdity had produced – from somewhere – a printed card. This he handed to Bill in exchange for the money, saying, 'You wouldn't mind, would you, filling out this card. It's a sort of survey we're doing, y'know, marketing and such, trying to find out who our clientele are . . .' He trailed off.

Bill looked at the card: 'Where did you first hear about us? 1. In the media 2. Personal recommendation 3. As part of a package holiday . . .'

'Of course,' he told the deluded hotelier, 'but if you don't mind I'll fill it out later and post it, I'm in a bit of a hurry.'

'Not at all, not at all – here's an addressed envelope for you. Make it easier.'

As he marched across the car-park to the car, Bill crumpled the card and the envelope into a ball and tossed it into a convenient bin. He also abandoned himself to unnecessarily carping laughter – the idea that this isolated spot would ever attract anything much besides passing trade, and the occasional shooting, fishing and drinking crew was as ridiculous as the ginger moustache.

Feeling the wind rising at his back impressed further how far Lybster was from anywhere – save the North Sea. Bill took off his jacket and chucked it on the back seat of the car. Then he swung himself into the front. He rammed the key into the ignition, turned it, and the car thrummed and pulsed into life. The CD chirruped – then some John Cage came on. With another negligent circling of his hand, Bill scraped the big saloon around a hundred and eighty degrees, and shot back up on to the A9, this time heading south.

For the next hour, until he saw the hitchhiker, Bill drove hard. There was something about the man in the pub at Lybster, the whole episode in fact, that unsettled him. There was that, and there was the sense that as the car plunged south – switch-backing over spurs, and charging down hillsides – it was taking Bill out of the underimagined world and into the world that was all too clearly conceived of, fixed in its nature, hammered into banality by mass comprehension.

Not that you'd know it thus far: the road still leaping and twisting every few yards, the gradients often one in ten or better. In mist, or rain – which was almost always – the A9 was simply and superficially dangerous, but shorn of its grey fleece it became almost frolicsome. So Bill thought, chucking the car in and out of the bends.

In rain you had little opportunity to pass even a car, let alone any of the grumbling lorries that laboured up this route to the far north; and there were many of these. It could slow the whole trip if you got caught behind one. Slow it up by as much as a half again. Even in fair conditions the only way to pass their caravans – they tended to travel in naturally occurring clutches, equally spaced – was to get up to about ninety on the straight, then strip-the-steel-willow of the oncoming traffic and the lorries themselves.

It was exhilarating – this headlong plunge down the exposed cranium of Britain. After twenty miles or so Bill had a spectacular view clear across the Moray Firth to the Grampians. The mountains pushed apart land, sea and sky with nonchalant grandeur; their peaks stark white, their flanks hazed white and blue and azure. Not that he looked at them, he looked at the driving, snatching shards of scenery in the jagged saccades his eyes made from speed-ometer to road, to rearview mirror, to wing mirrors, and back, over and over, each glance accompanied with a head jerk, as if he were some automated Hasidic Jew, praying as he went.

In a way Bill was praying. In the concentration on braking and accelerating, and at these speeds essentially toying with life and death – others' as well as his own – he finally achieved the dharmic state he had been seeking all morning: an absorption of his own being into the very act of driving that exactly matched his body's absorption into the fabric of the car; a biomechanical union that made eyes windscreens, wheels legs, turbo-charger flight mechan-ism. Or was it the other way round?

The wands of memories interleaved themselves with the sprigs of scenery, and then the whole hedge of impressions was further shaped and moulded by the music which poured from all four corners, before being flattened by the mantra of impulsion. Last night at the pub – the local doctor, Bohm, drunk – mouthing off about miracle cures for dipsomania – psychedelic drug rituals in West Africa, mystical twaddle – the walk home in the stiff wind, rain so hard it gave his cheeks and forehead little knouts. Now, on the road ahead, a passing opportunity, slow-moving old Ford Sierra, ahead of it two lorries and another two cars slightly further on, doing about sixty – a good seven hundred metres to the next bend. A bend beyond that allowed a view of more open road, but what of the hidden stretch? Calculate how much there was. Count: one, two, three seconds. Chance it. Rearview, Bam! Accelerator floored, wheel wrenched, back pressed back into seat. Leather smell. Vague awareness of oceanic chords playing – perhaps Richard Strauss. Indicator popping and tocking. Past the Ford. Past the first lorry. Up to eighty now. Bam! Shift rammed into third. Eighty now, nearing the bouncing butt of the second lorry. Fuuuck! There was a car. Now about a hundred metres off. Moving fast. Deathly fast. Check wing mirror. Dance the one-step of shock. Slide between the two lorries. Receive a fusillade of flashing and honking. Then – Bam! Back out again. Two hundred metres left of the straight – no view of the next stretch, just green tussocks, grey-green wall, strident black-and-white cow – keep it in third, will it back up . . . eighty . . . ninety . . . the ton. Fifty metres left – and the second lorry was cleared, evacuated, left behind as surely as a shit in a toilet in a motorway service centre. Left behind like the past, like failure, like regret.

Bill felt this marvellous sense of freedom and release as he cheated death and unslipped the surly gravity of the lumpen lorries. He felt it ten times between Borgue and

Helmsdale, fifteen between Helmsdale and Brora, then more and more as the road opened up and the hills retreated from the road, leaving it to flow and wiggle, rather than twist and turn.

A glimpse of Langwell House, gothic on its promontory, as he zigzagged through Berriedale; a proscenium framed shot of Dunrobin Castle as he wheeled past its gates and cantered down into the long spare main street of Golspie. And still the sun fell down, and still the road glimmered, and still Bill thought – or perhaps only thought he thought – of nothing. Past the Highland Knitwear Centre. How many sweaters had Bill bought in a lifetime of blandishment? Too many perhaps. One purple cable knit at this very shop – for a girl called Allegra. A diminutive blonde – too young for Bill. Then twenty-two to his thirty-five. She was all chubby bits, a dinky little love handle, who when stoned on dope became psychotic, fanatically washing her hands in the air like some method-trained obsessive. Bill had to talk her down every time it happened – and he didn't like taking his work to bed with him.

She gave head like a courtesan – like a goddess of fellation. She pushed down the prepuce with her lips, while her tongue darted round the root of his glans. One of her childlike hands delved in the lips of cloth that sagged open over his crotch, seeking out the root of him, juggling the balls of him. And this as the car motored along the banks of the Cromarty Firth, past the outcropping of cranes and davits at Invergordon. Even at the time Bill had recognised the automotive blow job as a disturbing concomitant to Allegra's manic laving. It was her way of placing him back under her control; he might have the steering wheel – but she was steering him, gnawing the joy stick.

It was Allegra's first and last trip to Orkney with Bill. Their relationship didn't so much split up as shatter some weeks later, when, at a dinner party given by middle-aged friends of Bill's, Allegra, drunk, had screamed, 'Why doesn't he tell you all that he *loves* going down on women, but can't stand to have them go down on him!' then thrown her vodka tonic in Bill's face, then attempted to ram the solid after the liquid. A lunge that Bill deflected, so that the crystal shattered on impact against the invitation-encrusted mantelpiece. The friends had plenty to talk about after Allegra and Bill had left.

As the car tick-tocked along the bleak street, Bill imagined the grey houses to either side populated with his past courtesans, his myriad lovers. It would be like some Felliniesque dream sequence. No, come to think of it, better to house the past lovers – there had to be at least a hundred of them – in Dunrobin Castle itself. It was so big there would be a room each for the more mature, and convenient dormitories for the young girls. Bill smiled at the thought of this perverse seraglio. But hadn't Fellini been right? Wasn't this the only possible psychic solution to the sense of hideous abandonment that the practice of serial monogamy imparted? To get them all in one place. It wasn't that Bill wanted them all sexually available – quite the reverse. But he wanted them in a context that made what existed between him and them, if not exactly important, at any rate viable. He wanted to feel that it had all mattered, that it wasn't simply animal couplings, mechanistic jerkings, now forgotten, now dust.

Taken with the fantasy, Bill allowed it to occupy him as he pressured the big car through the long avenue of trees that led from Golspie to Loch Fleet. Dunrobin Castle populated by all of his lovers, all of the women he'd ever had sexual relations with. The younger ones would handle the bulk of the domestic work. There was Jane, who was a professional cook, she could run the kitchens, with the assistance of Gwen, Polly and Susie. There would be enough women in their twenties to handle all the skivvy-ing, leaving the more mature women free to spend their time in idle conversation and hobby-style activities. Why, come to think of it, there was even a landscape gardener in Bill's poking portfolio; perhaps there was a case for not simply maintaining the grounds of the castle, but rede-signing them?

Even as Bill entertained this notion of a comforting castle, cracks began to appear in its façade. *All* of his former lovers . . . That meant not just Allegra, coming at him time after time with vitrified daggers, during the fatal attraction of cocktail hour, but other, still more unstable lovers, howling and wafting around halls and stairways. Worse than that, it meant his ex-wife; where would she come to roost? No doubt in an outhouse, from where, on dark nights, the sounds of screamed imprecations could be heard, blown in with the wind, and echoing around the drawing room where the others sat sewing, and Bill himself grimaced over another whisky.

And if there was to be room for the ex-wife, there would have to be room for other unsavoury characters as well. Despite himself, Bill urged the conceit to its baleful conclusion. The tarts – there would be room at Dunrobin for the tarts, the brasses, the whores. Bill imagined trying to keep them out – this delegation of tarts. Meeting them at the gates of the Castle and attempting to turn them back. 'But you fucked us!' their spokesmadam would abjure him. 'We demand room in the Castle!' He would have no choice but to admit them – and then the fragile concord of the seraglio would be shattered. The other lovers might have been prepared to accept sorority as a substitute for monogamy, but the tarts? Never. The tarts would swear and drink. They would smoke crack in the billiard room, and shoot smack in the butler's pantry. They would seduce the younger lovers and outrage the older. On cold nights Bill would find himself desperately stuffing his head beneath covers, beneath pillows, trying to shut out the sounds of their wassailing, as they plaited with the moan and screech of the wind.

On the long straight that bounced up the other side of the loch, Bill clocked the signs requesting assistance from the coastguard in the fight against drug smugglers: If You See Anything Suspicious . . . The image of gracious polygamy faded and was replaced by one of Bill beachcombing, prodding at shells with a piece of driftwood, his jacket collar turned up, its points sharp against his chilled ears. The oiled tip of his makeshift shovel turns up a corner of blue plastic bag. He delves further. Six rectangular blocks, each sealed in blue plastic and heavily bound with gaffer tape are revealed to be neatly buried. Bill smiles and gets out his penknife . . .

Another sign whipped by at the top of the rise: Unmarked Police Cars Operating . . . Spoilsports. No seraglio and now no mother lode of Mama Coca; no white rails for the wheels of the big car to lock on to; no propulsive, cardiac compression to take Bill's heart into closer harmony with the rev counter . . . He hunkered down once more, gripped the steering wheel tighter, concentrated on the metallic rasp of John Lee Hooker's guitar, which ripped up the interior of the car. Then came the roadworks. Then came the hitchhiker.

Bill braked, and looked for somewhere to pull over. About fifty metres further on there was a break in the earth-soft verge where blue-grey gravel puddled on to the roadway. Bill aimed for it, indicated, and then crunched the car to a halt. In the rearview mirror he could see the hitchhiker running towards the car, his pack bouncing, his poncho flapping, an expression of gap-toothed desperation on his face, as if he were absolutely certain that this offer of a lift was a taunt or a hoax, and that as soon as he was level with the car Bill would drive off guffawing.

The hitchhiker yanked the car door open and the fresh air and moisture and sunlight streamed in. 'Thanks, mate –' He was clearly going to converse.

'Get in!' Bill snapped. 'I can't stop here for long.' He gestured at the roadway, where the cars were having to pull over the centre line in order to pass. The hitchhiker threw himself into the front passenger seat of the car, his pack still on. Bill glanced in the rearview, indicated, lazily circled the wheel to the right, and rejoined the traffic.

For some seconds neither said anything. Bill pretended to concentrate on the driving and observed his captive out of the corner of his eye. The hitchhiker sat, his face almost against the windscreen, the backpack – which Bill now saw had a tent bag and roll of sleeping bag tied to it – was like a whole, upper-body splint, designed so as to force its wearer into closer contemplation of the road. A Futurist's corset.

'I'll stop as soon as I can,' Bill said, 'and we can put that in the back.'

The hitchhiker said, 'Thanks very much.'

He was – Bill guessed – in his late twenties or early thirties. His accent was Caithness, the sharp elements of a Scottish brogue, softened and eroded by a glacial covering of Scandinavian syllables. His black, collar-length hair was roughly cut. He wore the yellow nylon poncho, and under it a never-fashionable, fake sheepskin-lined denim jacket. From behind the distempered non-wool, poked the collar of a tartan shirt. The hitchhiker's breath smelt foully of stale whisky. His eyes were bivouacked in purple bags, secured by purple veins. He was unshaven. His teeth were furred. He had an impressive infection in the dimple of his strong chin – he wasn't bad-looking.

'Are you going far?' he asked.

'All the way,' Bill smiled, 'to London, that is.'

The hitchhiker grinned, and attempted – insofar as the pack allowed him – to settle more securely in his seat. It was the last question he asked Bill for the whole journey.

They were across the Cromarty Firth causeway and on the Black Isle before Bill found a proper layby to stop in. They both got out of the car and Bill rearranged the things on the back seat so that the hitchhiker could stash his pack. They were rolling again in a couple of minutes. Bill pushed the car up to seventy and then idled there, the index finger and thumb of his right hand holding the lower edge of the steering wheel as if it were some delicate surgical instrument. The rain ceased and the roadway shone once more. The muted CD played the current single by a hip guitar band. The hitchhiker drummed chipped, dirty nails on frayed, dirty denim.

'So,' said Bill after a while, 'where are you headed?'

'I'm going all the way too.' He hunched round to face Bill, as if they were casual drinkers striking up a conversation at the bar of the car's dashboard, 'I stop in Poole, Dorset, but I've a mate in Glasgow I want to see for tonight.'

'Well, I can drop you outside Glasgow, I'm heading straight on through and south.'

'That'll be grand.' The hitchhiker smiled at Bill, gifting him a sight of peaks of plaque. It was a smile that should be given at the conclusion of such a trip – not the beginning. 'Nice car,' the hitchhiker said, still smiling.

'Yeah,' Bill drawled, 'it motors. So, where're you from?'

'Thurso.'

'And what's the purpose of the trip?'

'I'm studying down in Poole, got myself on a computer course like. I had a reading week so I thought I'd get up to see my kiddies –'

'They're in Thurso?'

'Aye, right enough.'

The old 'fluence was still there, Bill thought. A couple of miles, a few questions insinuated in the right vulnerable places, and like some cunning piece of Chinese marquetry – a box with hidden compartments subtly palped – the hitchhiker's psyche would begin to open out, to exfoliate. They swung over the ridge of Isle and the car caromed on down, on to the dual carriageway. They emerged from a forest of scattered conifers and there, hunkered around its cathedral spire, Inverness gleamed.

'Inverness,' said the hitchhiker.

He even states the obvious! Bill snidely exulted.

'Did you come from Thurso this morning?'

'I did. After a bit of a session – if you catch my meaning.'

'Some mates saw you off then?'

'They couldna' exactly see me off – they were all pished malarkey. Five of the fuckers, all inna heap. So I tiptoed out. Got a lift right away across to Latheron, then down to Dornoch. Then I was walking in the bloody rain for four miles before you stopped for me –'

'It was difficult to stop. The roadworks –'

'Aye, right enough.'

'You've got a tent and stuff there?'

'In case I get caught short like – and have to spend the night on the road. I had to do that on the way up. I slept by the side of the road near Aviemore.'

'Wasn't that a drag?'

The hitchhiker snorted. 'I'll say. Come five in the morning the rain starts coming down holus-bolus, and then a fucking cow starts giving a horn to ma' flysheet. I was back on the road before dawn, with my thumb stuck up like a fucking icicle . . .' He trailed off and gave Bill another grimy grin. His stubble was blue.

Bill was emboldened to ask, 'So, you're fond of a drink then?'

The hitchhiker pressed the ball of his thumb into one eye socket, the middle joint of his index finger into the other. He kneaded and scrunched his features, answering from within this pained massage, 'Oh well, I suppose . . . perhaps more than I should be. I dunno.'

Bill grimaced. He looked for a turning on the left – the carriageway was still dual – when he saw a forestry track. He dabbed the brakes, indicated, lazily circled the wheel and pulled in. 'Slash,' he said.

They both got out. Bill left the car running. They both pissed into the edge of the woodland. Through steam and sun Bill examined his companion's urine. Very dark. Perhaps even blood dark. There was a touch of jaundice in the hitchhiker's complexion as well. Maybe kidney infection, Bill thought, maybe worse. Not that this would be necessarily pathological in any way. They drank like that in Thurso – as they did in Orkney.

Bill knew ten men under thirty-five on Papa alone who had stomach ulcers. In Dr Bohm's surgery there were forty-odd leaflets urging parents to check their children for symptoms of drug abuse. Absurd, when about the only drugs available on the island were compounds for ensuring the evacuation of bovine after-birth. Bohm also had one small tattered sticker near the surgery door, which proclaimed: Drinkwise Scotland, and gave a help-line number. This lad was, Bill reflected, quite possibly addicted to alcohol, without necessarily being an alcoholic.

When they were back in the car Bill reached back behind the young man's seat and pulled up the car bottle. It was half-full. 'Will you have a dram?' He sloshed the contents about; they were light and pellucid – as the stream of urine ought to have been. Bill appreciated the exact battle between metabolic need and social restraint that danced with the young man's features. He broke the spell by uncorking the bottle and taking a generous swig himself. Then he passed the bottle to the young man who was saying, 'Sure . . . Yeah . . . Right.'

The whisky went off like an anti-personality mine somewhere in the rubble-strewn terrain of Bill's forebrain. He flicked the shift into reverse and crunched backwards. He took the bottle from the young man and re-stashed it. He hugged the headrest and sighted down the road. Nothing. He banged the accelerator and the car twisted backwards, pivoting at the hips, rested on its rubber haunches for a second while Bill flicked the shift into drive, then shook itself and plunged back up the long hill. Twenty, thirty, forty . . . the turbo-charger 'gnunng'ed!' in . . . fifty-five, seventy, eighty . . . to either side the rows of orderly conifers strobed back; the gleaming road ahead twanged like a rubber band; the sky shouted 'Wind!'; the reggae music welled like beating blood: 'No-no-no-oo! You don' love me an' I know now –' Bill was feeling no pain. The young man was shouting something, Bill hit OFF.

'– arked cars –'

'What was that you said?' Bill's voice was precise and dead level in the instantaneously null environment of the car. It sounded like an aggressive threat.

'Y'know the police, man . . . the pigs . . . They have unmarked cars on this road.'

'I know.' Bill poked at the speedometer. 'Anyway I'm only doing eighty-five, they won't pull you till you get within a whisker of ninety – d'you smoke?' Without so much as twisting the thread of conversation, Bill had filched another joint from his inside pocket.

The whisky and the skunk opened the young man up. He skewed himself further in his seat, imposing more intimacy, and Bill began to feed him questions. His name was Mark. His father had been a marine engineer. Much older than the mother. The father was Viennese – Jewish. A wartime refugee, he designed some of the early SONAR systems. The mother died of cancer when Mark was eight, the father four years later. The father had had money but the estate was mismanaged by uncaring trustees. Mark and his brother ended up in children's homes. They were separated. Mark left school, got a job with a carrier's. Married, had two children and . . .

'Fucked up, I s'pose, right enough.'

'What's that?'

'With the kiddies like. Fucked up. Y'know, I was young – didn't know what I wanted. Still don't, I s'pose.' He gifted Bill another smile that had once – no doubt – been charming.

Bill had been waiting for this; this descent into the cellar of Mark's mind. The kids – his relationship with his kids – would have to be the trapdoor, the way down. Bill had pegged Mark as a bolter almost immediately. There was an aspect of bruised dejection about the young man which suggested someone who was willing to wound but afraid to strike. Someone who would say the unsayable and then attempt retraction. Someone whose capacity for self-love would only ever be manifested through attitudinising and narcissism.

Bill thought that he quite hated Mark already. He hated

the young man's willingness to be drawn out. His self-absorption. His tiresome lack of cool – he had told Bill four times while they smoked the joint how good the dope was in Poole, and how adept he and his pals were at obtaining it. Bill resolved to pump Mark for all he was worth. To gut the man's past, quarter his present, and draw a bead on his future. It was a game Bill had often played before – trying to find out as much as he could about someone he encountered by chance. Find out as much as he could, and – this was crucial – not give away anything about himself. Once the mark began asking questions themselves the game was over.

'It's difficult bringing up kids –'

'Specially with no dosh. Specially with no space, y'know. Space to think. I always thought there was more to me than just a driver. My father was a brilliant man. I couldn't find myself. Couldn't in Thurso – nothing there. And my wife . . . she didn't, sort of, get it . . .'

'Understand?'

'Right.'

'And it's better down in Poole? Did you go there directly?'

'Well, no. I bummed around the country, sort of, for a while. I mean, I set off aiming for Glastonbury that year – and then just sort of kept on. Got, well, ended *up* in Poole because of the Social –'

'Easier to claim?'

'Aye.'

They were well into the mountains and the clouds had come down. To the right the Monadhliaths, to the left the Grampians. The valley was a mile or so wide. Beyond the rough summer pasture the mountains did what they did best: mounting. Either the furred flanks of forestry, or the abrasive architecture of scree. Up and Up, until the indefinite, thrusting peaks made contact with the cloudy massifs lowered from above. Bill noted that the car was almost out of petrol. They would have to run into Aviemore.

'I'm going to run into Aviemore,' he said to Mark, who was humming along with the music, 'but we won't be stopping, we'll just grab some sandwiches and head on – have you eaten?' The young man was hitching. It was plain that he'd spent all of his money on booze the night before. This was Bill's opportunity to do him a real turn. Feed him up.

'Nah, really . . . nah . . . I'm all right.' The suitable case for charity suitably hung his face. Bill said nothing – he was looking for signs. Eventually one ran along the road towards them – it was a mile to the turn. The sign – as did most in this part of the Highlands – showed a turnoff diverting from the main road, lancing a boil destination, and then rejoining it. Bill mused on how like life this was; the temporary diversions that you attempted to make, which were always cut off, subsumed once more to the ruthlessly linear, the deathly progression. Bill thought of sharing this observation with Mark, but then thought better of it. Then he did anyway.

Mark pondered for a while, then factored himself in: 'Yeah, I feel that my whole life's been like that up till now. I haven't been doing what I should – I've been marking time.'

'Neat.'

'What?'

'Neat.'

'What?'

'Nothing.' They sat silent as Bill piloted the car through the outskirts of Aviemore. The place was still tatty despite the money that had recently been poured in. Most of the buildings were chalet-style, with steeply pitched roofs running almost to the ground. But the materials were synthetic; concrete and aluminium; asbestos and perspex. Every surface seemed to be buckling; every edge rucking up. 'Shit hole,' Bill said.

Seeing a biggish Texaco station, set back off the road, Bill lazily circled the steering wheel to the left and the car oozed on to the forecourt. He pulled up to the pumps, was out of the door with the petrol-cap key in one hand and a tenner in the other, before Mark had a chance to plan his arrival. The air here was a sharp embrace. Bill still vibrated with the road. The outside world was warped. It felt like leaving a cinema after a matinée, and coming out into the inappropriately bright afternoon.

'I'll fill the tank – could you go and get us three or four of those crappy plastic sandwiches they do – tuna, chicken, whatever . . . And some drinks, Coke, Irn Bru – yeah? And some fags. Regal blue. OK?'

Mark slouched off to the shop. If I give him enough things, Bill thought, he'll have to ask me about myself. He'll have to evince some curiosity about his benefactor. Bill wanted this. He didn't like his dislike of the young man, didn't like the way it was curdling in his gut – curdling it with still more bilious, watery gripes. If Mark would only ask him about himself the inquisition could be called off. They could chat normally, instead of this ceaseless interrogative chatter. Eventually silence would fall – not companionable, but not alienated either. In due course he would drop the young man off, on a slip road, about ten miles outside Glasgow. They would part and forget.

Spasmodically, Bill clutched the handle of the pump, until the attendant hit the flashing button on his console and the petrol began to glug. Perhaps Mark had done a flit, a new bolt, Bill couldn't make him out in the shop. It wouldn't be a bad score for the lad; a bit of whisky, some dope, a tenner, a ride, why not duck out now while he was ahead? Then Mark appeared from the back of the shop, where the customer toilets were, and Bill allowed himself the luxury of feeling a little guilty, imagining that he had misjudged human character.

Back in the car Mark struggled with his seatbelt while they rolled back out on to the road. 'They'd no tuna, but I got a bacon one, and chicken with corn . . . and . . . smoked ham.' He displayed the plastic-packed chocks of sandwich to Bill, as if he were about to be asked to perform some visio-spatial test with them.

'Have you got a Coke?'

'Aye.' Mark passed it to Bill, but not before thoughtfully opening it.

Bill drank the Coke and drummed the wheel. They puttered between more, mutant chalet-style blocks of tourist flats, then past a shopping parade, then out into the country again. Bill didn't say anything until they were heading south on the A9 once again. Then he sighed, cranked the big car up to eighty-five, overtook a convoy of Finnish campervans which were struggling up a long gradient, and said, 'So, did you see much of the kids when you were up this time?'

'It was . . .' Mark was struggling with a recalcitrant piece of ham; gristle in a tug-of-war between bread lips and flesh lips. 'It was . . .' Bill decided to ignore the appetitive recovery. 'Difficult, y'know. I've nowhere to take them, and I'm not happy hanging around her place – not that's she's keen or anything. I took them to the park a couple of times . . . and for tea.'

Either the clouds were descending, or the road was still rising, because turbulent clumps of vapour were falling down from the dark passes, and scudding a couple of hundred feet above the road. Bill put on the headlights, full beam. 'Was it a long time since you were up before then?'

'I hadn't been back before.' Mark let this fall from between chomping jaws, then grimaced. 'Ach! It's not like me.'

'What's that?'

'To be saying so much.'

'Really?'

'Ach ye-es, well, I dunno . . . I was always a bit of a tearaway, y'know –'

'I gathered.'

'Nothing grievous, but this and that, y'know, telling a few tall ones to the Social, doing a few chequebook and card jobs. So I was always good at . . . y'know . . .'

Y'know, y'know, y'know? What could this young man imagine about Bill? That he knew everything? That such a nonce word had become Mark's asinine catch phrase, begged the very question the answer to which it assumed. The more 'y'know's filled the car, the more Bill felt certain that he did know – and bridled from the truth: 'Lying?'

'Yeah, I s'pose. There's a way of doing it –' He grinned. 'A technique almost. It's like job interviews –'

'Job interviews?'

'Yeah. If you don't want the job, you tend to do well in the interview. It's the same with lying. People always make the mistake of trying to make someone believe what they're saying – but that's not the way. You've got to not care whether they believe – and they will. I'm pretty good at it, if I say so myself. Not that I lie now though.' He was gabbling. 'I don't have to any more – don't need to . . .'

But he had lost Bill, who was no longer listening to the content of what Mark said – only its form. Bill was listening to the emotional shapes that Mark was making. In the rising and falling of tone, the bunching and stretching of rhythm, he was able to discern the architecture of Mark's past history: the outhouses of unfeeling and evasion; the vestibules of need and recrimination; the garages of wounding and abuse. All of it comprehensively planned together, so as to form a compound of institutionalisation and neglect. Bill honed his ears, concentrating on this shading in of a sad blueprint. The young man's actual *pride* in his mendacity – that would have to be one part bravado, one part a lie and one part the truth. Nasty little cocktail. Nasty little dilemma for the two of us, imprisoned in a car, speeding through a mountain pass. Bill hunkered down more against the comfortable padded extrusion of the door, letting his weight rest on the inside handle. He scanned Mark out of the corners of his eyes; a series of quick penetrating glances, as ever interleaved with shards of scenery, fragments of road. He really was rough. The fingers nicked and burnt: pus-ridden here – browned there, the knuckles fulsomely scabbed. He might not be altogether *compos mentis* – this hitchhiker, awarded to Bill by the journey, like an idiotic prize – but that made him all the more potentially dangerous.

'Potential for people, like me, to do all sorts of things . . .' Mark had veered on to the subject of the Internet. It appeared to verge most of his discourse. 'Don't you think?'

'Oh definitely,' Bill replied, surfacing, and used the hiatus to ask for the chicken sandwich, before getting back down to the drive, getting back down to the questioning.

Past the turning for Kingussie, past the A86, forking away to the west coast and Fort William, the big car bucketed on along the darkening road, as the autumn afternoon curled about the mountains. Bill kept the speed up – because he had no speed. The last of the Dexedrine had been used for the drive north. It was unwise for him to blag any more for a while. More than unwise – fucking foolhardy. So, on this mammoth drive Bill would have to depend on caffeine and ephedrine pills. Hideous shit he hadn't scoffed since revising for school exams. Feeling himself flag and sopor welling up from the road, Bill scrabbled in the pocket of his jacket, located a couple of the bitter little things, washed them down with a mouthful of flat Coke. Mark was talking about what served him as a love life.

'If you've had bad experiences it affects you. I dunno – maybe I'm not so good on the trust end of things . . .' Bill realised he was referring, preposterously, to his capacity for trust – not his trustworthiness. 'So I keep my distance. Jennifer' (that was the new girlfriend) 'did move in for a bit, but I felt crowded. We couldn't see eye to eye. The place was too small. She wouldn't give me my space – like my wife. Always crowding me, getting on my case about . . . stuff. We're still seeing each other though . . . though it's not quite so full-on . . .'

Bill thought he could probably decipher this completely now. Mark was abusive – like many of the abused. Back in Thurso was a wife who had cowered when one of those barked hand-battens was raised; and in Poole it had been the same. Bill heard hysterical flutings of heterosexual discord in his inner ear: Mark and the nameless women, pleadings and beratings like vile duets. The hitchhiker harped on about the harpies.

By now they were coming down off the mountains. The land turned a greener, tawnier hue by the mile. The isolated shuttered lodges were being replaced by scattered habitations, farms carved out from the heathery hillsides. But as if to taunt the occupants of the car, who were, after all, coming in from a kind of cold, the rain now recommenced. Bill flicked the stalk, the wipers did their thing intermittently, then steadily, then rapidly. And by the time they were passing the turning for Pitlochry the land, the road and the sky had been boiled up into a vaporous stock. Turner, Bill thought, would have painted this greying haze, had he been alive to suck the butt-end of the twentieth century.

Mark was talking about the Internet again. About how a friend of his – an acquaintance really, had set up a small service provider and software technical-support company. The friend was letting Mark spend time on his equipment, learn his way around it. The friendship, Bill surmised, was actually just as virtual as a Windows window. Mark was there under sufferance – if there at all. But Bill wasn't really thinking about this, he was remembering a woman he'd bedded in Pitlochry. A wannabe thesp, up for the summer theatre festival. Bill had motored through and caught her in an execrable production of *Lady Windermere's Fan*. Funny that – a bad production of Wilde. Funny how bad direction, bad acting, bad sets and costumes were the dramatic equivalent of monkeying with the controls on a television, so that the picture became over-contrasted, or too dark. In this case the effect of the monkeying was to produce leaden vulgarity, rather than frothy and sophisticated farce.

After desultory applause he had cornered her in her cubbyhole dressing room. The smell of silk, satin, crinoline and powder was sharp, overpowering. She'd giggled as he pushed up her skirts . . .

'We didn't realise he had a stash in there. We just went in to get these tapes back, but we found it in his room, so we took it. It turned out it was his whole stash. He paid us upwards of two hundred to get it back – a decent score.' Mark was, Bill realised, talking about another rip-off. He'd slid from contemplating that mundane world of electronic encoding, to the airily fascinating world of Poole bedsits.

'So.' Bill lit a Regal with the lighter he now held, permanently crushed, between palm and steering wheel. 'Did you take any of the smack?'

'God, no! I wouldn't do that! Bit of puff, fine – bit of whizz when it's about, but I don't want to fuck up – I've seen what that shit can do to people.'

Bill inwardly grinned. What more could a heroin addiction have done to this young man? Make him leave another family? Make him lie more than he had already? Make him a more self-satisfied and still less reflective petty thief? Bill doubted it.

They were past Perth and heading down the long valley towards Gleneagles and Stirling. The country was still green here, with the stubbly residue of crops catching, with a shimmy of light, the occasional burst of sun from between cloud banks. The hills had pushed back still further from the road, and the farmhouses were trimmer, better kept, more on show. The changed landscape dampened the mood in the car; the evocations of domesticity, whipping by in the slipstream, reminded both Bill and Mark of the queer accommodations they had made with life. Bill felt like a drink.

He could visualise – quite clearly – the slopping level of whisky in the car bottle. He wanted to stop and have a piss and then a decent pull. Tramp down the memories that his cross-examination of Mark was dragging to the surface. But Bill didn't trust Mark at all now. He wouldn't feel safe leaving the car running while he splattered on the verge.

He could all too clearly imagine the sound of the door slamming at his back, the car's wheels crunching, spattering gravel. His own anguished cries as he turned, and ran up the road, his cock still spluttering pee as he contemplated loss of car and everything else. And he wasn't even insured for theft. Bill really hated Mark now. Hated him for being pathetic – and a threat; at one and the same time.

A layby came by. Bill dabbed the brakes, lazily circled the wheel. The car ground to a halt. Bill yanked up the bottle of Campbelltown from its sleeve of medical journals. He unscrewed it, took a deep pull and passed it to Mark, who looked at him warily, took a slug and passed the bottle back. 'You're not bothered by the pigs then?' he asked.

'Of course I am,' Bill replied tartly, 'who isn't? But that's the last before Glasgow – I'll not risk going head-to-head with them.' He checked the rearview and side mirrors, lazily circled the wheel to the right, then pushed home the accelerator, like the plunger of some 300 cc hypodermic. The big car summoned its inertia and banged back up on to the crown of the road. Bill felt the bladder of mistrust push its toxic cargo back against his pelvis. He resigned himself to the sensation. Better score more distraction.

'So, what'll you be doing with this mate in Glasgow then?'

'I dunno, not too much. We certainly won't be drinking single fucking malts.' He grinned at Bill in a way he hoped was rueful. 'More like single fucking pints. He's on the sick – my mate. But I've got a few quid, I promised him a bit of a night. It'll be the same as our normal routine. Do a few cans at home. Down to the pub for a few. Then a carry-out; and then the racing –'

'Racing?'

'We-ell, not racing exactly. It's just a thing we do – we've always done – when I'm in Glasgow. My mate – he's got these old Tonka toys, y'know?'

'Yeah.'

'Not the little one – the jeeps and that. But the big ones, the ones kids can sit on and push along wi' their feet. Y'know, the big earth movers and that?'

'Yeah.'

'Once we're right bladdered we get them out. There's one each – an earth mover and a dump truck, but we always have a little scrap over who gets which. The dump truck's faster, but it has a dicky wheel – comes off at speed. Anyway, we get 'em out, like I say, and we go racing down Sauchiehall Street. Y'know Sauchiehall Street?'

'Yeah.'

'Aye – well, you'll know it's got a good long slope to it then, just right. Like a sort of ski-jump effect, y'know. Anyway, it's a right good laugh. All the folk coming out of the pubs cheer us on; and if one of us runs into a feller, there's always a ruck of some sort. Good laugh – great *craic*!'

Mark was clearly gingered up by this, this prospect of a drunken race seated on toys long since outgrown. His eyes were wide – so that Bill could clock all the yellowed rim of them. His grin gaped; his sour mash breath blanketed the car. Bill lit the last of his pre-rolled joints and took a big pull of flowery smoke. Mark was still puffed up, but Bill's silence about the Tonka-toy trials was clearly unnerving him.

Eventually Bill spoke: 'Tough, tough toys for tough, tough boys,' he said.

'Whassat?'

'You remember – don't you? Or are you too young? It was the advertising slogan for Tonka toys. The telly advert was all set in a sand-pit and there would be this drumming – tom-toms, I suppose – and the various Tonka toys would come into view, all of them self-propelled. No drivers – of any scale at all. Then the drumming would go to a kind of peak, while one of the Tonka jeeps bounced over the terrain, and a voice would say "Tough, Tough Toys for Tough, Tough Boys!" in *very* stentorian tones – you remember?'

'No, I can't rightly say I do.' Mark was downcast.

Perhaps, Bill thought, I shouldn't have upstaged his anecdote, or maybe he's embarrassed because he doesn't know what stentorian means. They drove on in silence, passing the joint between them.

They were leaving Dunblane behind on its promontory of green, when the rain, which up until then had been confining itself to irregular bursts, clamped down in earnest. As Bill pushed the big saloon up on to the M9 motorway, curtains of near-solid precipitation were pulled to around them. The world disappeared into an aqueous haze. Bill sat forward in his seat and concentrated hard on the driving. There was so much water on the road that any sudden braking would result in an aquaplane. And the skunk – which never troubled him in clear weather – seemed to slick his brain, so that an injudicious thought might result in a psychic aquaplane. He tried a few more conversational forays with Mark, a few more insinuating questions, but the hitchhiker had clammed up. He'd shot his wad with the Tonka toys anecdote. Either that, or – and the apprehension of this made Bill peculiarly uneasy – Mark was coming to an awareness of the extent to which he'd been filleted; of how much Bill had managed to get out of him, while rendering nothing of his own in return.

What must it feel like, Bill considered, to have given

that much of yourself and got so little in return? It was a version of psychic rape. It was a dishonest employment of his own neglected analytic abilities. It was an abuse of someone who had never agreed to be a patient. It was like trying to get a whore to come. It was an obscenity – a violation. Bill kept silent, piloted the car through its new, turbulent element.

Past Stirling with its folly wavering through the rain. Every time Bill went by he swore that one day he would stop, climb the tower, preferably with a woman. It looked like the tower's summit might be a good place to make love. Or at any rate fuck. The rain was worse now – almost solid. And the traffic was heavier – in every respect. Enormous articulated lorries pummelled the carriage-ways. Bill began to bite the insides of his cheeks. By the time they passed Falkirk, and joined the A80 for a spell, the conditions were truly dangerous, and the big car was wallowing along at between thirty and forty.

There won't be much racing tonight if this keeps up,' Bill said, trying to leaven the atmosphere. But all he got from Mark was a grunt.

Bill couldn't get the Tonka-toy racing out of his head. He could picture it only too well: the drunk ragamuffins at the top of the road, their outsize toys clutched between their tattered bejeaned legs. The knots of men and women spilling on to the pavements from pubs and clubs. And then the bellow to begin. The acrylic wheels skittering and scraping on the paving. The sense of accelerating on nothing as the stabilising legs retract. A biff here, a bash there, and all the time picking up speed. The racers' jerky perspectives disclosing only the onrush of the street . . . How will it all end, if not in tears? Tough, tough toys – for tough, tough boys.

'I can't drop you right in Glasgow –'

'Whassat?' Mark had to shout over the drumming of the downpour and the thrumming of bass. Bill killed the CD.

'I can't drop you right in Glasgow, I was going to let you off when I got on to the M73, but –' Bill remembered the confused pack, the cheap plastic poncho. 'I couldn't do that in this rain – you'd be soaked.' Mark gave him a look as if to suggest that this was all that people like Bill ever did to people like him. 'What would you say to my dropping you in Motherwell and then you can get the train in from there – it'll only be a few quid . . .'

Mark looked at Bill, his expression heavily freighted with the lack of a few quid more than the very few quid he had; and the eternal recurrence of people's assumption that he might be capable of making good the deficiency. Bill thought of Mark's night out, the cheap drinks scrounged; the dregs drained; a crumb of hash on a pin head trapped beneath a milk bottle; perhaps solvents or fights towards dawn. Bill ambivalently relished the opportunity to say, 'Look, it's no bother to me – a few quid. I'll stump it up . . . and well, who knows, maybe you'll have the chance to pay it back in the future.' Bill presented Mark with the grin of an inverted Cheshire cat – it was gone long before Bill was.

'I wouldna' want to impose –' said Mark, with the easy non-assurance of someone who had been doing just that for years.

'It's no problem – no worry.' Bill wanted to go on with this mini litany of reassurance, to say that there would be no *pain*, no *poverty*, no *want* of any kind. That Mark and he would be reunited after the storm had spluttered to a finish. That they would find themselves in a field, verdant with opportunity, growing with cash; and that the two of them would smoke skunk and drink whisky. Make fiscal hay while the sun shone.

But instead Bill said nothing – simply drove; and as the prow of the big car parted the downpouring waves he envisioned Sauchiehall Street, the tough, tough toys, their tough, tough riders. Surely with this offer of money Mark would ask him something – his *name* even. But no.

They splashed past the slip road for the M8 and central Glasgow. By the time they reached the Motherwell exit of the M74 the rain hadn't simply thinned – it had gone altogether. The road ahead was mirror-bright once more; the verges painfully green. Even the outcrops of housing in the middle distance appeared sluiced into cleanness. See The Difference With Flash-floods. If only this will hold, thought Bill, knowing full well it wouldn't. He began making those same, implausible calculations of hard driving he had made on the road out of Thurso that morning. It was four-thirty now, drop the hitchhiker by five. He might be in the region of Manchester by eight, Birmingham by ten, home by midnight – wherever that was.

They were puttering up the hill into Motherwell, then they were channelled into the switchbacks of the one-way system. The inhabitants of the old steel town had taken the break in the rain as a signal to sally forth. There was a preponderance of wheeled shopping bags and thick overcoats among the precincts. Eventually Bill found the entrance to the station and pulled in. He twisted sideways in his seat, while Mark, galvanised by arrival, yanked open his door, swung out, opened the back door and commenced reassuming his confused backpack. Bill managed to extract a tenner from his tight pocket; a tenner so worn and soft that it felt like the pocket lining. 'This should do it,' he said to Mark. The hitchhiker looked at the money as it were no more than his due – a reasonable prophylactic, Bill tacitly agreed, to the shame occasioned by receiving charity.

'Are you sure?'

'No problem, really, no problem at all.'

'Well, thanks for that, really, thanks . . .' Mark dried, perhaps conscious of a hole in his gratitude; a hole where a name should have been inserted – but it was too late for that now. 'I dunno – maybe some time –'

'Whenever, really – whenever.' Bill did his negative Cheshire cat act again.

'And thanks for the lift, and the smoke . . . and the dram –'

'Really, no problem, good to have company. I wish you luck with all of your endeavours. A bright young man like you – you'll come through.' Sounding portentous no longer seemed to matter. It was better to pull out this Capraesque bullshit, rather than allow Mark to wallow in the gathering realisation that he was an unthinking, unfeeling drone. That he could take a lift from a man, smoke his dope, eat his food, drink his whisky, and then take his money, all without even asking him his name.

The hitchhiker stood, one foot on a newly laid kerb, the other on the wet asphalt of the roadway. His pack was back on his back, his poncho caught the wind and billowed: the spinnaker for a solo yacht on a round-the-life race.

Bill leaned across and addressed him through the lowered passenger-door window. 'And as for the dosh – don't worry about it. I hope there's a couple of quid left over – you'll need some oil for the racing tonight –' Bill heard Mark try and cut across this final imprecation, but the big car was already rolling, and the blunt hand was already circling, and the bloodshot eyes were already checking, and the bored ears were already adjusting to the thrum of bass.

In the rearview mirror Bill saw Mark jerk the pack into a more comfortable position and head towards the station entrance. It wasn't until he was back on the M74 and rolling south, at speed, that Bill considered what it might have been that the hitchhiker was trying to say.

Food, who needed it? It just made you shit more on these sedentary migrations. Best not to bother. Best not to think about rest either. Those signs that whip by in the already hazy periphery of vision:

T...A...K...E......A......B...R...E...A...K...
T...I...R...E...D...N...E...S...S......K...I...L...L...S.

And what would rest be like anyway? Bill had tried that option, sagged across the wheel like a human air bag, in some forlorn service-station car-park. Or Welcomed Inn to seven hours of thrashing in thin duvets, then tea-making in the chill dawn, rearranging individual plastic cups of UHT milk on a little ledge, before putting on his pants, his jacket, driving again.

No, stopping was out of the question – there had already been an unscheduled halt at Mrs McRae's. But that was only to be expected . . . by the time the *Ola* got into Scrabster it had already been eleven . . . and there was no point in pushing on with that savage headache . . . or that savage tremor. Did he perhaps have a savage tremor now? Bill held one hand free of the steering wheel and watched its level, relative to the horizon of the windscreen itself, which, as he honed in on it, gulped up a hundred metres of road and a chunk of hillside. No, no tremor in particular. Bill groped for a couple more Pro-Plus pills in his jacket pocket. He lit another cigarette. He boosted his speed, overtaking a lorry, undertaking a panel van in the fast lane, ratcheting the big car up to ninety-five as he hovered back to within sideswiping distance of the central barrier. Strip-the-steel-willow!

Bill liked this section of the drive. To have slipped away from Glasgow so surely, and now to bucket down Clydesdale with the last of the afternoon sun bouncing over his shoulder, and the hills of the Ettrick Forest opening up to the south-west. It was also an entrance to another hinterland – the Borders – and suitable that night should meet day here as well.

But, Christ! Bill was tired. And ever since he'd dropped the hitchhiker in Motherwell, dropped him back into his own particular sink of anonymity, he had felt troubled. It was a mistake to have picked up the hitchhiker. *He* certainly hadn't appreciated the gesture. No, not a gesture – actually an *altruistic act*. Or was it that the hitchhiker had got his measure all too well? He wasn't that stupid. He had been genuinely affronted by the inquisition, resolved to give nothing real at all – spun Bill a line. 'Genuinely affronted'! What an asinine expression. Bill laughed at the asininity and then tried to surf a little more on his own hilarity. He tried to imagine that he was high – and lighthearted. It didn't work.

Darkness was welling up from the road; to the west it flowed from the valleys. Bill switched the lights back on to full beam. I'll be cosy in my little light tunnel, he joked. He had stopped at Mrs McRae's because he was sick with drink. He had more or less gone up to Orkney this time because he was sick with drink. He didn't like doing locums – he couldn't hold any other kind of job down. Not any more. He knew what genuinely affronted him – Bill did. What genuinely affronted him was the vigour of his fingernails. They kept on growing despite everything. Even now, the pallid fingers wrapped around the steering wheel each had their own dear little crescent of new life –

and new dirt. Only something as dumb as a fingernail could go on growing in this hellish environment. Take skin, for example. Take the skin on Bill's ankles – Bill had. Bill had picked and plucked and even strummed the ulcerating skin on his ankles, and it had rewarded him by generously suppurating. That was skin for you – very intelligent stuff. Didn't go on growing after death, like hair or nails.

The hitchhiker had had this information encoded in his own lousy, drink-raddled body. In that they were alike – in that and perhaps a lot else as well. Bill thought of how workable, how trustworthy, his denial of his own drink problem usually was. It was like a handy, movable bulwark that he could position in front of any one of the dark corridors leading away from his self-awareness. The hitchhiker – Bill shouldn't have picked him up. He'd broken the rhythm of the journey; he'd made Bill late. He'd fucked with the bulwarks. Ha! Late for his own funeral. No – his own *cremation*. In Hoop Lane, opposite the Express Dairy. When Bill was young he thought that everyone had died here, that everyone was burnt here – at Golders Green Crematorium – their essence disappearing in the form of charcoal smoke issuing from a red-brick tower, into a grey sky. Now Bill knew he had been right.

And now, in the gathering gloom, Bill felt all pushed out of shape. His method of dealing with himself depended on carefully negotiated transitions from being alone to being among others. Hence Mrs McRae – who didn't, of course, count. Hence also Anthony Bohm, who was no threat to anyone; least of all – with his swollen liver more or less *propped* on the bar – to Bill, or any other physic-fond physician for that matter.

The encounter with the hitchhiker had turned Bill

about. He had mentally castigated the hitchhiker for his abusive relationships – but what constituted such an abuse? He knew what constituted such an abuse. The 3 a.m. rows that cranked up and then cranked down and then cranked up again; the siren song of emotional fracture. He knew all about them, just as he had full cognisance of the serial, parallel monogamist's lifestyle. No, no socialese, call a fucking spade a spade. He fucked around – like a spade. Grasped his haft and planted it where he would. At the Felliniesque conversion of Dunrobin Castle it wouldn't simply be a case of wassailing whores causing trouble – the whole emotional Utopia, the whole fantasy of inclusion was just that – a fantasy.

Bill's life was now – and he realised this groping in the dark for the car bottle, as the big saloon whipped through the roundabout and on to the A74 – based, established on exclusion. Every hysterical evasion, every late-night session rubbing up the whisky bottle, until Mr Blubby, the drunken genie, emerged – it was all coming back to him. He took a slug, and in his hurry to get the bottle up and down without leaving go of the wheel, managed to slop several measures on to his chest. He was tired – and yes, perhaps it would be worth admitting it to himself – just a little drunk.

No time to consider that now. Heads down, no non-sense, mindless boogie. Hone in on the music – ignore the background screech of the Furies, who pursued him: 'Bill! Bill! Why did you do it/say it/go there/lie/come back/treat me like this!' He pumped up the CD. He bit down on another caffeine lozenge, hoping the bitterness alone might make him alert. It wasn't working. The road was doubly blurred. He rubbed one ulcerated shin against the other. He chomped the inside of his cheek. He pinched the

fat on the inside of his thighs with his unabashed fingernails. Eventually he took to slapping himself. Big, open-
handed clouts. First one with the left, then one with the
right. Left to left and right to right. Each blow gave him a
few seconds of clarity, another hundred metres of onrush-
ing progress.

And as the big car bisected the night, drumming past
Lockerbie, ignoring the blue signs that blazoned: Carlyle's
Birthplace, and eventually gaining the M6 – which was lit
for its first few miles, a tarmac chute – Bill gutted the
carcass of his own life. He pulled out the entrails of
neglect, and the gall bladder of resentment; he removed
the engorged liver of indulgence, and excised the kidneys
of cynicism. He fumbled in the cavities of his body for his
heart – but couldn't find it.

The big car plunged on. No longer a chimera, a meld
between man and machine, but merely a machine, with a
ghost loose in it somewhere. Desperately Bill shuffled his
pack of shiny memories, of *al fresco* lovemaking, of
dramatic hill scenery, of . . . his son. Who would be
what – around five now. Not very clever that. Not clever
at all – to have not seen your own child for two years.
Three years. It had been three years.

That had been the shabbiest of the accusations he
had laid against the hitchhiker – the one of neglect.
Bill knew all about neglect. He knew all about unanswered phone calls, crumpled-up letters, torn postcards.
People said they didn't want children because they
didn't want the responsibility. But if you didn't take
responsibility for them – how could you have it for
yourself?

About forty minutes later, at Shap in the Lake District,
at the point where the M6 really did begin to feel as if it
were plunging inexorably downhill, down to the south,

down to London, the ghost that was piloting the machine took a long final look in the rearview mirror, before lazily circling the steering wheel to the left and turning into an inexistent layby.

DESIGN FAULTS IN THE VOLVO 760 TURBO: A MANUAL

'. . . bearing in mind the fact that everyone hides the truth in matters of sex . . .'

> – Sigmund Freud,
> 'My Views on the Part Played by Sexuality
> in the Aetiology of the Neuroses'

1. Instruments and Controls

Welcome to the terrifyingly tiny world of the urban adulterer. Bill Bywater has been snogging with a woman called Serena. Giving and receiving as much tongue as possible – exactly at the point where Sussex Gardens terminate, and the streams of traffic whip around the dusty triangular enclosure of trees and grass, before peeling away in the direction of Hyde Park, or Paddington, or the M40.

Bill has been snogging – and the adolescent term is quite appropriate here – in a way he remembers from youth. Not that the palpings of lip-on-lip, tongue-on-lip, and tongue-on-tongue have been any less accomplished, or plosively erotic, than we have come to expect from the man. It's just that Serena has recently had an operation on a benign cyst in her cheek. Bit of Lidocaine. Slit and suck – two stitches. Bosh-bosh. 'Perhaps it would be wise' – the surgeon had said, admiring the creamy skin of her cleavage, the standing into being of her ever-so-slightly large breasts – 'if you were to avoid using your mouth for anything much besides eating over the next week or so?'

He was right to make this statement interrogative – almost verging on the rhetorical, because Serena hardly uses her mouth for eating at all, preferring dietary supplements and cocaine to get by on. Serena used to be an 'it' girl – but now she's 'that' woman. A socialite – she went to a finishing school in Switzerland where they taught her to fellate. She'd set her cap at Bill months ago. Not that he wasn't ripe for it.

Serena says, 'I've had a small operation on my cheek . . .' The eyelashes perturb the polluted air, monoxide and burnt rubber. 'Try and be gentle with this side –' She caresses her own elastoplasted cheek. Their bodies marry. Her thighs part slightly to receive the buttressing of his thigh. Her lips begin to worry at his mouth – so adept Bill wonders if they might be prehensile. He allows his hands to link in the region of her coccyx. A thumb lazily traces the rivulets and curves between her arse and the small of her back. She moans into his mouth. The traffic groans into his ear. He concentrates on stimulating the side of her which isn't numb.

As he is snogging, Bill is acutely aware of the time: 6.30 p.m.; the place: Sussex Gardens, W2; and the implied logistics: his wife, Vanessa, cycles home every evening along Sussex Gardens, at more or less this time. It is not unlikely that Vanessa will see Bill snogging with Serena, because Bill is – he acknowledges with a spurt of dread – at least sixty feet high. He bestrides the two lanes of bumpy tarmac, his crotch forming a blue denim underpass for the rumbling traffic. Vanessa will be able to see him – this Colossus of Roads – the very instant she jolts across the intersection of the Edgware Road, and commences pedalling down Sussex Gardens.

Caught bang to rights, caught snogging with this slapper . . . His only defence, the fact that she's a little dolly of a thing compared to him. He's holding her aloft in one hand, clutching her wiggling torso to his huge, bristly cheek. He's having to be so damn gentle, tasting with his forty-inch tongue the sweetness of her two-inch bud. Her white satin shift dress has ridden up over her hips. She isn't wearing any tights – her pants are white, with an embroidered panel over her pubis.

'Bill!' Vanessa shouts up from below – she's ramming her front tyre against his foot, the knobble of uncomfortable bone protruding above the edge of his moccasins. 'Bill – what are you doing!?'

'Doing?' He squints down at her, as if she's caught him in an inconsequential reverie – stagnantly considering the cost-effectiveness of double glazing, or fully comprehensive insurance. 'Doing?' He looks at the writhing, half-stripped woman in his hand, and then sets her down, gingerly, on the far side of the road from his wife. 'Oh *her*, or rather – *this*. It's just a doll, my love – you can't possibly be jealous of a *doll*.'

Couldn't be jealous of a doll, but might well be jealous of Serena who is not only a doll, but who has also, predictably, been a model. Bill, feeling the laser beams of his wife's gaze burning through buildings, fences, filing cabinets, people, had broken the embrace – which was getting nowhere. Or rather, it was getting somewhere only too fast. What could he do with Serena, short of hiring a room in the Lancaster Hotel for half an hour?

No, that would show up on his credit card statement. They were too old for Hyde Park bushes, and the Volvo 760 Turbo was out of the question on account of various design faults.

Serena had been having a session with her therapist, who had his consulting rooms on Sussex Gardens. Bill had arranged to meet her by her car. A metal rendezvous. Serena had a Westminster permit – Bill didn't. He couldn't find a meter for aeons – he imagined her growing old, her face wizening, an old apple on a draining board. When he did eventually find a space – by the needle exchange Portakabin on South Wharf Road – he had neither pound coins nor twenty-pence pieces. He wanted to ejaculate and die – simultaneously. He stopped one, two, three passers-by – got enough to pay for twenty minutes' snogging. Park up the Volvo – and grab a vulva. Pay for space – space to live.

The minutes tick away in her wounded mouth. Until – confident that at any minute he'll get a ticket – Bill breaks from Serena. 'Call!' they call to each other as he staggers back across the road and disappears in the direction of Paddington Station.

Not that he's out of danger yet. Bill starts up the Volvo and savours its clicking, ticking and peeping into life. But when he pulls away he realises – given that he has absolutely no justification for being in this part of London, on this day, at this time – that the car is grotesquely elongated. When he turns right out of London Street and on to Sussex Gardens, the back end of the vehicle is still in Praed Street. When he reaches the lights on the corner of Westbourne Street, his tail end is still blocking the last set of lights, causing traffic in all four directions to back up, and engendering a healthy tirade of horn-accompanied imprecations: 'Youuuu fuuuucking waaaanker!'

Deciding that the only way he can escape detection – given that he's driving an eighty-foot-long vehicle – is to head for the Westway flyover, Bill turns right. As he circles the triangular enclosure where he snogged with Serena, he is appalled to see that the back end of the Volvo is passing by on the other side. He looks through the rear windows of his own car and can see sweet wrappers and medical journals scattered around on the back seat. Jesus! Astonishing how ductile these Volvo chassis are – they know what they're about over there at the Kalmar Plant. Know what they're about when it comes to building an eighty-foot extrudomobile like this, that can be seen clearly from a mile away . . .

Bill Bywater, feeling the Volvo concertina back to its normal length, as he gains the anonymity of the motorway flyover, scrabbles in the breast pocket of his shirt for a cigarette. He lights it with a disposable gas lighter. The dash lighter has long since gone. Bill airily lit a fag with it a year or so ago, waved it gently in the air, and then threw it out the car window. One of the design faults – although hardly limited to the Volvo 760 Turbo – was this lack of a tether.

Another was the ashtray itself. This was accommodated neatly enough, in the central housing of the dash, but it was impossible to pull the tray out at all unless the shift was in drive; and fully out only if it was in first gear. The implications of this stagger Bill anew as he struggles to insinuate his ash-tipped fag into the small gap. Could it be that the car *cognoscenti* at Kalmar intended this as an anti-smoking measure? It hardly made sense. For the ashtray couldn't be opened at all when the shift was in park – implying that you should only smoke, and even empty the ashtray, when the car was in motion.

The Volvo is passing Ladbroke Grove tube station,

doing around seventy. Bill can see commuters tramping the platform. And anyway – even if the operation was technically difficult – he did at least know how to empty the ashtray. The manual expressed it quite succinctly: 'Empty ashtrays by pulling out to the limit and pressing down the tongue.'

Bill was masterful at this – he could even avoid the cyst.

2. Body and Interior

Bill has arranged to meet Serena at a pub in Maida Vale. It's a barn of a gaff on Cunningham Place – so prosaic it might even be called The Cunningham. It's the night of a vital World Cup qualifier for England, and the city soup is being insistently thickened by cars, as the spectators head for their home terraces. The driving is stop-start – and so is the parking. Eventually, he finds a tight space on Hamilton Terrace. He cuts in well enough the first time, but the space is so confined that he has to turn the steering wheel in the other direction, then back, then reverse again, each time gaining just a few inches more of the precious, temporary possession.

With each rotation the power steering 'Eeeeeeyouuuus' – a fluid, pleasurable kind of whine; and with each dab on brake, or plunge on accelerator, the rubber limbs buck, receiving pressure or its release. 'In-Glands! In-Glands! In-Glands!' his pulse chants in his temples. Bill feels exposed – in this act of taking the space; worries that he may be observed, censured. When he's finally got himself and the car properly berthed – no more than six inches to front and aft – he lunges out the door, giddy in the hot, sappy, fume-tangy evening air. But there's nothing; only an old woman with secateurs in a front garden; the roar of traffic from the Edgware Road; a Tourettic man – gnome-like with a spade of grey beard – who high-steps it over the domed camber of the road, legs smiting his chest, whilst he expels a series of sharp 'Papp-papp-papp!' sounds.

Bill is reassured. In a London uncaring enough to ignore such blatancy – the Tourettic looking as if he were on a run-up to jumping clear of his own nervous system – Bill's own peccadilloes *not even consummated, as yet*, can hardly be of any interest at all. Still, it takes him five minutes of walking up the road, patting his pockets, retracing his steps to see if he has forgotten anything, or dropped anything, or illegally parked the car – only too easy to do in a city where the controls of adjoining zones are radically different – before he resigns himself to the concrete reality of the rendezvous. He is going to meet Serena – this time he might fuck her.

Serena is sitting on one of the four trestle-table-and-bench combinations that occupy the dirty oblong of paving in between The Cunningham itself, and the low brick wall that borders it. A very believable terrace – for London. There are metal ashtrays with beer spilt into them, there are crisp packets wedged in the tabletop cracks, there are sunshades poking through two of these tabletops. One advertises Martini – the other is in tatters. The compression of boozing bodies within the cavernous boozer is already considerable; the baying of the clientele and the baying of the Wembley crowd – relayed by a giant-screen television suspended from the ceiling – are echoing one another. The beery exhalations surge from the double doors of the pub; which are propped back, so as to allow the T-shirted multi-lung to draw in another great gulp of exhausted air.

Bill considers that this rendezvous is taking place within a spatial gap – the Edgware Road/Maida Vale hinterland –

and, more importantly, a temporal one. 'I can't stand all this nationalist sporting triumphalism' – he has been priming Vanessa the five days since he avoided Serena's cyst – 'it's going to reach a hideous climax . . . And then what – when they lose there'll be a national depression for days. I can't stand it. I want to opt out.'

Of course, what Bill really wants to opt out of is any situation of *bonhomie*, of excitation, that might embrace them – and tighten up the vice of fidelity. Bill has been working on his dissatisfactions with Vanessa for weeks now – building up a comprehensive dossier of her awfulness. Without this adulterers' manifesto Bill knows he'll be incapable of being remotely serene – with Serena. It would only take one embrace, one shared apprehension, for him to have to abandon his plans. Therefore, why not excise this possibility *and* use the time available.

'Shit! It's all shit!' he had cried an hour or so before. 'I can't stand it – I'm off out. I've got to find somewhere – anywhere where nobody's concerned about this fucking football match!' He then grabbed his car keys from the hall table, performed an uninteresting arabesque in the process of snatching up the CD face-off and his mobile phone, before slamming the door and sprinting off up the garden path. Vanessa, who was sat marking spelling tests, wondered what the hell her husband was on about – she wasn't remotely interested in the football international; and their two-year-old son was, somewhat proleptically, already at his grandmother's.

'Hi!' says Serena – who cares nothing for Bill's predicament, who indeed positively savours it. 'I thought you wouldn't make it.'

'Traffic – parking.' He fobs her off with his key fob. 'Have you got a drink?' She downs the rest of her sea breeze and downs the glass.

'No.'

He shuttles in and out of the bar over the next half-hour. Serena has four more sea breezes – a nicely paradoxical drink for this landlocked Saragossa. Bill struggles to keep his alcohol intake down; tonight has undoubtedly seen the inception of a special Metropolitan Police Task Force to deal with adulterous drunk drivers. Every time he thinks she isn't looking – he checks his watch. The seconds are ticking by towards half-time. In the meantime they edge closer as well.

Serena is wearing a black suede miniskirt. It has six brass buttons to fasten it at the front – but the three bottom ones are undone. Serena is wearing a cream silk blouse and no bra. Serena never wears tights in summer – her legs are too good. Each time she leans forward Bill sucks her nipples; each time she leans back he runs his bent-back index finger up the front of her pants. Not.

Bill dives into the public bar of The Cunningham and edges through the crowd of passive dribblers. 'Awwwww!' they cry – awed by some feat of failure. It takes several such 'awws' and accompanying pokes in the ribs for Bill to gain the far side of the public bar, and the stairs down to the toilets. In the toilet he releases the trap of his flies and the grey hound of penis comes out frothing. Painful – peeing with an erection – Bill has to force himself into alarming postures in order to lend his urine to the giant ceramic ear. While he's doing this he reflects on the paradoxical sense of control offered by reckless driving.

That's what he needs – to get Serena away from the pub, get her in the Volvo, take her for a spin. There's a vanity mirror set into the passenger-seat sunshade – she'll like that. And there'll be no chance of being observed by anyone who knows either of them – or Bill's wife. Even if Bill's wife were to suddenly manifest herself in the Volvo – Serena could hide in the glove compartment, as any other adulterer might hide in a cupboard. She really was a doll.

3. Starting and Driving

It takes the same brake shoe-shuffle to extract the Volvo (overall length four metres and seventy-nine centimetres) from the parking space. Bill, as he circles the steering wheel back and forth, wishes he were coming rather than going – because he could then make some crack to Serena, analogise the parking space and *her* space.

They pop up on to the crown of Hamilton Terrace and Bill turns the big car to the north. He is conscious of Serena on the seat beside him, her thighs slightly parted, her trunk slightly tilted in his direction, a tip of pink tongue between her scarlet lips. 'How's the cyst?' he forays – they have yet to snog.

'Better!' she laughs, a horrible, expensive, phone-your-divorce-lawyer kind of laugh. She is – Bill reflects – an awful, venal, unprincipled and deeply alluring woman.

Bill turns right into Hall Road and then left into Abbey Road. He's driving fast – the decision to leave the pub had been mutual. He had said, 'It's getting insane in there – looks like they'll be going to a penalty shoot-out. Let's get out of here, go somewhere where there's neither sight nor sound of football, hmm?' And she had said, 'If you like.'

The streets are emptied of traffic – the whole city is inside, watching the match. Bill banks to the right, to the left, he feels the weight of the car shift beneath him like a body. He concentrates on the whine of the transmission and the thrum of the engine. He pokes at the CD and a track with a suitably heavy bass line begins to underscore the tense atmosphere in the car. 'Drive smoothly, avoid fast starts, hard cornering and heavy braking . . .' What the hell do they think anyone wants a Volvo 760 Turbo for, if, as the manual suggests above, it's inadvisable to drive the car with any alacrity?

At Kalmar – where Bill knows from his careful reading of the manual, the Volvo 760 Turbo is built by dedicated teams of workers, rather than by an unconscious and alienated assembly line – they presumably have no need of the car's maximal performance capability. In the sexually tolerant atmosphere of Sweden, the Volvo has evolved as a highly safe vehicle in which to transport the promiscuous. If you're about to start an affair with a fellow worker at the Plant, you simply say to your wife, 'Bibi, I've decided that I must make love to Liv. I shall take the estate today – and a clean duvet!' Whereupon she replies, 'Of course, Ingmar, but remember, "Protective bags should be used to avoid soiling the upholstery" . . .'

'You seem preoccupied?' Bill wouldn't have believed that anyone could actually say this whilst toying with her silken *décolletage* – but Serena just has.

'Mmm . . . з'роэс зо, work, y'know '

'Yes! Your work.' Serena stirs her languor into an animated whirl. 'What's it like being a shrink? Have you got any really weird, disturbed patients? D'jew think I'm crazy?'

Bill tilts the car up on to Fitzjohn's Avenue before replying, 'Which of those questions do you want me to answer first?'

'Oh, the last, I suppose . . .'

Christ! The woman knows how to toy – she's a world-class toyer. 'Why on earth do you imagine that you're crazy?'

Serena takes her time answering. She chafes her thighs together so slowly that Bill cannot forbear from imagining the minute accommodations of flesh, hair and membrane that are going on behind the three-buttoned curtain covering her lap. Eventually, when they are level with Lindy's Pâtisserie on Heath Street, she comes back with, 'Bluntly, I find I have to have a really good orgasm every day,' and gives him an amazing smile, her teeth so white and vulpine, her gums so pink.

Bill feels the sweat burst from his armpits like spray from a shower fitment. He grips the wheel so tightly that as the Volvo bucks across the junction with Hampstead High Street, he feels he might wrench it clear off and twist the O of metal, foam and plastic into an involved pretzel shape. Kerrist! He's thinking about adultery in Hampstead – it's gone this far, he keens inside; my life has plunged into a prosaic – prolix even – vanishing point.

At Whitestone Pond they stop in order to allow a man with black-and-white striped trousers to traverse the zebra crossing. Serena doesn't appear to notice this – but Bill does. Bill finds he is noticing everything: the golden micro-fleece on the nape of Serena's neck; a model yacht on the pond, tacking neatly around a floating Coke can; to the right of the road the Heath, and beyond it, collapsing waves of concrete and glass and brick and steel – maritime London. 'When you say "a really good orgasm" ' – Bill chooses her words carefully – 'do you mean good in a moral sense?'

Serena breaks into trills and even frills of laughter – if that's possible. 'Tee-hee-hee, oh no – not at all! *I* mean a ripping, snorting, tooth-clashing, thoroughly cathartic orgasm, one that makes me feel as if every individual nerve ending has climaxed. *That* kind of good orgasm.'

'Oh, that kind.' Bill feels certain he's damaged the turbo unit. He habitually does everything to the Volvo's engine that – according to the manual – he shouldn't. He races it immediately after starting, before the cold oil has had a chance to reach all the lubricating points. Worse than that, the engine has also been turned off when the turbocharger was at high speed – with the risk of seizing or heat damage – although, admittedly it wasn't Bill who'd done it.

It was Vanessa. She managed to lean right across Bill, tear the keys out of the ignition and throw them out the window of the car and clear over the parapet of the Westway, as the Volvo was ploughing along it at seventy. When they had coasted to a halt, Vanessa threw herself out as well. No one likes to be made a fool of.

Bill parks the car in the small car-park off Hampstead Lane, diagonally opposite to Compton Avenue. They walk out on to the Heath. A light breeze is blowing up here and within seconds it's dried their sweaty brows, cooled their sweaty bodies. They embrace and Bill feels Serena's hair being blown about his chops. It's the closest he's ever been, he realises, to a shampoo commercial.

They walk on, stopping every few yards for more snogging and groping. Bill is certain he has never had a more turgid erection in his life. If he flung himself forward on to the macadamised path, his resilient member would simply bounce him back up again. If he took his trousers off and scampered across the grass he would, to all intents and purposes, be indistinguishable from the famous statuette of Priapus, his penis as large and curved as a bow. Good orgasm, ha! Great orgasm, more like.

On top of Parliament Hill they take their bodies to a bench that faces out over the city, and sit them there to listen to its peculiar silence. From the direction of Gospel Oak a man comes running up the hill. Even from three hundred yards away Bill can see that he's wearing an England football shirt. The man is clearly in some distress; as he nears Bill becomes aware of labouring breath and pumping arms. He comes up to them like someone about to deliver news of a bad naval defeat by the Persians. But instead of collapsing he props himself against their bench saying, 'Iss gone to penalty shoot-outs – I couldn't cope any more.'

He's a small plump man, with a bald pate fringed by a neat horseshoe of grey hair. Clearly football is his life. 'I got meself this fucking big Havana – to celebrate wiv.' He displays the stogie to them, clamped in his humid paw. 'But now I dunno, I dunno, I can't cope –'

'We came here to get away from the football,' says Serena.

'Me too, me too,' the man puffs back.

'Actually' – Bill takes a certain delight in this savage betrayal – 'I bet we'll be able to hear the result from up here.' On cue there's an enormous roar from the city below. 'There we go, that was one goal.'

The three of them wait for two minutes, then there's a second eruption of roaring from the metropolis. They wait another two minutes and . . . nothing. Worse than nothing – a negative roar, a sonic vacuum in which a roar should have been. 'They've missed one . . . the fuckers . . . they've missed one . . .' The little man is destroyed, ripped asunder. He grinds the Havana into the grass with his training shoe, then he heads off back down the hill.

Five minutes later Bill and Serena are rutting in a copse.

4. Wheel and Tyres

It is four days later and Bill Bywater sits at the desk which occupies most of the half-landing in his Putney house.

Vanessa likes to be by the river; Bill rather wishes she was in it. Bill thinks it suitable that his study should occupy this in-between place, neither up nor down, because he has an in-between kind of psyche – especially at the moment. This is now the terrifyingly tiny house of the urban adulterer and Bill moves about it with incredible subtlety, acutely aware that every movement – from now on and for the rest of his natural life – will constitute a potential, further violation.

Bill sits at the desk and contemplates the Volvo 760 Owner's Manual for the year 1988 – perversely enough the year of his marriage. He has reached the section entitled 'Wheels and Tyres'. Bill smiles manically – he's lost his grip – and reaches for the Tipp-Ex. On the opposing page there's a neat pen-and-wash drawing of a 1957 Volvo Amazon, captioned accordingly. With great deliberation Bill applies the little brush with its clot of liquid paper to the word 'Volvo' and smiles, satisfied by its deletion. It is approximately the hundredth instance of the word that he has dealt with, and soon the manual will become an opaque text, the arcanum of a vanished religion.

As he leafs back through the pages, Bill is deeply satisfied by the small white lozenges of Tipp-Ex smattering them. They look like the results of pin-point accurate ejaculations. Bill, like Freud, has never repudiated or abandoned the importance of sexuality and infantilism, and with this unusual action he is attempting to reorient his sexuality through infantile handiwork. Bill is working hard to convince himself that by eradicating the word 'Volvo' from the manual, he will also annul his obsession with Serena's vulva, which has got quite out of hand.

In the copse she made Bill take off all of his clothes – and all of her own. At last his hands got to go on stage and open her curtain skirt. He shivered despite the summer heat and the close, dusty rot of desiccated shrubbery. 'What's the problem?' she laughed at him, cupping her own breasts, stimulating her own nipples. 'No point in worrying about the cops – we're in it already.' Their clothing made an inadequate stage for the performance that ensued. Bill could never have guessed that such a sexual Socrates would prove so satisfied a pig; she snorted and truffled in the musty compost. They had fucked five times since – top 'n' tailing each other at the top 'n' tail of each day.

Again and again Bill scans the preamble to the section, which admonishes him to 'Read the following pages carefully', but his eyes keep sliding down to the subheading 'Special Rims', what can it mean? On page 67 there are directions for changing wheels, and a photograph of a young woman doing just that. The caption reads: 'Stand next to body.' Bill finds this distracting, but not as much as he does the boldface line further down the page which reads: **'Make sure that the arm is lodged well in the attachment.'**

Bill sighs and throws down the Tipp-Ex brush. It's no good, it's not working. Instead of the deletion of the word 'Volvo' cancelling out thoughts of Serena's vulva, it's enhancing them. The firm, warm, lubricious embrace of living leather; the smell of saliva and cigarette smoke; the twitter and peep of the CD – a soundtrack for orgasm. Perhaps, Bill thinks, perhaps if I get to the very root of this I'll do better. Perhaps if I delete the word 'Volvo' from the car itself it will do the trick?

Serena has mastered a trick. She can apply ever so slight pressure to Bill's indicator levers and she can effortlessly flick his shift into drive. Serena has undoubtedly read and absorbed the manual. Bill wouldn't be at all surprised to learn that she knew exactly how to grease the nipple on the retractable-type towing bracket. That's the sort of woman she is, as at home in a family car like the Volvo 760, as she would be in a sportier model.

Bill crouches by the radiator grille. The tarmac is so warm on this summer evening that his feet subside a little into the roadway. In his right hand Bill holds a pot of Humbrol metal paint, in his left a brush. He is carefully painting out the word 'Volvo' on the maker's badge of the car. He hears a riffle of rubber wheels and the fluting of a toddler, and turns to see that Vanessa has come up beside him, pushing their son in his buggy.

'Bill' – how can a voice be so cram-packed with wry irony (or 'wiferonry' as Bill awkwardly compounds it – to himself) – 'what on earth are you doing?'

'Whaddya' think?' he snaps.

'I don't know – that's why I asked.' The toddler's eyes are round with anxiety; his life is already characterised by these tonal conflicts between giants, Gog and Magog smiting his Fischer-Price bell.

'I'm getting rid of all the instances of the word "Volvo" on this fucking car – that's what I'm doing.'

'Dada said the F word.' The toddler doesn't lisp – his voice is high and precise.

'Dada wants to rid himself of the F word,' Vanessa pronounces sententiously.

'How true, how true . . .' Bill mutters.

When the buggy and its cargo have disappeared inside the house Bill straightens up; he has arranged to meet Serena in the pub in St John's Wood, and more importantly – he's covered. He holds a seminar at the Middlesex Hospital every Wednesday evening at this time, so Vanessa won't be curious about his absence. Bill stashes the paint and brush in the cardboard box of car impedimenta that he keeps in the boot of the ex-Volvo. He strolls up the path and opening the front door with his key shouts into the crack, 'I'm off!' and at the same time snatches up the CD face-off, his mobile and a sheaf of lecture notes he has to drop off for Sunil Rahman – who is giving the seminar. To Vanessa, who is feeding the toddler in the kitchen, this irruption of sound is just that – an odd kind of effect, as of a train window being opened while passing through a tunnel at speed.

In the ex-Volvo, waiting at the lights by Putney Bridge, Bill dickers with the servos that alter the angle and rake of the driver's seat. One of the servos is on the blink, and if he presses the button too much the seat tilts forward and to the left, threatening to deposit him face down, dangling over the steering wheel, in a posture all too reminiscent of how Bill imagines a suicide would end up after making with a section of hose and watering the interior of the ex-Volvo with exhaust fumes. 'Jesus!' he exclaims out loud as the lights change. 'I've got to stop this!'

Proceeding up Fulham Palace Road Bill faffs around with nodulous buttons until he manages to get Serena's number. He clutches the purring instrument to his ear and hears her recorded pout. When the time comes he leaves a plaint in place of himself: can't make it, lecture, car trouble . . . later. This isn't, of course, the first time that Bill's bailed out of this kind of situation, nor, he suspects, will it be the last.

The lecture notes dropped in reception at the hospital, Bill wheels the big car up on to the Westway and heads out of town. There's only one place for him now, Thame, and only one person he can speak to, Dave Adler, proprietor of the Thame Motor Centre – Repairs and Bodywork Our Speciality. Dave has worked on Bill's Volvo for many years now – ever since he gave up psychiatry. Dave sees no intrinsic design faults in the Volvo 760 Turbo itself, rather he is inclined to locate them in the driver.

Conversations between the two men usually go something like this:

Dr Bill Bywater: Dave? It's Bill.

Dr Dave Adler: Yeah.

Dr BB: There seems to be something wrong with the transmission . . .

Dr DA: Yeah.

Dr BB: The car isn't changing up smoothly, it sort of over-revs and then – well, *surges*.

Dr DA: Have you checked the automatic transmission fluid?

Invariably Bill hasn't checked it, or the windscreen reservoir, or the oil, or the brake fluid, or indeed any of the seething, bubbling liquids that course through the car's blocky body. This will provide Dave Adler with an entrée for a sneer about how ridiculously cavalier Bill is about his car, and how if he would only pay attention to maintenance he wouldn't run into this trouble.

While Bill smiles to himself at the thought of the unscheduled lecture he will receive this evening when he turns up in Thame, the ex-Volvo rumbles down off the flyover and heads west into the soft heart of Britain.

Forty minutes later the car rolls to a halt in a dusty lane that snakes away from the market square of the small Oxfordshire town. The high wooden doors of Dave Adler's garage are shut and chained. Dangling from the hasp of the lock is a peculiar sign which Dave uses in lieu of a more conventional one. The sign reads: 'BEARING IN MIND THE FACT THAT EVERYONE HIDES THE TRUTH IN MATTERS OF SEX – WE'RE CLOSED.' Bill guffaws to himself, albeit a little wearily.

Meanwhile, in Putney, Dave Adler lowers himself carefully into the inspection pit of the Bywaters' marital bed. He has the necessary equipment and he's intent on giving Vanessa Bywater's chassis a really thorough servicing. As far as Dave Adler is concerned a car is a means of transport, nothing more and nothing less.

THE NONCE PRIZE

1.

Danny and Tembe were standing in the kitchen of their house on Leopold Road, Harlesden, north-west London. It was a cold morning in early November, and an old length of plastic clothesline was thwacking against the window as the wind whipped it about. The brothers were cooking up some crack cocaine; Danny worked the stove while Tembe handled the portions of bicarb and powder. On the kitchen table a deconstructed boom box – the CD unit, speakers and controls unhoused, connected only by a ganglion of cabling – was playing tinny-sounding drum 'n bass.

Tembe had heard an item of gossip when he went to buy the powder off the Irishman in Shepherd's Bush three hours before, gossip he was now hot to impart. 'Yeah-yeah-yeah,' he said, 'sheeit! Those fuckers jus' sat in the fuckin' house an' waited for the punters to come along –'

'Issat the troof?' Danny cut in, but not like he really cared.

'I'm telling you so. The filth were smart, see, they come in an' do the house at aroun' eleven in the morning – like the only fuckin' down time in the twenty-four. Bruno and Mags was washing up an oz in the kitchen – Sacks was crashed out with some bint in the front room. They got one of them jackhammer things, takes the fuckin' door to

175

pieces, man, an' then they come in with flak jackets and fuckin' *guns*, man, like they've got the fuckin' tactical whatsit unit out for this one –'

'Tactical firearms unit,' Danny snapped, 'thass what they call it – but anyways, wasn't Bruno tooled?'

'Yeah – and some. The blud claat had a fuckin' Saturday night special, .22 some motherfucker built from a fuckin' starting pistol. You recall I tol' you that Bruno shot that nigger Gance and the bullet bounced of his fuckin' rib – that was this shooter. Anyways he didn't have no time nor nuffin' for that cos' they was on 'im in seconds, gave him a good pasting, nicked his fuckin' stash, nicked about a grand he had in cash, an' then tol' 'im he had to front it up while they nicked all the fuckin' punters.'

'And did he?'

'Yeah, man. Solid. He had no choice. He sat there by the fuckin' door an' greeted them all in. Jus' imagine it, man, you fink you're goin' to score a nice rock, you're all didgy about it, all worked up an' that, pumping, right, an' you get to the fuckin' door, in a right state, only to get fuckin' nicked! Silly motherfuckers! The filth got twenty of them – that's that Bruno out of the fuckin' crack business –' and Tembe, no longer able to contain himself at the thought of this busted crack house, like a ship of fools grounded off the All Saints Road, burst into peals of unrestrained laughter; a laughter that to Danny's over-sensitive ears sounded peculiarly harsh and insistent.

To cut the flow Danny waved the bottle he'd been cooking the crack up in in front of Tembe's face. 'Lissen,' Danny said, 'now you've tol' me hows about I get to have my fuckin' get up an' that – yeah?'

'Yeah, all right, no fussin', yeah. Keep it mellow like . . .' Tembe fumbled around in the mound of crack that sat drying on a wad of kitchen towelling, his finger picked a peck and he passed it over. 'There you go – thass at least three hits, bro', get it down you an' then fuck off an' that.' Danny wasn't paying any attention to this, he'd already fumbled out his stem from where he kept it, tucked in the top of his right boot, and was crumbling a pinch of crack into its battered end. Once the stem was primed he lit the blow torch and commenced smoking.

Tembe regarded him with quizzical contempt. 'Y' know I mean it,' he said, putting on his most managerial of tones for this troublesome employee. 'I want you doin' those City drops like *now*, man. Those boys want their shit nice an' early. If you're done by one, you can pick up another 'teenth – do the bitches at the Learmont. I'll sling you some brown in all –'

'How much?' Danny snapped, he was still holding down the hit of crack.

'A bag – whatever.'

'In that case,' he spoke through the gust of exhalation, 'you do the fuckin' portioning – and I'll' – he snatched up a roll of clingfilm from the work surface – 'do the fuckin' wrapping.'

Two hours later Danny was limping down Aldergate. It was raining and he was soaked through. About the driest things he had about his person, Danny reflected bitterly, were the rocks of crack housed in his cheeks, each one snugly wrapped and heat-sealed in plastic.

'Do the City,' Tembe impatiently ordered and off Danny had to go, clanking down the Bakerloo Line to Oxford Circus, and then clanking on along the Central Line until he reached Bank. On the fucking tube, the *tube*, not even a cab to ease his lot. And when he got to Bank it was the fucking foot slog. Up to Citibank, the stupid plastic jacket he had to wear flapping in the wind and rain, the defunct radio attached to its lapel banging against his collar bone. Then get the fucking Jiffy-bag out in the vestibule. Spit a couple of rocks into it. Seal it. Up to fucking reception: 'Delivery for Mistah Fuckin' Crack-Head Banker.'

'Fine, if you leave it right here I can sign for it –'

'Sorry, it's a special whatsit thingy – he's gotta sign himself, yeah?'

'Oh right – sure, I'll ring his extension.' She looks through Danny at a Monet reproduction while he waits, finger-drummingly bored. And then here he comes, Mistah Fuckin' High Wire Act, tripping across the quarter-acre of carpet tiling without a care in the world, on his own little personal conveyor belt, which is carrying him straight to a seventy-quid Nirvana.

'Is that for me? Thank you. Where can I sign – there?'

You can sign wherever you fucking please, asshole, because this biro doesn't work and this bit of paper is just that.

'Thanks again – and do give my regards to Mr Tembe.' He rolls away again.

Fucking pin-stripe suit, fucking old school tie. He won't be looking so fucking dignified in five minutes' time, Danny internally sneers as he slops his way back to the lift, sitting in a fucking toilet stall, pretending to do a shit while he sucks on a pipe made from a crushed Coke can. Silly cunt.

In Aldergate Danny paused to envy a dosser. The young white guy sat in the doorway of a travel agent's, surfing to nowhere on a piece of old packing case. His blue nylon sleeping bag was pulled up to his armpits, leaving his arms free for entreaty. He looked, Danny thought, like some enormous maggot that had crawled into this niche in order to metamorphose, possibly into a crack-head banker.

Danny gave the dosser a fifty-pence piece, and savoured the shock on the young man's face when he realised he had successfully begged from a black guy not much better off than himself.

Good karma, Danny thought to himself as he slopped on down the road. Give to those worse off than yourself and the Fates will look kindly on you. Nowadays Danny was increasingly drawn to consider the attitude of the Fates to almost anything he did. The Fates had to be consulted as to which sock he should put on first when he got up; which boot he should tuck his stem into before leaving the house; and which side of Leopold Road he should walk down on his way to the tube.

Danny appreciated – with a deep, almost celestial clarity – the fact that the Fates were very much a product of the ten or so rocks of crack he was smoking every day. For one thing the Fates often appeared in his mind's eye as tall, wispy, indeterminate figures, their forms actually *composed* by gossamer wreaths of crack smoke. However, if Danny honed in on them, their miasmic covering fell away to reveal truly terrifying, djinn-like figures – the towel-heads from hell. Bearded, turbaned, wearing long grey-and-black robes, and carrying mutant, nine-foot-long Kalashnikovs.

The Fates kept him company – they were the bears that would savage him if he stepped on the crack. But if he maintained those good high stimulant levels, the Fates would keep counsel with him, warn him of the filth round this corner, or some Yardie cunt Danny had stolen from round the next. Of course, Danny didn't really *believe* in any of this, it was simply a magical soundtrack to his life; but then the Fates were very similar in their manifestation to Danny's crack habit itself – both were paradoxical addictions to something intrinsically frightening and unpleasant. He shifted the wads of plastic in either cheek, with a motion akin to rinsing with mouthwash; then he delicately palped each one with the tip of his tongue.

Danny conducted this internal stock-taking at least a thousand times a day. In his left cheek was his own stash – in his right was the merchandise. Usually, when Danny set off from the house in the morning, the right-hand cheek would have around twenty-five rocks in it, and the left five. Five rocks to take him through five hours of tube rides and walking around the City pretending to be courier, a cowboy without a horse. Ducking into a kha- zi, or an alley, or a fucking hole in the wall, every quarter- hour on the quarter-hour to smoke the poisoned flour. Out with the stem; out with the lighter; crumble finicky crumble as the Fates gather at the periphery; crowding in, a press of dirty beards and muttering; the recitation of arcane fundamentalist texts, decrying the existence of Danny; dirty grey nails reaching out to rend him – then blown away, extinguished, blanketed by the first rich gush of smoke from his nozzled mouth.

Five rocks equalled twenty pipes – one every fifteen minutes. Enough time while the gear was still doing its thing for him to slop to another financial institution, make his drop, slop on. Enough time – if he eked it out right- eously – for Danny to avoid a clanking comedown on the Central Line, seated sweating in a strip-lit cattle truck, along with the rest of his hetacomb. All too often, how- ever, Danny's lop-sided chipmunk visage began to balance itself a little early in the day, the right-hand cheek getting delved into a little more than it should. And on those occasions Tembe would withhold the bag of brown at the end of the shift; or even – if he was feeling particularly managerial – even a measly taste. And Danny would have to accept this – accept the rack of shit his life had become.

How had it come to *this*? Danny bit down on the cyanide capsule of the past as he turned into London Wall, heading for London Bridge and the offices of Barclays De Zoete Wedd. How had he ended up being a runner for his dumb little brother Tembe – or 'Mr Tembe' as he was apparently known to the denizens of the Citibank futures department? Dragging his drenched carcass around these terrifying caverns of commerce, feeling his life blood, his manhood drain away, and with only the Fates to keep him company. Danny knew, of course, the answer: he had touched the product.

Whether this had occurred before or after the exhaustion of the seam of crack Danny had discovered in the basement of Leopold Road, he did not wish to acknowledge. The mother lode of crack had certainly been too good to be true – and now it no longer was. Whether Danny's estimates with plumbers' rods had been inaccurate at the outset, or the bulk of the crack had simply been washed away, corrupted by drainage and seepage, was besides the point. All that mattered was that after a couple of years of very high living the seam was gone, and at around the same time Danny, feeling wrung out by the experience, had taken his first pipe of crack and discovered what he had always suspected; that, in this most unnatural of pursuits, he turned out to be a natural.

Corresponding mysteriously to an episode in their childhood, the two brothers now found themselves on a seesaw, Tembe coming down to the ground, while his older brother shot up into a psychotic sky. For, as Danny cranked up the go-go candy, doing first three, then five, then sixty pipes a day, so Tembe decided that enough was enough and stepped on the shit once and for all.

In fairness to Tembe, contrary to the expertise of a

thousand counsellors, psychiatrists, politicians, church-men, and the parents of teenagers who had died from ecstasy overdoses, he found it astonishingly easy to step back through the door of non-perception. 'Never did like the shit anyways,' he explained to members of the posse, hanging out on the traffic island by Harlesden tube, drinking Dunn's River and riding the dossers. 'I jus' did it cos it was like *there*. Gimme a spliff anna beer any day; I can do up a ton of sensi a day an' all it do to me is to make me more righteous, more irie an' that.'

Being more righteous and more irie for Tembe largely consisted in a switch from unbridled crack consumption to quite remarkably efficient production and distribution. As Danny gibbered his way through the peaks and troughs of the crack storm, no longer the master puppeteer – merely a puppet on a pipe, so Tembe took up the strings that fell from his numb fingers. Little brother grabbed the clien-tele and set big brother – once so fucking arrogant, so high and mighty – to work.

Whereas Danny the non-user had always felt at worst indifferent, and at best friendly towards the munificent mannequins, Tembe the former user felt nothing but contempt for them – especially if they were white. 'They have every opportunity, every fuckin' break an' all they do is smoke this shit. They have no respect for themselves – I tell you, they actually *deserve* to be crack-heads, they should give me their money an' that, because they're really *donatin'* it, donatin' it to a righteous cause.'

The righteous cause was Tembe's black Saab 9000, with full skirts, fairing, personalised number plate etc., etc.; and feeling irie for Tembe was equivalent to feeling silk shirts between his shoulder blades, and the weight of an entire wardrobe of American, gangsta rap-style suits hanging from them. Tembe brought a fervour to his materialism that was almost messianic, as if, having pissed thousands of pounds up the wall, he was determined to wring out bricks and mortar until he got it all back again.

'You're too fuckin' fly, boy,' Danny had admonished him, as they sat, Tembe beering and spliffing, Danny piping and cracking, in front of the Saturday-afternoon racing. With Darkus long gone – all that was left of him was a hair-oil stain on the ancient antimacassar of his armchair – Danny, preposterously, was adopting some of the old man's avuncular manner 'You go strutting roun' the fuckin' town, making out like you're some big mutha-fuckin' dude. Thass the way you bring the heat down, man; all the fuckin' heat – an' not just the filth, the Yardies, the Turks, the Essex boys, the Chinese . . . even the fuckin' *Maltese*. You need to maintain a low fuckin' profile, look respectable an' that –'

'Yeah, yeah, yeah, t'chew!' Tembe sucked his cheek disdainfully. 'You taken a decco at your fuckin' profile recently. It ain't just *low*, big brother – it's in the fuckin' gutter.'

Danny had had to admit that his terminally stringy vest, caked dungarees, and flip-flop footwear that wasn't flip-flops was hardly the acme of respectability. He shut up and applied himself to the business of acquiring more blow-torch burns on his hands. And now, replaying the conversation in his echoing inner ear as he slopped through the oppressive, grooved runnel of Lothbury EC2, it occurred to Danny that the Fates were undoubt-edly responsible for this bizarre vice versa, and that even these intimations of doom and destruction – which were nothing if not routine – were, on this particular day, awfully germane portents.

Poor Danny – as he crouched in a service entrance of the Bank of England, servicing his own entrance – he couldn't possibly have known which, precise, words had been portents (they were, as it happens, 'Maltese' and 'low profile'). And although the Fates were temporarily routed in the direction of Aldgate – stashing their AKs, pocketing their false Korans, gathering their ghostly robes about them as they went – at the precise moment, some five minutes later, when Danny flotched into the lobby of Barclays De Zoete Wedd, his head uncluttered by magical thinking, his nemesis was touching down at Heathrow.

Skank, who for the purposes of this business trip had sensibly adopted the work name 'Joseph Andrews', had certain inflexible views about air travel: it was against the law of God, and it terrified him. 'You tek de bird,' he would lecture his fear-hobbled audience, 'de bird have feathers, it have light bones. Pick a bird up – feel it weight in your hand. Feel how *sui-ta-ble* it is for flyin' – because God made it that way. But you tek de plane. De plane is made of metal, it shaped like a bullet. It may go up high in the sky, but one day it falls back to eart'.'

Skank dealt with his fear of flying by coshing himself insensible for the duration with a Rohypnol; but as the wheels bumped and then glued themselves to tarmac, he was wide awake, and clutching the hands of the two small children who were sitting either side of him so tightly that they did his screaming for him.

The children came courtesy of one of Skank's employees, as did their mother, who was, purely recreationally, the wife of the real Joseph Andrews, a Pentecostalist minister who had absolutely no idea that she was in so deep with crack, that she was in still deeper with the Yardies; and that it followed they'd pay her to take a little holiday to her sister's in London. After Dorelia had gone, Joseph had no idea where his passport was either.

Joseph Andrews, a.k.a. Skank, entered the immigration hall with his two pseudo kids still tightly clasped. His 'wife' walked demurely a few paces behind him carrying the hand luggage. When he reached the counter he put the two green Jamaican passports directly into the officer's hand. The officer scanned the face in the photograph – same celluloid dog collar, same v-neck pullover, same serviceable black jacket – then scanned the face in front of him once more. Skank bore an expression of bleak sanctimoniousness, utterly befitting a man who believed in the full weight of the Lord's Providence.

'Is this the address you'll be staying at during your stay, Reverend Andrews?' asked the officer.

'Thass right, my sister-in-law's in Stockwell.'

'And the purpose of your visit, Reverend?'

'Y'know, catching up with the family, friends –'

'But you won't be doing any work?'

Skank fixed the officer with an inquisitorial eye. 'I don't consider the Lord's work to be work as such, but since you ax' I will be preaching at the Stockwell Temple –'

'Of course, of course, that's quite all right, Reverend.' And with a cursory glance at the children and their mother, and then at their passport photographs, he waved the party on. The next entrant in line came to the desk and proffered his passport.

A young man had been circling the arrivals' pick-up zone for some time in a Mercedes saloon, when Skank and the Andrews emerged from the terminal. He pulled up to the kerb and they got in. As the car sped down the exit ramp Skank yanked off the stiff dog collar, and in one fluid motion removed the Glock which was stashed in the glove compartment. He checked the magazine and put the automatic in his jacket pocket, then turning to the driver said, 'So, what de word, Blutie?'

'The word is good, Skank,' the young man replied, flashing a gold 'n gap grin.

'Then *drive* blud claat.'

Skank dropped the Andrews in Stockwell and went on, heading for the East End. As the big merc. splashed through the low-rise high density of South London, the big dread carefully removed what remained of his hairy finery from beneath a wig and a flesh-coloured bathing cap. Turning to Blutie, Skank said, 'De blud claat gone done make me shed me locks, y'know. It's not enough for him to steal – he have to mek a man shed 'im locks. And for why? Jus' to pay some fucker – jus' to pay him!'

'It's the way here, Skank. The Chinaman said he'd happily farm the contract for you – but you gotta come in person to hand over the dosh – shows good faith an' that.'

'T'chew! I call it rank stu-pid-ity, boy. If de chink knew we was settlin' a hundred thousand-dollar score mebbe he'd want more for hisself.'

'Undoubtedly,' said Blutie – who liked the sound of the word.

'As is, wa' he charge for us to rub out dis piece of shit?'

'Two hundred quid.'

'Two hundred pounds! Sheeit! Life is cheaper than fuckin' Trenchtown in this place.'

'You ain't tellin' no word of a lie, Skank, but see here.' Blutie shifted in his seat and spread his hands wide on the steering wheel. 'You've got to 'preciate that the Chinaman isn't taking out a contract on London for us, it's more like he's selling on the debt. The enforcer we're going to meet *wants* the contract. He thinks he can extract a fair wadge out of Danny – thass London's moniker now – before he does the how's your father –'

'But he gua-ran-tee to kill 'im, right? He gua-ran-tee to shoot the little fucker, yeah?'

'He's solid – the Chinaman says so.'

It was unfortunate for Skank that he didn't know as much about the Chinaman as he did about revenge. Skank's revenge on Danny wasn't a dish eaten cold – it was well nigh frozen. It had been five years since the three keys had gone missing in Philly, and all that time Skank had bided, waited. He picked up bits of information here and there and husbanded them; he put irons in the fire and tended them. Eventually the poisonous tree bore fruit, the Chinaman, a long-time associate of Skank's, told him that a black crack-head from Harlesden, who smoked regularly in his house, had told him in turn, about a crew on his manor who were outing much better than average product.

The Chinaman found this interesting enough in itself – it was always wise to keep abreast of the competition. But more interesting still was the thumbnail c.v. the crack-head supplied of the two brothers who ran the operation. Apparently, the older brother, who went by the name of Danny, had been in the army. But more than that, he had gone into the army after a trip to Jamaica. A trip to Jamaica in the late eighties.

It was the only down time in the twenty-four when the big merc. bearing the big dread pulled up in front of the old house on Milligan Street, in back of the Limehouse Causeway. 'Wa' de fuck's *that*?' enquired Skank, seeing the Canary Wharf Tower for the first time in his life as he got out of the car.

'Offices,' Blutie replied. 'I'll park the motor.'

Skank was ushered into the mouldering gaff by a child,

who might have been the Chinaman's granddaughter, or even his great-granddaughter. They picked their way through the warren of interconnected rooms and found the old man in what could have been a kitchen, had it not been for the presence of a large steel desk and two filing cabinets, in addition to sink, fridge and vomit swirl-patterned lino tiles. 'Please!' he exclaimed, getting up from behind the desk. 'Please to be welcome to my office, Mistah Skank!'

'Please,' Skank countered, 'jus' Skank is suff-ic-ient. So iss all offices roun' hereabout now?'

'Oh yes, oh yes, plenty change, big new dewelopment. Plenty offices. Plenty office workers. Plenty office workers who need help –'

'So, busyness is good then?'

'Busyness is excellent! This is an enterpwise zone –'

'Issatso.' Skank couldn't help feeling that the China-man's efficiency and zeal was undercut by his working apparel, a dirty terry-towelling bathrobe, but he hadn't come to talk about that. 'I've got de two hundred – have you got my man?'

'No problem, no problem –' He broke off and called into the next room, 'Mistah Gerald, would you come through, the Jamaican gentleman has arrived.'

Certainly the Chinaman liked to think that Gerald was a run-of-the-mill enforcer. But the Chinaman's mind was not unlike his place of business, a bewildering agglomera-tion of different spaces housing deeply incompatible contents. And as in each of the rooms of the Chinaman's bizarre den – one set aside for opium smoking, the next for crack, a third for ecstatic gibbering – each of the compart-ments of his mind featured a different belief system, an incompatible truth, another story.

Even Skank felt a chill run down the back of his neck

when Gerald walked into the room. He was a small man with hardly any shoulders; his face wasn't so much warped as entirely twisted to one side, as if the wind had changed at the precise moment Gerald had been hit with a hard right cross. He had on a blue nylon anorak of the kind children wore in the sixties; set on his head was an obvious toupee. Set beneath the toupee, and shining forth despite the violent moue was a visage of absolutely uncompromising vapidity and bloodlessness; a face like the belly of a toad. This was not a man with ordinary feelings – or perhaps any feelings at all. Accompanying Gerald was a boy of about fifteen, the same height as his master – for clearly, that's who Gerald was – pipe-cleaner thin, ginger-haired, freckled, and wearing an identical blue anorak. They both had flesh-coloured rubber gloves on.

Skank cleared his throat, 'Errm . . . Gerald.'

'Yes.' The voice was blank as well.

'Dis man 'ere say you can deal with my prob-lem.'

'Yes.'

'Do you know where de fellow lives?'

'Not necessawy,' the Chinaman interjected. 'The man who told me about him – he'll bring him here tonight. He's had a little twouble with the police – it wasn't hard to persuade him.'

'Good. Den what?' Skank had folded his arms and was regarding Gerald critically. The blank man unzipped his anorak without speaking and flipped it open. A shotgun, cut down so that there were only three inches of the barrel and half the stock left was dangling from a hook inside it. Skank said nothing. Gerald zipped the anorak up again.

Blutie came into the room and handed Skank an envelope, which the big dread handed to the Chinaman. The Chinaman handed it to Gerald. Skank shook hands with the Chinaman, nodded to Gerald and he and Blutie left the room. Skank didn't take a full breath until they were back in the street.

2.

Bruno and Danny sat on the stairs of the old house in Milligan Street husbanding the last crumbs of Bruno's crack. It was around midnight. Bruno had sworn to Danny that he'd be generous with the shit – even though he was buying. But inevitably, now that they were down to the penultimate hit they were beginning to squabble. 'Sheeit!' Bruno exclaimed. 'Thass loads more than my last – take a bit of it off, man!'

'No way!' Danny replied. 'You said I could have a big one to finish on – then there's that for you.' He pointed at the crumb of white stuff that remained lying on a piece of plastic on the dusty stair. 'Iss no help that we've only got this poxy fuckin' bottle.' Danny gestured with the pipe they were using, which had been crudely fashioned out of a miniature Volvic mineral-water bottle.

'You should've brought your fuckin' stem, man,' Bruno retorted.

'*You* should've brought *your* fuckin' stem 'n all.' And to put an end to the pathetic quarrel, Danny sparked his lighter, applied it to the heap of fag ash and crack set in the tin-foil bowl, and commenced drawing on the biro stem.

At that moment a large party of people – perhaps six in all, entered the hallway at the foot of the stairs. The Chinaman met them himself, ushering in their leader – a large, heavy-set man wearing an expensive 'crombie – with much bowing and scraping. The four other men who shuffled in behind were clad in various degrees of fashionable suiting, and together with them was a quite beautiful young woman in a very short skirt. Danny wasn't paying any attention, but Bruno pegged them as West End media types, out for a night's drug slumming.

The party, led by the Chinaman, commenced tramping up the stairs past the crack smokers. They all ostentatiously averted their eyes from the spectacle of Danny, drawing for all he was worth on his final pipe of the day, except for the last man to pass, a fat type with oval glasses smoking a cigar, who squinted down at the pipe in Danny's hand and sneered, 'I prefer Evian myself.'

Danny stopped drawing on the pipe, and together with a plume of crack smoke spat at the man, 'Whassit t'you, cunt!' but Bruno laid a hand on his arm and muttered, 'Safe, Danny.' And he let it lie.

Not for long though. After ten minutes had elapsed and together with them the last vestiges of Danny's hit of crack, he began to appreciate the full awfulness of his position. He was hideously strung out. He'd done three rocks more than he should have during his morning's sodden tramp around the financial institutions. He managed to deliver twenty rocks to the bitches at the Learmont and the ones in Sixth Avenue, but it hadn't been quite enough to mollify Mr Tembe, who had cut his evening hit of brown to a mere smear. So Danny now had the rumbling beginnings of heroin withdrawal to contend with, as well as the hideous trough of a crack comedown. He hated sitting on this filthy staircase, waiting to summon the energy to stagger down, stagger to the tube, clank all the way back to Harlesden, face the derision of his squeaky-clean little brother: 'Thass whappen when you smoke the shit, man, give it a rest . . .' And all the way the Fates walking with him, whispering and cachinnating, ordering him to tread there, breathe here, spit there, unless he wanted to be eviscerated by destiny. But what

Danny hated most of all, right here and now, was the dissing the fat white cunt had given him.

Danny leapt to his feet, ran up the stairs, barged through the door of the room the party had disappeared into. He didn't take any time to register the occupants – who were smoking opium, contorted by the sloping ceiling of the attic room into various cramped postures – he merely picked out the fat ponce and gave him a smack in the mouth. Then it was back down the stairs and straight out the front door, to where Vince, the China-man's Maltese minder, who had witnessed Danny's sudden departure, was waiting.

Vince delivered a deft karate chop to the back of Danny's neck which felled him instantly. Crack had winnowed away the muscle that Danny had put on in the army – the huge Maltese could lift him by the scruff of his jacket using only one hand. Vince carried Danny as if he were a kitten, down the area steps. At the bottom he pressed him up against the wall, and when Danny began to come round – his flickering eyes providing him a view of Vince's repugnant nose, which had been sliced in two during a knife fight and crudely sewn back together again – Vince began, almost tenderly, to press down on his cartoid artery.

Two minicabs pulled up to the kerb and the West End slummers emerged from the house. The party got in to the cars and they drove off. Shortly afterwards a vomit-coloured Austin Maxi pulled up and Gerald and his boy got out. Gerald was about to go up the short flight of steps to the front door when he saw Vince and his unconscious kitten in the basement area. Gerald jerked his head significantly in Danny's direction, and Vince, enjoying the conspiratorial silence of the very ugly, wordlessly did his bidding. By the time he'd carried Danny back up to the street, the rear door of the Maxi was open.

Vince slid the body on to the seat and without even giving Gerald so much as a backward glance, reentered the house.

Gerald and the boy got into the Maxi. The boy was driving. They drove off to the north, heading for Clapton.

Sixteen hours later, at around three in the afternoon, Danny regained consciousness. He was lying on dirty linoleum. The first sensations he had on awakening were the smell of the stuff, and the thrumming weight of his head, mashing his cold cheek into the floor. Danny groaned, coughed, spat and sat up. The room he was in might once have been an office – there were a couple of cheap wooden kneehole desks set against one wall, a battered filing cabinet against the other. The office must have also been a shop of some kind, because there was a large front window. However, this had been completely boarded up on the inside and the only light in the place came from the chinks between the planks.

Following one of these wavering beams to its destination on the back wall, Danny saw that this was entirely covered with a papering of posters. He squinted at them through the gloom. They all featured photographs of children. The photos were obviously family snaps that had been blown up and reproduced in black-and-white – Danny could see the individual dots composing the images. Then he read the lettering and realised, with an access of dread, what they were. They were posters appealing for help in the search for missing children.

Danny scrambled to his feet. He felt an awful thickening and distortion in the already unpleasant atmosphere of the room. He could smell something sickly, yet faecal. A dollop of vomit came into the back of his mouth. He could see a tartan blanket thrown over something in the dark corner, only three paces away. Danny knew what the thing was before he lifted the blanket – and then he knew for sure.

It was the mutilated corpse of a six-year-old white boy. Danny registered blond hair, pulped features, cut throat. There was a lot of blood. The child's hands and feet had been severed and left beside the corpse, which was naked from the waist down. The last thing Danny took in before he began, simultaneously, to puke and scream, was that the little boy was wearing a bright sweatshirt, featuring a decal of the character Buzz Lightyear from the film *Toy Story*.

Yes, Gerald, who by this time was heading west, to Bristol, was no ordinary enforcer, as the Chinaman well knew. Just as his accompanying boy – whose name was Shaun Withers – was not really a boy at all, but a twenty-year-old violent retard. Gerald and Shaun had met each other on the treatment course for sexual offenders at HMP Grenville. Day after day they had sat together in group-therapy sessions where sincere psychiatrists urged them to give voice to their most keenly desired fantasies of rape, abuse, torture and murder, in the hope that this would enable them to gain the merest sliver of objectivity about their conditions.

Gerald and Shaun managed to achieve very considerable objectivity about their favourite shared fantasy – the abduction, buggering, torture, mutilation and eventual murder of a young boy, the younger the better. They resolved to join forces and make it a reality as soon as they were released. Gerald got out first – he had been serving a two-year stretch for indecent assault – and went back to his home town of Bournemouth. But the local paper there had already published a picture of him the day before, and printed the address of his house. Gerald found that the constant posses of vigilantes screaming abuse outside, and the flaming, petrol-soaked rags shoved through his letter-box, rather cramped his style.

Gerald left Bournemouth and headed for London where he lost himself in the immemorial city's stygian under-world. He worked sporadically for the Sparks family in Finsbury Park, collecting debts for them and when neces-sary inflicting a beating. But generally he kept quiet, moved his digs every month, and bided his time. Six months passed before Shaun was released after completing his three-year stretch for rape. In London he joined Gerald, who already had the elements of a plan in place.

Shaun had spent the last year of his sentence, at Gerald's behest, cheerfully allowing himself to be buggered by the ex-cop who was the boss of the nonce wing. The ex-cop had gone down for corruption and was desperate not to be sussed as a queer. Shaun guaranteed to keep this informa-tion to himself in return for a little assistance with getting back on his feet once he got out. The assistance he most required was a reasonably roomy set of premises where he and his good buddy Gerald could resume their activities. The ex-cop had to oblige. It transpired that he had the lease on the offices of a defunct minicab firm on the Lower Clapton Road. The place was boarded up and had no electricity or water, but it had several rooms, and most importantly a back entrance that wasn't overlooked. Gerald and Shaun took the keys while making sincere expressions of gratitude.

They found the boy in a playground a mile away in Stoke Newington; his name was Gary. It took only minutes for the two men to persuade the six year old to accompany them to their house for some sweets and videos. He got into the Maxi almost gaily and chattered away as they drove carefully back to the cab office. For Gary was not simply neglected and unwanted – he was also being abused already. Shaun and Gerald found this out when they got him inside and took his clothes off – his little arse was cratered with cigarette burns. The burns were the work of his mother's sadistic boyfriend. The same boyfriend who had bought him the *Toy Story* top.

Still, despite this, Gary was blond and slim and almost pretty. Gerald and Shaun managed to have plenty of fun with him over the next ten days or so, but then he became a bit of a drag. He was incontinent, he wouldn't eat, he'd lost his freshness, and the two men began to argue about who should have the task of washing him in between sessions. And Gary didn't even struggle satisfactorily any more, he just whimpered. Worse than that, Gerald had already clocked the profusion of missing-child posters that had gone up in the area, and he'd read in the local paper that the police were conducting exhaustive house-to-house questioning. It could only be a matter of time before the knock on the door came.

Gerald decided that what they needed was another body, someone to take the rap. Then, through the Sparks, he heard about a Chinaman in Limehouse who had a contract that needed enforcing. 'Just the ticket,' Gerald said to Shaun. Gerald never spoke much, but when he did he invariably retailed such hackneyed turns of phrase. When the two men came to heaving Danny's unconscious body into the office, and stuffing the downers down his throat, and removing the semen from his seminal vesicles with a long hypodermic, Gerald referred insistently to him as the 'thingummyjig'.

And that's how the thingummyjig came to be in the boarded-up cab office in Lower Clapton Road, screaming and puking on a cold November afternoon. But he didn't have to suffer his terror and revulsion alone for long.

Gerald and Shaun had thoughtfully phoned the local constabulary, shortly after quitting the premises.

Three months later, and ensconced on the nonce wing of Wandsworth Prison, Danny had plenty of leisure with which to reflect on the awesome apathy that had gripped him during those few minutes in which he waited with dead Gary for the door to the cab office to be kicked in by the police. Granted, he still had enough downers in his system to make a polar bear sluggish; and granted he had the smack withdrawal and the crack come-down underlying this fateful torpor, but even so there was a genuine acceptance of his fate – or rather his Fates.

They thronged the corners of the dark room, their gloomy robes brushing against the missing-children posters, their grimy turbans scratching the polystyrene ceiling tiles. The Fates muttered and chuckled over the child's corpse, and for the first time since they emerged from the cracks in the corners of the world to keep him company, Danny could clearly understand what they were saying. The words 'low profile' and 'Maltese' and 'set-up' and 'Skank' were there; along with 'fool' and 'crack-head'. And in the dark room, perfumed by psychopathy, Danny acknowledged that his nemesis had come back to haunt him.

It was just too smooth – and too inexplicable otherwise. Bruno offering to front him an evening's rocking in the East End. The big, ugly Maltese who had given him a careful twice-over when they arrived at Milligan Street, and then the same fucker, choking the sense out of him after Danny had given that lairy git a smack. Now he was here, obviously many hours later, and there was blood on his hands. Danny, unlike anything else graphic in the room, had been neatly framed.

For, there was not only blood on his hands, it was under his nails and in his hair as well. Some of it was his own — some was Gary's. This, when it was also neatly catalogued at the trial, was damning enough; as were Danny's dabs on assorted implements: knives, hacksaw blades, screwdrivers etc., revolting etc . . . . But worse, far worse, was Danny's semen in the little boy's anus, Danny's semen in the little boy's throat. These were facts that thankfully weren't published in the newspapers, although they remained in Danny's deposition papers, when the corridor was frozen and he was hurried down it on his way to the nonce wing.

The police were amazed by Danny's quietism when they arrested him. Since he put up hardly any resistance, they administered a minimal beating. It was the same as he was shuffled from one nick to the next over the next nine weeks. It didn't matter what they screamed at him, or how they slapped him — he wouldn't rise to it. Eventually they gave up — it was no fun punching a bag.

Danny's lawyer, a young white woman, was perfectly prepared to attempt a proper defence of her client. She may have been inexperienced, and have had as little knowledge of Danny's world as she did of the dark side of the moon, but she could see that none of it added up. Danny had no form as a sex offender, and was too old to have suddenly blossomed into such an evil flower. He might have no alibi, and no willingness to go in search of one, but there was no effective circumstantial evidence against him either. This was an organised killing, but the police could find no signs, other than forensic, that it had been Danny who'd organised it. And anyway, why organise a murder so comprehensively, then fail to remove yourself from the crime scene in time?

None of this mattered though. None of this could fly in

the face of that semen, which Gerald had so artfully extracted, then inserted. And none of it could be challenged if Danny remained, as he did, listless, silent, surly, showing no indication that he wanted to substantiate his – purely formal – plea of not guilty.

For Danny the trial was a series of unconnected, almost absurd, impressions. At the Crown Court in Kingston, the police who had arrested him stood about in the lobby, smoking heavily in their short hair and C&A suits. Danny mused on how peculiar it was that they always looked more uniformed when they weren't. The gold-painted mouldings of fruit bordering the ceiling of the large hall jibed with the freestanding, cannister-shaped ashtrays that pinioned its floor. The court usher was black, and had more than a passing resemblance to the late Aunt Hattie. The prosecuting QC was white; he affected a large signet ring, a watch chain and a clip-on bow tie. He reminded Danny of one of the punters he used to serve in the City. As he waited each morning with the Securicor guards for the expensive charade to begin, Danny would look for sympathy in the eyes of a large portrait of Queen Caroline – and find none.

Sitting in the dock for day after day, Danny was acutely conscious of the need not to look at anyone. The jury were ordinary people, who, in the struggle to appear mature at all times, ended up seeming far more childish. Especially childish in the way that they beamed hatred at Danny given half a chance. The public gallery was, of course, out of the question. Instead Danny concentrated on the peculiar, double-jointed ratchets that were used to open the high windows in the courtroom. And for hours he would lose himself in the texture of the vertical louvres that covered those windows.

Danny came to during the judge's summing up: It was

for the jury to decide what they believed; it was up to them
to assess whether the witnesses were telling the truth; it
was important that they accepted the judge's direction in
matters of law, but it was for them to decide in matters of
fact. The judge was careful to acknowledge that they
might decide to believe *this*; but on the whole he thought
it far more likely that they would prefer to accept *that*. So
he cut up the cake of justice and handed out a slice to
everyone saving Danny.

The jury were out for such a short time that it was
difficult to believe they'd done anything save walk into the
jury room, chorus 'He's guilty as hell' and walk straight
back out again. Even the judge was impressed by their
alacrity – and the prosecuting QC positively glowed. It
was three in the afternoon when the scrap of paper was
passed by the foreman to the clerk, and then by the clerk
up to the bench. All morning the court had been directly
under the Heathrow flight path, and each damning sum-
mation by the judge was accompanied by the roar of
another 747, bearing another six hundred people and
escaping earthly confinement at six hundred miles an
hour. As the judge took the scrap of paper Danny heard
an almighty boom, and peering through the gap in the
louvres behind the judge's shoulder, he saw the white
needle of Concorde lifting off into the grey sky.

Danny's sentence was life. With a minimum recommendation that he serve twenty years.

His solicitor managed to grab a few minutes with him in
the holding cell. 'You'll have to ask for protection,' she
told him. 'With your offence and sentence you have no
choice – otherwise you'll get a pasting. But do everything
you can to get off Rule 43. If you come to your senses and
want to fight this, want to appeal, it will go far better for
you if you've protested at your sentencing all along, and

the best demonstration of that is that you refuse to admit you're a nonce. Never admit you're a nonce – you're not a nonce, are you, Danny?'

Danny gave the young woman a long, level look for the first time since he'd met her, then tonelessly replied, 'No.' Then two Securicor men came into the cell, cuffed him and led him out.

For Danny the next two weeks were as confused as the last two weeks before his rendezvous with Gerald. With its elision of day and night, its muddling of time and distance, and its random acts of senseless departure, the Prison Service did its best to replicate the lifestyle of the drug addict. Outside the court Danny was bundled into a blacked-out category 'A' Securicor van. The inside of the van was divided into sixteen individual cell-lets, eight each side. Once he had been locked into his cell he was there for the duration of an eighteen-hour day, every day, for a fortnight. The cell window was blacked out, so that the outside world was doused in permanent night-time; and the door was solid to the ceiling. Inches in front of Danny's face there was a metal grille which ran from waist-height to the roof of the van. Should Danny have chosen to do so he could have communicated, through this grille, with his fellow traveller in front. And if he'd been prepared to twist around in his seat he could have done the same with the prisoner behind.

Danny chose to do neither. He sat still, listening to the catcalls of the inmates and the imprecations of the guards. When the van stopped he heard the slop and slurp of the shit and piss in the covered bucket between his shins. It didn't feel like any kind of an indignity – this; after all Danny was a nonce. A nonce, a sickening, shitty, pissy nonce. The lowest of the low. Danny had been around enough to hear the stories about what happened to sex offenders inside. He knew about juggings and shivings and socks full of pool balls. He had heard tell of how the 'normal' offenders plotted to get their hands on nonces; how even a fairly lowly crim' – a crack-head, a larcenist, whatever – could vastly improve his status by doing a nonce. Behind those high walls slathered with anti-climb paint there was only ever one season; an open one for nonces.

So Danny kept silent, lest he give himself away, and listened to the constant yammering of his fellow prisoners. Every time they stopped at another nick and there was an exchange of personnel, the questioning would start up: 'Who're you?'; 'What're you in for?'; 'Have you got anything bottled?'; 'D'jew know Johnnie Marco?' and so on.

Every day, late, the van would halt for the night and the shackled prisoners would be led into another shower block, ordered to strip, doused, and then locked away for a few hours in holding cells. Then, with dawn still far off in this winter wonderlessland, the cell door would be whacked open, they'd be shackled again, marched out to the van, loaded, and driven off.

After a few days Danny became conscious of the fact that almost every prisoner in the van, at some point during the day, would realise that he knew one of the other prisoners in the van. Further, all the prisoners in the van seemed to take this for granted: 'Issat so-and-so?' they'd call out, and when it was confirmed that it was, they'd try and ascertain what it was that had happened to so-and-so. Had he done a screw? Had he been on the block? Had he been nicked for drugs? Gradually it dawned on Danny that this snail's-pace progression in the jolting miniature cell actually was a form of incarceration for these men; and that the prison van itself was a special kind

of institution. The prisoners who were moved so relent-
lessly were the troublemakers, the bolters, the ex-barons,
and presumably those like Danny himself who required
rigorous sequestration.

Danny began to wonder whether he would serve all of
his twenty years being shunted around the country in this
fashion, with nothing to read save his deposition and no
one to talk to at all. Along with this creeping suspicion
came another, curiously ambivalent intimation. The Fates
had gone – or perhaps they'd never existed at all. No
longer did Danny have to indulge in peculiar twists of
magical thought in order to protect himself from the
malevolent djinns, there was no point – his fate was worse
than death already. Not only had the Fates gone, but his
stomach had ceased to gurgle and void itself, his armpits
had ceased to drip cold sweat and his appetite had – grossly
inopportunely – returned in force. Danny was clean.

With cleanliness came an indignation that burned inside
Danny like a whole body dose of clap. Granted he'd
ripped off Skank, and granted that he'd been due a
comeuppance, but this? This! To be framed as a nonce!
No, it couldn't be, Danny would do anything, adopt any
stratagem to clear his name. He remembered what the
solicitor had said after the trial; that he should do all he
could to avoid getting stuck on the nonce wing – that
would have to be his first priority. He would tell the
governor – he remembered that every new inmate had an
interview with the governor – that he didn't want protection, he didn't want to be segregated.

All of this Danny firmly resolved on the thirteenth day
of the van. But the following morning, when the van
pulled up for the fifth time, and to his blinking surprise
Danny found himself standing outside the high brick wall
of HMP Wandsworth, his resolve began to drain away.

It continued to drain away as Danny was inducted into the prison. The screws who showered him, printed him, issued him with his kit, and then led him through the curiously empty reception block seemed so uncustomarily unaggressive that they were almost solicitous. Danny, of course, didn't say anything to them save for 'Yessir' and 'Nossir', but when he was ready to go on to the wing, one of them muttered 'Poor fucker', and he couldn't forbear from asking, 'What's up?'

The screw, who was white moustachioed and close to retirement, shook his head and looked straight at Danny before answering, 'You'll see.'

There was no enigma to this arrival. Danny was led across a yard, in through one gate, across another yard and in through the end door of A Wing, the first of the five 'spokes' that comprise the Wandsworth panopticon. It's possible – but unlikely – that had Jeremy Bentham, the originator of the panopticon prison design, seen Danny's welcome at Wandsworth, he would have felt that his ideas had reached an effective fruition.

Bentham conceived of the panopticon, with its five spoke-like wings, projecting from a hub-like central hall, as an evocation of the all-seeing eye of God. He had hoped that the inmates of the five wings, constantly aware of their observation from the central hall, would apprehend within the architectonic of their own imprisonment the true nature of the relationship between God and Man. Certainly, Danny felt the presence of an all-seeing eye as he walked down A Wing, a screw to his rear and another in front, and then walked through the central hall and on down E Wing to his final destination. But this was an all-seeing eye made up of many hundreds of other eyes, an all-seeing eye that also possessed hands, hands which were all banging cutlery against the bars of their cells. And there were all-shouting mouths as well, row upon row of them. They kept pace with Danny as he marched through the gauntlet of hatred. 'Nonce! Nonce! Fucking nonce!' they all screamed, and every ten shaky paces Danny heard a more personal, targeted remark like: 'We'll get you – you fucking nonce!'

By the time Danny reached his allotted cell, on F Wing, he was blanched with the sweat of terror. 'We thought we'd put you two together,' said the screw, gesturing through the doorway of the cell he'd just unlocked, 'given that you're both black geezers and that.'

Inside the cell a fat black man was sitting on a bunk. He looked up from something he was writing on a pad of paper, gave a broad grin and said, 'So, you're the famous Clapton cab killer.'

And that's how Danny came to meet Fat Boy, the mentor from hell.

3.

'Yah man!' said Fat Boy, 'I've got it on damn good authority – you're gonna get jugged, an' right here, on the fuckin' nonce wing, tomorrer –'

'B-but this is – I mean we're *all* fuckin' the same here, how can anyone think they have the right.'

'The right! Ha-ha-ha! Rights he talks about. That's real fine; you, the fuckin' Clapton cab killer, talking 'bout rights. You – a fuckin' monster who tortured and sexually abused a six-year-old child for days before killin' 'im and cuttin his fuckin' hands and feet off! Sheee!' Fat Boy ran his finger around the omega sign he had shaved into the hair at the back of his neck before continuing. 'You've got a nerve, man. Right here, right now, you're regarded as

one of the badarsed of the badarsed in the whole fuckin'
nick. And, since this wing is the fuckin' clearing house for
every single fuckin' nonce in the whole country – it means
you're one of the baddest arseholes there is.' And Fat Boy
went back to running his finger around the furry groove of
his omega sign; a nervous tic, which, in a few short hours
had driven Danny closer to distraction than anything else
he'd experienced since going down.

Danny slapped the linoleum with the soles of his shoddy
canvas shoes. 'So,' he asked after a while, 'who's gonna do
the sodding jugging, then?'

'Waller, he's gonna do it. He's an ex-cop, see, an' he's
the fuckin' baron in here right now. He an' another bent
copper, name of Hansen, between 'em they've got the
whole fuckin' wing sewn up. Any given time they've got
five hundred and forty Rule 43 prisoners on 'ere. That's
five hundred and forty to tax. They've got the drugs,
they've got the money, they say who goes on an' who goes
off the wing, an' naturally they organise the fuckin'
juggings.' Fat Boy snuggled into the bunk a little
more, drawing his chubby legs up into a tenth-lotus
position, before continuing to impart wisdom, like some
grotesque sadhu. 'See, yer nonces are basically a law-
abiding lot, an' cowardly to boot. It comes natural to
them to do whatever a copper says – whether 'e's bent or
not, see? And anyways these coppers are 'ard fuckers,
man, real 'ard fuckers –'

'Well, I'm no fuckin' battyboy myself,' Danny spat.
'An' I'm no nonce neither. I'm gonna see the fuckin'
governor today, right? They've gotta let me, right? An'
I'm gonna say I don't want no protection nor nothing –'

'Yeah-yeah-yeah-yeah,' said Fat Boy, as if he'd seen it
all before – which he had, 'an' I'm no nonce neither –
leastways not a fiddler or a fucker – but let me tell you,

man, as a favour like, there's only one fuckin' way of doing *your* stretch an' thass right here. Forget going over there, you wouldn't last seven seconds. An' anyway, he won't let you, not until you build up some trust wiv' 'im, then he might let you go, but only as a fuckin' *tout*, mind. No, you've got a jugging coming, man, an' the only fuckin' hope in hell you have of avoidin' it is sittin' right here in front of you in the shapely shape of yours truly, Mistah FB, the moderator, the negotiator, the secretary general of the United Nations of Nonce.'

Fat Boy relaxed his legs and swung himself up. He waddled to the door, poked his jug head out and checked the landing in either direction, then he waddled back to the sink in the far corner and removed one of the tiles on the splash back; behind it there was a stash of – among other things – chocolate bars. Fat Boy took one out and replaced the tile, securing it with shreds of Blu-Tac. Turning back towards Danny he held the chocolate bar up and said, 'Snickers?' Danny ignored the offer. 'Whadd'ya' mean *you're* not a nonce?'

'I'm not.' Fat Boy bit deep into his Snickers.

'Well, are you filth then?'

'Nah! Course not! I'm doing a fuckin' "nyum-nyum" five for supplying child porn, right? It's not my kick, you understand, but where there's a market . . . "nyum-nyum" . . . I could probably get away wiv' being over there – I've got friends an' that, but it suits me well enough to be on the nonce wing on account of the business opportunities, see? I'm on to a good "nyum-nyum" earner here an' thass why I can help you out, stop you getting a fuckin' jug of boilin' water and fuckin' sugar poured over your fuckin' nonce bonce.'

'What's the earner then?' Danny asked, seemingly contrite.

Fat Boy saw Danny was in earnest and sat down on the opposite bunk again, brushing fragments of peanut, chocolate and toffee from his ludicrously inappropriate, loudly patterned Hawaiian shorts. 'You know what's it that envelope you carry everywhere wiv' you?' His voice was queasily intimate and lubricious.

'W-what? My deposition, you mean?' Danny reached instinctively for the brown envelope – he had been told that it was a disciplinary offence not to know where it was at all times.

'That's the one – wass innit?'

'I dunno, my statements, trial evidence an' stuff –'

'Trial evidence, right, trial evidence!' Fat Boy snatched the envelope from Danny's hand, and before he could protest had opened it and scattered the contents on top of the bunk. Fat Boy sorted through the slew of paper with both hands. 'See, here's your original statement, here's the filth's, here's psych' reports an' bullshit, an' here's bingo!' He had a smaller manila envelope in his browner hand, from which he pulled a sheaf of photographs. As he examined each one and tossed it on to the blanket, Fat Boy gave a helpful commentary: 'Mug shot of you, 'nother one . . . ah, here we go, crime scene, exterior, day – worth a few bob; crime scene interior – worth a few bob more; and here's the real spondulicks, victim at crime scene – one, two, three, four of 'em. Oooh! Ugly man, ugly – good angles as well – *and* the fuckin' icing, an' old shot of the victim, ahhh! Ain't he sweet, lovely *Toy Story* top – !'

'Gimme that!' Danny snatched the photo from Fat Boy and grabbed the rest of them as well. He began stuffing them all back into the envelope, whilst almost shouting, 'You sick fuck! You sick fuck! Thass your earner is it, is it?' Fat Boy recoiled, his new cell mate might have looked skinny and run down but the boy's reflexes were damn fast. Danny ranted on: 'You sell this shit, do you? Issat it? You sell this shit to the nonces, oh man! Seen I caan't believe it. Blud claat!'

'An' the fuckin' address.' Fat Boy acted unperturbed. 'What?!'

'The address, some fucker will pay well for little Toy Story's address. They get a kick out of it – the nonces do, sendin' tapes an' shit out to the victim's family. Yeah, they get a real kick out of it. You could cut it either way, man – a package deal, address, shots, the lot, or parcel it off. Given your rep' man, *half* your bag will get you off the jugging, an' then there's a bit of a profit to be 'ad. Bit of puff, bit of brown, I can even get you a rock if you fancy one, whaddya' say? If you want to cut a deal wiv' Waller – I'm your man. I'm the deposition king of F Wing an' thass the troof.'

Danny had finished packing the envelope. Still holding it he stood and walked the two paces to the end of the cell. There was a foot-square, heavily barred window set near the top of the wall. Danny gripped the bars with one hand and dangled there for a while, allowing the strong currents of nausea that were passing through his mind gently to twist his body this way and that. He tilted his face over the sink in the corner and didn't so much spit into it, as allow the saliva to fall from his mouth. Christ! He'd known he was going to encounter men who would revolt him, men who had done unspeakable things, but Fat Boy's parasitism on the nonces' perverted desires was even worse. To think that he might be banged up in here with the omega man – who was at it again as Danny dangled, his fat finger rasping through the nappy hair – for hours, then days, then months, then years. The two of them sleeping and shitting only inches apart, their breath, their farts, their very thoughts commingling. Danny retched and a cable of phlegm tethered him to the plughole.

There was a cough and a rasp of boot outside the cell. The screw who had escorted Danny on to the wing was standing there. He clicked his heels, wiped his moustache with the back of his hand and intoned, '7989438, O'Toole, the Governor will see you now.'

'O'Toole! Hahaha! O'Toole, that's your *handle* is it, man.' It was inevitable that Fat Boy would appreciate a feeble pun. 'O'Toole! Not enough you should be coon and nonce, you're a Mick into the bargain –'

'Shut it, Denver,' snapped the screw at Fat Boy; then he jerked his head at Danny, who disentangled his fingers from the bars, wiped his mouth and shuffled out of the cell. Before heading off along the landing Danny poked his head back into the cell and sang in a reasonably tuneful falsetto, 'You fill up my se-enses like a night in a forest/ Like a sleepy blue ocean –' and then he was gone, leaving the omega man without the last word.

The screw marched Danny along the iron catwalk of the landing; one pair of feet banging with boot-shod authority, the other slapping ineffectually. In the awful, silent drum of the nonce wing theirs were the only beats. To their left and twenty feet below, the ground floor of the wing was more or less empty, no association going on in this least sociable of areas. Bats were neatly aligned on the ping-pong table, balls racked on the pool table. To their right, cell doorway after cell doorway presented a vignette of a nonce standing, a nonce sitting, a nonce writing, a nonce obsessively brushing his teeth. There was no soundtrack save for their footfalls on the landing; it was like a black-magic lantern, or the advent calendar of the Antichrist.

When they reached the grey-painted iron stairway Danny cleared his throat and rasped, 'Sir?'

'Yes, O'Toole.'

'Will we have to go right up those two wings, sir, the way we came like – I mean to get to the Governor?'

The screw pulled up and faced Danny, giving him a proper screwing out – it was his trademark. 'No, son, we won't. That was your initiation; every inmate who's going into protection is led through those two wings. It satisfies the inmates who aren't protected.' The screw was still screwing him out. Danny couldn't believe it, the old fucker was for real; he was talking to Danny as if Danny were a human being.

'An' you don't hold with it . . . sir?'

'No, I don't. This is meant to be a showcase nick now, run by the POs, but don't believe it, lad, the cons still have a big hold here. Mind yourself.' And they descended.

The Governor of HMP Wandsworth, Marcus Peppiatt, was considered a high-flyer in a hierarchy that positively thrived on Icaruses. Since his graduate entry Peppiatt had fully justified his rapid ascent through the ranks. While Assistant Governor at Downview he had nobbled a skunk-growing operation in the prison infirmary. At Blundstone in Norfolk, where he assumed the gubernatorial position, he had put a stop to a situation where the bulk of supervisory visits was supervised by the inmates themselves. Then came the appointment to Wandsworth, in theory a great step up.

But Peppiatt was only too aware that the old Victorian panopticons such as Wandsworth remained the dark-star ships of the prison fleet. It was an irony screaming into an eternal void that these five-winged whirligigs, built to embody an ideal, were the very real centres of eruption in a volcanic system. Peppiatt's appointment came in the wake of fifteen inmates seizing a JCB that had been brought into an inside yard for construction work. They'd battered nine prison officers and seriously assaulted three civilian workers. The only thing that prevented them from ramming their way through the gates and taking off across Wandsworth Common, batting promenading matrons to either side as they fled, was their inability to get the earthmover into reverse gear. The Home Office could manage reverse gear; they fired the then governor.

Marcus Peppiatt was a liberal – in a strong sense. He believed in a prison system that embodied rational, utilitarian principles, not that far removed from those enjoined by Jeremy Bentham himself. Indeed, Peppiatt had gone so far as to set his ideas on these matters down in a book entitled *Rational Imprisonment*. Several copies of this tome were stacked in a shelf behind the Governor's desk. The spines of the books were blue, with the words 'Rational Imprisonment' picked out in a particularly virulent yellow. When, as now, the Governor was seated behind his desk, his head became aligned with the shelf in just such a way that, to a viewer in the position of 7989438, O'Toole, he appeared to be ensnared by his own slogan.

'7989438, O'Toole, sir,' said the old human screw with the white 'tache.

'Thank you, Officer Higson.' The Governor hunched forward over his blotter. 'Could you wait in the outer office to escort the inmate back, please, I don't think we'll be long. Deposition?' This last was aimed at Danny, who passed across the envelope. The Governor extracted the folder inside and began to scan the contents. So this was the Clapton cab killer. He scrutinised the original mug shot of Danny; one that displayed to full effect the vapid, lost expression which had led the prosecutor at Danny's trial to descend to the banality of evoking the banality of evil. To the Governor it contrasted remarkably with the alert, tense, angry expression on the face of the young black man who stood in front of his desk.

The Governor placed both his hands palm down over the contents of Danny's deposition, as if he could staunch the blood of the victim inside. 'Well.' He regarded the psycho. 'You're on F Wing now, O'Toole, and if you behave you'll stay there indefinitely.'

'Sir?'

'Yes.'

'I don't want no protection, sir, I want to be on an ordinary wing.'

'Is that so, O'Toole.' The Governor got up from behind his desk – a standard-issue, large-scale, dark-wood, gubernatorial item – and began to pace the office like the public-school headmaster he so closely resembled. Danny's eyes paced it along with him: over to the window (bars on the outside, mesh on the inside, people don't realise that it's the staff as much as the inmates who're in jail). 'I expect you got a worse initiation on your way from Reception to F Wing than most, O'Toole . . .' Wheels away from the window, hand scrabbling in wire-wool hair. 'You're a convicted sex killer, O'Toole, and your victim was a child; there are at least a thousand men in this prison who, given the chance – left alone with you in this office, for example –' Moves over to the smoked-glass door, grey-flannel legs scissoring, shuts the door eliminating the riffle of computer keys in the outer office. 'Would happily wring the life out of you with their bare hands.' Moves back behind the desk and sets himself down, steeples his fingers erecting a small church over the deposition and addresses Danny from this fleshly pulpit. 'I'm not so sure that I'm not one of them.'

Danny wasn't impressed. The army had taught him how to square up to authority in the right way, directly but without any attitude. They didn't like attitude. 'But, sir, if I'm on F Wing for my own protection how can you explain the fact, yeah, that the man I'm banged up with has jus' tol' me I've gotta sell him that' – he stabbed a finger at the deposition on the desk – 'if I don't want to get jugged.'

At this the Governor sat up straight and was rationally imprisoned once more. 'I see, yes, your deposition. And what's the name of your cell mate, O'Toole?'

'The PO called him Denver, sir, but he styles 'imsel Fat Boy.'

'We know about Denver, O'Toole –'

'It's bloody sick, sir, sick, the man's floggin' the pictures of victims an' that, floggin' them to the nonces. He say they even get the victims' addresses and send tapes and shit to them. It's *bad*, sir, it's n-not r-right.' Danny stuttered to a finish, and took a step back, aware of having overstepped a mark and attempting practically to correct it.

The Governor was quite beautifully perplexed, 'I see, sick, is it.' He'd heard of the righteous lack of conscience of paedophiles; he'd even witnessed plenty of it, but this was ridiculous. 'I suppose it's sicker and *badder* than what you've been convicted for?' He'd tapped the barrel. Danny commenced gushing.

'I didn't do nothing, Governor. Nothing. I'm not a nonce – I've never interfered with no kiddies, no way, not ever, man. No, man – you gotta believe me, sir, I been set up. I was a crack dealer, see? For years like, an' I worked for this man in Trenchtown. He sent me the powder an' I had a crew in Philly, US of A. We'd cook the shit up and flog it, see? But I nicked a couple of keys off of him, this

Yardie called Skank. It's him what done this, framed me up. You gotta believe me, I can't be with those nonces, I'll lose all respect, man, respect for myself, whatever —'

'Appeal, O'Toole.'

'Whassat?'

'You will be wanting to appeal.'

'Yes, sir, of course, but first off I gotta get off of the nonce wing.'

The Governor looked at a pair of crossed miniature sculls that had been left on the far wall by his predecessor. Next to them was his own Plexiglass-encapsulated Mission Statement. He could just about make out bullet point four: 'Inmates should be regarded as potentially viable economic contributors, even while in a punitive environment.' Next to this was a photograph of the Governor's freshman year at Loughborough; a long, pale, spotty swathe of humanity, curiously vague at one end because twenty of them had run round behind the stand while the camera was panning, so as to appear in the picture twice. The Governor's eyes returned to Danny's. 'Anything is possible, O'Toole.'

'Sir?'

'It's not impossible for you to get off F Wing — if you really want to.'

'Yeah, but Fat Boy says only as a tout — an' I believe him . . . sir.'

'Tout's an ugly word, O'Toole, but anyway that's not the point. You're in it up to here; even if you don't get attacked because you're a sexual offender it would appear more than likely that this man Skank will still want you dead, right?'

'Even so, sir, even so, I ain't no nonce, I need my respect, my self-respect —'

'You need a friend, O'Toole, and a very well-connected one at that.'

'I've gotta get off the wing, Governor.'

'You've *got* to listen – are you prepared to listen?'

'Course.'

'Good. Well, for now do just that. Do *only* that, and we'll see what we can do, and, O'Toole.'

'Sir?'

'Do something useful while you're here. It's quiet enough on F Wing, there's work available, there are courses available. Show me you can make something of yourself; show me you're worth it. Got it?'

Danny nodded. The Governor signalled that the interview was at an end and was about to call for the PO when Danny butted in. 'Sir?'

'Yes, O'Toole.'

'What about the jugging, sir, what about Fat Boy, he says it's this ex-copper, Waller, he's the one that's gonna do me.'

'I see.' The Governor shuffled Danny's deposition together on the blotter, and handed it to him with a smile the bitter side of wry. 'Well, everybody has to save their skin, don't they, O'Toole?'

'Sir?' Danny couldn't tell if this was fuckwit racist dissing or what.

'I'll leave it to your conscience.'

Back on F Wing Danny cut a compromise deal with Fat Boy. All the shots, even the one of the boy's corpse, but no address. The boy was dead now – and he didn't even know he was; but the living knew everything.

In prison, in the English winter, the word crepuscular acquires new resonance, new intensity. You thought you knew what permanent dusk was like – you knew nothing. For here and now is an eternity of forty-watt bulbs, an Empty Quarter of linoleum, and a lost world of distempered walls. It's an environment of corridors and walkways, a space that taunts with the idea of progression towards arrival; then delivers only a TV room full of modular plastic chairs and Styrofoam beakers napalmed by fag ends. In this sepia interior the nonces move about reticently, unwilling to trouble the gloom. There's even a certain modesty in their demeanour, a modesty that flowers in the exercise yard, where their efforts to avoid one another and create zones of inner protection within their non-fraternity become almost courtly.

Danny was absorbed into this mulch of humanity with barely a ripple. It was as Fat Boy had said: the nonces were a law-abiding lot. Indeed, abiding was their main strength. While the idiots over in the panopticon lost their heads, hung from the bars ranting, disdained pork, took up Rastafarianism, went on dirty protests and generally fought time's current, the nonces abided in their isolated gaol, shat out from the body of the prison, marooned in the desert of its own perversion.

The nonces abided, trading photographs of their victims like soccer stars. They were largely family men, community-charge payers. Many had had travelling occupations – salesmen and such. They saw themselves as avuncular – and had often introduced one another to children as 'uncle'; they were generous, and had frequently been apprehended by the police, carrying toys, looking for a child to give them to. The nonces abided and contemplated the sick society that denied its own desires and by extension theirs. They were big fans of *The Clothes Show*, and would be found in the TV room in silent ranks on Sunday afternoons, muttering about the obscene thinness of the teenage couture models, and how it shouldn't be allowed. They also enjoyed *Children in Need*.

The nonces abided, plotting certain revolutionary acts that would enable them to advance the cause of noncery. They factored in social hypocrisy, but on the whole still considered that things would have changed by the time they got out, attitudes would have matured. Their 'liberation' of certain youthful citizens would be seen as just that: the freeing of tender souls into the warmth and *bonhomie* of a full relationship with someone older. Much older.

There were some malcontents. A small posse – perhaps twenty in all – who gathered along with Waller and Higson outside the POs' office on the ground floor. Here, the tough, bent ex-cops would swagger, showing their nonce acolytes the most effective way to punch out a screw. It worked – everybody was suitably intimidated.

But Danny found he could cope. He cultivated sleep when lock-up came round. He would withstand an hour of Fat Boy's vapid, con-man blether, before pointedly wrapping the anorexic pillow round his head and diving for the bottom. Fat Boy still came on to him, of course. There were the endless wheedlings over the address, and the ceaseless exhortations for Danny to apply for a visiting order: 'When yer gonna get a fuckin' VO, O'Toole?'

'When is never, Denver.'

'Come on, O'Toole, one good bottler and we'll be flush for months. Come on. They say you can't bottle at Wandsworth – but that's bullshit, I done it loads of times. All you's gotta be is blatant like – just shove it up your jacksie right in front of the screw, all nonchalant like –'

'I'm not getting a VO, Denver – I don't want no fuckin' visitors.'

'I know *you* don't want a fuckin' visitor, but there's friends of *mine* that might like to visit you, get acquainted an' that. Come on, O'Toole, you tol' me you used to like a bit of smoke . . .'

'Used to' were the post-operative words. No longer was this the case. The inmates of F Wing were subjected to random drug testing as much as those in the rest of the prison. A smoke of dope would get you a positive test result after two weeks; although, with hoe-downing, honking irony, smack or crack would be out of your system in hours. It was as if the authorities were doing everything in their power to inculcate a vicious, hard-drug culture in the prison system.

Danny took the long view and eschewed the puff. He didn't want to lose his remission, even though he was scheduled for release in 2014. And with the smack and crack evacuated from his body, and the Fates exiled, no more potent now than the dust balls which blew along the corridors, Danny knew that class As were off the menu as well. He began to work out again, stretching and slamming his body back into high tensility. He lobbied for work and got a cushy number: eight hours a week turning the poles for birdhouses. The work was pernickety, repetitive and economically useless; the birdhouses were shoddy and barely paid for the materials used to make them. It reminded Danny, in its very essentials, of the way he, in the depths of his crack addiction, had ceaselessly combed the carpets of Leopold Road on the lookout for lost bits of rock.

But the work and work-outs got him away from Fat Boy and the cell. Because after lock-up, when he plunged into sleep, the Terrors were waiting for Danny. The Fates had always had a certain sang-froid, a certain disdain for their own haunting, but the Terrors were hams, pure and simple. They screamed at Danny, ringed him round with their gaping mouths, tier upon tier of them, like the landings of the wing, and every single one ejaculating nothing. The nothing of imprisonment, the nothing of a dead life, the nothing of a millennial come-down. Towards dawn Danny would usually awake, wrung out, more exhausted. He would essay an unambitious wank – two score tugs and a plash against the sheet – then wait for the darkness of the cell to be infused with the darkness of another day.

Danny was waiting for the Governor to be in touch, to give him his break. He remained scrupulously low-profile, muttering 'sir' to the screws if they spoke to him, and shuffle-slapping out of trouble whenever he saw it coming at him, along a rumbling walkway, or around a distempered corner.

One day, about two months after he'd arrived on the nonce wing, having taken receipt of a compartmentalised lunch tray mounded with mashed potato and little else, Danny found himself scrutinising the list of educational courses pinned up outside the POs' office. It was a tatty little codification of tatty little opportunities. There was a carpentry class, if you wanted to brush up on birdhouse construction; and a music appreciation course, if you felt that Albinoni might soothe your soul. All in all there were eleven different classes offered. Danny sucked the inside of his cheek and considered the possibilities. Presumably this was what the Governor had meant went he talked of Danny 'making something' of himself; perhaps if he undertook one of the courses the Governor might hear of it and moderate his attitudes accordingly. Best to do a vocational course – that would go down well. At the very bottom of the list there was a course called 'Creative Wiring', taught by a Mr Mahoney. That sounded OK to Danny – it must, he thought, be to do with electrics and stuff. If he could add a few more skills to what he already knew about DIY, Danny would have the beginnings of a trade. The course kicked off that week on the Thursday afternoon, an hour before lock-up. Danny resolved that he would be there.

4.
The Nonce Prize

Danny got permission from Officer Higson to go up to the Education Room. He walked along the ground floor of the block, eyes down, avoiding any eye contact with his fellow prisoners. Not that Danny worried about the nonces any more, and he certainly didn't perceive them as a sexual threat. The first few days he'd been on the wing, he'd been certain that every second he was on association, or in the exercise yard, or in the queue for food, the perverts were eyeing him up from behind, assessing his potential role in some deviant playlet. Danny could swear he felt their corkscrew gazes, like static electricity on the nape of his neck. But Fat Boy disabused him of this notion, as he had of so many others. 'Na, na, you're wrong there. You gotta look at it this way, O'Toole; even yer rapist is incapable of any real straight sex, and yer nonce is doubly incapable. For a nonce to want to butt-fuck you, well! It wouldn't really be a perversion, as such, you'd 'ave to say that 'e was cured!'

At the end of the block Danny took the stairs up to the Education Room. F Wing, although built later than the panopticon, was still constructed along the same severe lines. However, at either end of the landings there were several storeys of miscellaneous rooms, piled up higgledy-piggledy. Here the noxiousness of Victorian architecture, unconstricted by utility, burst forth into duff mouldings and depressing finials. This was Gormenghast Castle converted into an old people's home.

Danny spiralled his way up glancing into rooms as he went. Here was a therapy group – there an early-release group. Knots of nonces sat about reassuring each other that everything would be all right – for them. Danny climbed on. At the very top of the staircase he found the Education Room. He paused outside and glanced through the window set in the door. Inside there were four battered desks; three of them had old manual typewriters set on them, and the fourth an equally primitive word processor. Two of the desks were tenanted, one by Sidney Cracknell, the other by Philip Greenslade.

These were a couple of the most reviled nonces on the wing – nearly as reviled as Danny himself. They were both serving life, Cracknell for running a children's home in the way he thought best; Greenslade for a Clapton cab office-style abduction, torture, rape and murder of an eleven-year-old girl. They were physically diverse types. Cracknell was so warped and wizened, it was difficult to imagine anybody entrusting a gerbil to his care – let alone a human being; whereas Greenslade had the affable, open-featured countenance, the white hair, and twinkly blue eyes of a gregarious West Country publican. Which he was. Danny thought it a coincidence, if not an especially remarkable one, that they should both want to be electricians.

Together with them in the room was a third man, who had to be the teacher. He was big, at least six feet four, and standing with his back to the door. He had a hip-length leather jacket on and black jeans. When he turned, Danny was confronted by a face that was the essence of Ireland: two big pink ears; full, sensual red lips; a blob-ended Roman nose and a knobbly forehead. The man's waxy complexion suggested that his potato-shaped head had been buried in a field for some months; while his broad shoulders and solid stance implied that he might have dug it up himself. He was probably around forty. He had deep-set, curious grey eyes which radiated intelligence and ferocity in equal measure from beneath an overhang of thick brown quiff. As he watched him, the man trained these eyes on Danny, then crooked his finger. Danny entered the room.

'And you are?' The man's voice was quite high, but crisp and assured, with the merest whiff of an Irish accent.

'O'Toole, sir.'

'No sirs here, *Mister* O'Toole. I prefer the title "Mister". I am *Mister* Mahoney – I assume you know *Messrs* Greenslade and Cracknell?'

'Err, well, yeah, sort of . . .' Danny wanted to say 'by reputation', but didn't think it would go down well. As it was Cracknell was already tittering at him.

'Please, Mister O'Toole, be so good as to take a seat. We are a small convocation, but I hope we'll prove a productive one.' While Danny shuffled behind a desk the Irishman ran on. 'I myself hold with the Alcoholics Anonymous dictum regarding these things – wherever two students of creative writing are gathered together, it's possible to hold a class.'

Cracknell tittered some more at this quip, and Greenslade managed an amiable-sounding grunt, but Danny chimed up, 'Mister Mahoney?'

'Mister O'Toole, how may I assist?'

'Did you say creative *writing*?'

'That's right.'

'Thass like stories an' that?'

'Stories, short or otherwise, that are part of cycles or standing alone; novellas of all kinds and genres; novels even – although for the beginner I would counsel against attempting the longer narrative form; in a word: a tale, and you, Mr O'Toole, the teller. Hmm?'

Danny thought carefully before answering. The wiring/ writing mix-up would make him a laughing stock for weeks, the running gags on the nonce wing had incredibly weak legs. And anyway, writing was a proper thing to do, writers – Danny thought – could make good money, especially if they wrote ads and stuff like that. The Governor might well look kindly on Danny's burgeoning writing career, let him off the nonce wing and give him protection from Skank's associates, one of whom would undoubtedly be waiting for Danny in the main prison.

'Mister Mahoney, this course, I mean, does it like . . .' Danny struggled to find some new words, Mahoney forbore from assisting. 'I mean will it like look *good* . . . I mean so far as the Governor's concerned.'

Cracknell was openly laughing now, but Mahoney silenced him with a glare. 'Mister O'Toole, I cannot speak for the Governor in this matter, or the Home Office in general. I don't believe they have an espoused position on writing as an aspect of rehabilitation. What I can tell you' – he slapped the desk in front of Danny to emphasise his easy articulation – 'is that *every single one* of the inmates who has completed my creative writing course has obtained a positive benefit from it. I'm not claiming to have produced an Henri Charriere, who after twenty years on Devil's Island had the singular success of publishing two bestselling novels, and having himself portrayed in the film version of one of them by Dustin Hoffman, but I've had my modest successes. One of my students last year is now being regularly published, and the year before we had a runner-up in the Wolfenden Prize for Prison Writing. That got a lot of good publicity for Wandsworth, and the then governor certainly looked very kindly on *that* inmate, got him the transfer he wanted to a cat. B, integrated nick, hmmm?'

Danny was convinced – he said, 'Will Smith.'

'I'm sorry, Mister O'Toole?'

'Will Smith. I mean, he'd have to play me in a film based on my prison experience – leastways I never seen that Hoffman blacked up nor nothing – in a skirt, granted, but never done up as a black geezer. A few years ago it'd have to be Wesley Snipes, but now it's gonna be Smith. The man's got more 'umour an' that, more sex appeal.'

There may have only been three students in Gerry Mahoney's creative-writing course, and they may have all been sex offenders, but despite that they managed to exemplify the three commonest types of wannabe writer. Greenslade was the relentless, prosaic plodder. Mahoney had read a story of his already, while they waited for other aspirants. It was suitable for a fourth-rate Lithuanian women's magazine, with its contrived characters, mawkish sentimentality and anachronistic locutions: 'And so it was . . .', 'The pale fingers of dawn . . .', and 'Deep in his heart . . .' all featured on more than one occasion. The only thing to indicate that this story was written by a man with an unconscious as dark as a black hole was the peculiar absence of affect. The author might have felt for his creations in the abstract, but on the page he manipulated them like wooden puppets, like victims.

Then there was the warped Cracknell. He was another stereotype – the compulsive scrawler. Once Cracknell got going, he couldn't rein it in. He'd been the first to arrive at the Education Room, dragging up the stairs with him – he walked with a particularly convoluted fake limp, the substance of ongoing and unsuccessful petitioning to the European Court of Human Rights – two heavy shopping bags full of hideous manuscript. 'My novels,' he'd puffed as he came in the door. 'I mean, I say novels, but really they're all part of the same big thing . . . like a . . . like a –'

'Saga?' groaned Mahoney, who had seen the like of this many times before. Cracknell positively beamed.

'Yeah, *saga*, that'd be the word, although it's not like there are a lot of Vikings and trolls and what have you in my novels; these are more sagas of the distant future – Oh! I like that, that's good, "Sagas of the Distant Future", that could be on the spines of all of them, with the individual titles on the covers, or perhaps the other way rou –'

'And what would you like me to *do* with these sagas, Mister Cracknell?' Mahoney had his hands on his hips and was observing Cracknell unpack his literary load, with such a baleful expression that his brows were not so much knitted as knotted.

'I'd be much obliged, Mister Mahoney – given that you're a published writer and that – if you'd give me your opinion.'

Mahoney flipped open the cover of the first of the eighty-five narrow feint exercise books Cracknell had piled up. Inside there was a furious density of manuscript: thirty words to the line, forty lines to the page. The handwriting was viciously regular, backward-sloping, and utterly indecipherable. Doing a quick calculation, Mahoney reckoned there had to be five million words in the exercise books – at least.

'You see,' Cracknell continued, 'these books here – one through twenty-seven – deal with the first three thousand years of the Arkonic Empire; and books twenty-seven through to forty cover the thousand-year rise to power of its arch rival, the Trimmian Empire. What I'd like is some gui –'

'Do you like writing, Mister Cracknell?'

'Pardon?'

226

'Is it the writing itself you enjoy, Mister Cracknell; or is it merely a way for you to fill your time?'

'Well, it certainly does fill my time. The bloke I share my cell with, he gets a little irritated now and then, because after lock-up it's out with the latest exercise book, open it up, and I may end up writing all night! By torchlight! I find it restful y'see –'

'That's as may be, Mister Cracknell, and I'm sure there is considerable merit in your sagas of the distant future, but as far as here and now is concerned, I'm not going to read them.'

Cracknell was dumbstruck, appalled. He nearly left the class forthwith, taking his literary tranche with him. He muttered about inmates' rights, about requests to the Governor, and finally about the possible envy of a certain Irish writer who might not be quite as fluent as Cracknell himself. Mahoney was unmoved. When, following Danny's arrival, he came to address the class as a whole, Mahoney set out his curriculum in a series of bold emphatics:

'Gentlemen, I appreciate Messrs Greenslade and Cracknell bringing me their work to read, but in my class we shall start from scratch, from the beginning, and proceed in an orderly fashion to the end. During this course you will write one short story, gentlemen, of between four and six thousand words. That's it. That's what we will focus on. Writing a story is deceptively easy – and deceptively hard. I don't want you to run before you can walk. I'm not going to be looking for fancy time-scales, unusual settings, or stories that take place entirely within the mind of a stick insect.' He paused and gave Cracknell a meaningful look. 'And nor will I be satisfied with stories which feature unbelievable characters in unreal settings.' The look was directed at Greenslade.

'Your stories should be about something you *know*, they should be written in *plain* language, and they should have a *beginning*, a *middle*, and an *end*.'

These last assertions were punctuated by Mahoney turning to the clapped-out whiteboard at the front of the room, and writing the three words on it, each with an eeeking flourish of a marker pen. 'Beginning, middle, end,' Mahoney reiterated pointing to the words in turn, as if he half expected the three nonces to sing along. 'When I'm at the beginning I should know where I am, and the same goes for any subsequent point in the story. A story is a *logical progression* like any other. For the next twenty minutes or so I should like you to think about a subject for your story and write me a single paragraph about it.' As he said this Mahoney moved between the three of them depositing pieces of paper and biros. 'A single paragraph' – Crackell got the look again – 'that tells me *who, where, what, why*, and *when*. That's all, no fancy stuff. Got it?' And with this the big Irishman plonked himself down in a chair, put his feet up on another, pulled a small-circulation left-wing periodical out of his jacket pocket, and commenced reading.

Twenty minutes later Mahoney identified the third stereotypic wannabe in his creative-writing course: the writer who can't write. Danny had just about managed a paragraph, but the sentences composing it infrequently parsed, and the individual words were largely spelt phonetically. Mahoney, however, did find to his surprise that Danny had genuinely fulfilled the assignment. His projected story had a beginning, a middle and an end, it had recognisable characters, and it was set in a milieu Danny clearly knew well. Mahoney looked down sympathetically at his newest recruit to the fount of literature. 'This isn't too bad, Mister O'Toole. I like the idea, although I'm not so sure how you're going to handle the triple cross over the coke deal, but you can get to that later. Are you serious about giving this a try?'

'Well, yeah, s'pose,' Danny muttered – Mahoney hadn't taken this trouble with the other two.

'In that case I would be obliged if you'd stop behind for a couple of minutes.'

When the repugnant duo had shuffled off down the stairs, each secretly satisfied that *he* was the most talented writer in HMP Wandsworth, Mahoney turned to Danny with a new and more serious expression on his broad pink face. 'You've got to get your spelling and grammar up to speed,' he said. 'It's no good having good ideas – and I can see you've got those – if you can't express them. I don't want you to take this the wrong way, but I've got two course books here designed to help adults with their literacy – with their reading and writing, that is. I'd like you to have at look at them. If we're going to make a writer of you, Mister O'Toole, you need to have a good command of basic grammar, hmm?'

Danny didn't take it the wrong way; he had decided a while before something quite momentous – he liked Mister Mahoney and wanted to please him. And within a matter of a fortnight Gerry Mahoney discovered something rather momentous as well – Danny O'Toole had genuine talent as a writer.

Danny chewed up the adult literacy course and digested it with ease. By the time the next class came round he was able to hand in to Mahoney all of the completed exercises. Mahoney gave him another book for a higher standard. Danny also began to read – and read at speed. He invested all of his birdhouse earnings to date in a torch and a supply of batteries. Then, after lock-up each afternoon, he proceeded to read his way through every single book available in the meagre nonce-wing library.

In the army Danny had read Sven Hassel, and on the outside he'd occasionally toyed with a thriller, but he'd never devoured print like this. He read historical romances and detective stories; he chomped his way through ancient numbers of the *Reader's Digest*; and he scarfed vast quantities of J.T. Edson westerns, with titles like *Sidewinder*, and *Five Guns at Noon*. As he read more and more Danny found himself essaying more difficult texts – the old dusty linen-bound books with the oppressively small type that were crowded on the bottom shelf of the library cart. So he came to read Dumas and Dickens, Twain and Thackeray, Galsworthy and – and an especial favourite – Elizabeth Gaskell.

Reading, for Danny, triggered an astonishing encephalisation. Not that he was stupid before – he was always sharp. But the reading burst through his mental partitions, partitions that the crack had effectively shored up, imprisoning his sentience, his rational capacity, behind psychotically patterned drapes. The alternative worlds of nineteenth-century novels enabled Danny to get a hard perspective on his own world, and to interpret his own life honestly. And there was more, much more. Danny, it transpired, also had an ear for prose. He could assay a line of English for its authenticity – the effectiveness with which the writer had psychically imprinted it – at the same time as he could parse it. As it was to crack addiction, so it was to literature – Danny was a natural.

After a month Gerry Mahoney began to bring books in for his favourite pupil, augmenting the tattered basics of the trolley with selections from his own library. Mahoney thought that Danny, being black, might prefer black literature. So he lent him James Baldwin ('Queer anna' coon – thass a turn up!'); Ralph Ellison ("That brother is *angry*, man – he's feelin' it all the time!'); Toni Morrison

('Yeah, yeah, yeah – but I did fill up a bit at the end.'); and Chester Himes ('Wicked! The man's a contender, funny, sharp, and he knows his shit – the fucker did time!'). Contemporary black writers appealed to Danny as well. He particularly admired the coolness of Caryl Phillips's prose and the quiet, lyrical anger of Fred D'Aguiar, but to Mahoney's enduring astonishment, the literature that Danny really liked was altogether different.

Danny liked the Decadents. To be more precise he adored tales of unnatural pleasures and artificial worlds. He devoured Maldoror; he cantered through *À Rebours*; and he spotted that *Dorian Gray* was sadly derivative. Within four months, with Mahoney's prodding, Danny was seriously translating *Paradis Artificiel* – and enjoying it. Not that any of this leaked into the story that Danny was writing himself; here he remained very much Mahoney's own acolyte. The story was set in Harlesden; it featured a protagonist not unlike Danny himself; it had the mandatory beginning, a middle Danny was attempting to slim down into an elegant waist, and an end that both of them agreed was an absolute stonker.

Already, even before the spectre of the prize came to haunt them, there was an exacting rivalry between the members of the writing class. Greenslade, who had once had a poem about his cat ('Oh beautiful cat/That makes me happy/Why can't you use your flappy . . . ?') published in the *Rainham Advertiser*, considered himself streets ahead of the other two when it came to the actual business of being a writer. 'Professionalism' was his watch word; and he would interrupt Mahoney's discourses on dialogue, or description, or development, to share his latest information on available grants, or royalty scales, or subsidiary rights. In fairness to Greenslade it has to be admitted that he *did* actually conform to most of the attributes of a British writer of his age (late fifties), without having had to go through the tedious business of actually publishing books, and then seeing them fade out of print, like dying stars.

Living stars were Cracknell's preoccupation. Mahoney had bullied him into attempting a short story, because that's what the class was all about, but Cracknell's subject matter – five thousand years in the history of the Printupian Empire – proved difficult to manage effectively in the abbreviated form. Rather than taking this personally – something he was incapable of, along with ordinary sympathy – Cracknell saw the whole thing in terms of genres. Science fiction – as its name implied – was the way forward, the way of the future. Anyone who continued to write sublunary tales was dealing in the worn coinage of mundanity. Not that Cracknell could have put it that well himself, he simply interrupted Mahoney's flow from time to time in order to observe that this or that sci-fi writer had long ago exemplified the point the teacher was making, and could they move on?

Moving on remained in the forefront of Danny's mind. His new-found absorption into literature wasn't about to sway him from his course. Danny still burned with a fervour; he wanted off the nonce wing, then he could appeal, clear himself, get free. Fat Boy, who was quite happy where he was, thought the piles of paper that trailed though their cell were quite ridiculous. 'You wanna get a transfer, right?' he wheedled Danny.

'You know that, Fat Boy, you know that damn well.'

'An' you fink that all this reading and writing's gonna get it for you?'

'Maybe – I dunno.'

'One good bottler, my man, one good fucking bottler. Half an ounce of gear – a quarter even; and you'd be out of here. That old man Higson, yeah?'

'Principal Officer Higson?'

'Yeah, yeah, yeah, *Principal* Officer Higson, that's the one. He's an old-style PO, knows the form, right? Now, a couple of years ago it would've taken a poxy grand, but given inflation an' that, and given that you're near the beginning of your sentence – which always makes it look a bit fishy – he says he can manage it for two.'

'Manage what?'

'Your fucking transfer, you moody little git, your fucking transfer!'

'Two grand?'

'Wake up, will you, O'Toole? I can't make it any clearer; you come up with two K for old Higson an' he'll recommend your transfer to the Governor. You'll be in a fully integrated, cat. C nick before you can say knife. And the only fucking writing involved is one poxy letter – instead of all this bollocks.'

But Danny stuck with the bollocks and then Mahoney announced the prize. It was another Thursday afternoon in the Education Room, and the three grown men were leaning – cheeks cupped in hands, elbows jammed below – on their desks like adolescents. 'Gentlemen,' said Mahoney in his high, faintly mocking tones, 'I think I mentioned to you at the outset of this course the existence of a competition for prison writing. It's called the Wolfenden Prize, it brings the winner guaranteed publication in an anthology, five hundred pounds, and considerable esteem.' Mahoney pulled some entry forms from his briefcase and handed one to each of them, whilst continuing. 'It's awarded for the best submitted story of between four and six thousand words. So, gentlemen! You can see that there was method in my madness; that there was a reason why I was so insistent on beginnings, middles and ends. I think all of you have the ability to be potential winners.'

Mahoney fixed all of them in turn with his gimlet gaze, and each of them thought he was referring to them alone. 'And entering the competition will bring our course to a natural, effective end, by enabling you all to learn the absolute importance of' – he began eeeking on the white-board – 'deadlines!'

Greenslade, preposterously, accused Danny of nicking his ideas. Cracknell, ludicrously, imagined Danny was appropriating what passed for his style. Tensions ran high. There were two weeks to go before the entries were due in, and during that time the three men studiously avoided one another. This wasn't easy, given that they all had to type up their manuscripts in the same room. Danny was acutely conscious that he'd managed to avoid any trouble on the nonce wing until now; but he sensed that Greenslade wouldn't hesitate if he thought that a strategic jugging was all that lay between him and the literary laurels.

Mahoney attempted to defuse the rivalry: 'I'm aware that the three of you feel very competitive about this, but I urge you to remember that there are at least ten men in this prison who will be entering for the Wolfenden, let alone the tens of others that will be entering in other nicks. And anyway, when you write you are competing only against yourself and posterity – there can be no living rivals.'

Mahoney certainly believed this, but he also believed that Danny was a genuinely talented young man who really deserved a break. He'd read Danny's story and it was streets ahead of most of the stuff currently being published. He'd never discussed Danny's crime, or sentence, to do so was taboo, but Gerry Mahoney didn't believe for a millisecond that he was a nonce.

Cal Devenish had agreed to judge the Wolfenden Prize for Prison Writing in the way that he agreed to do so many other things – without thinking. It sounded like a worthy cause, and there was something sexy about the whole notion of prisoners writing. Perhaps Cal would discover another Jack Henry Abbott, and become tied up in an infamous correspondence like Norman Mailer? What Cal hadn't factored in was the actual reading of the entries, set against his own fantastic indolence.

The shortlisted entries had arrived about three weeks before. Cal signed the courier's docket and leant them against the radiator by the front door. They were still there, a bulbous Jiffy-bag full of unimaginable pap. Cal groaned. It was a sharp, cold morning in early April, and he was scheduled to present the prize the following afternoon. He'd been awoken at nine sharp with an apposite alarm call: it was the secretary of the visitors' board at Wandsworth Prison, where the prize giving was to be held: 'Mr Devenish?'

'Yeah, what? Yeah, right?' Cal was gagging on consciousness.

'I'm sorry, I didn't wake you or anything?'

'Naw, naw!' Cal had been having a dream of rare beauty and poignance. In it, he had awoken and tiptoed downstairs to discover that the novel which he had been procrastinating over for the past two years had been completed during the night and lay, neatly word-processed on the desk. On picking it up and beginning to read, Cal was delighted to find that it was just as he had conceived of it during the long hours of not writing – but far far better.

'It's John Estes here, I'm the secretary of the visitors' board at Wandsworth.'

'Oh – yes.'

'We're very much looking forward to seeing you tomorrow –'

'Me too.'

'I wondered if it might be possible at this stage, Mr Devenish, for you to give me some idea of your decision regarding the winner – and the runners up?'

'Decision?' Cal floundered in his slough of irresponsibility.

'As to who's won the prize?'

'Is there any particular reason, Mr Estes?'

'Well, the thing is, as you may be aware, Mr Devenish, a lot of prisoners get transferred, and we wanted at least to be sure that the winner would be actually in the prison when you came tomorrow.'

'Oh I see, that does sound reasonable . . . the thing is, I was about to reread my short shortlist when you called. I should have an idea about that before the end of the day; may I call you then?'

Cal took the secretary's number down and hung up. Christ! It wasn't as if he didn't have enough other things to do today. He swung himself out of bed and, naked, stamped down the stairs of the mews house into the main room where he worked. Cal's desk was thatched with an interesting rick of unpaid bills, unanswered letters, notes for unwritten articles and unwritten books. As if to garnish this platter of ennui, almost all the sheets of paper, the desk itself, the computer and the fax machine had Post-it notes stuck to them recording never answered phone calls. Cal groaned and headed for the Jiffy-bag; at least with the formidable excuse of judging the short-story competition he could hold the rest of the obligatory world at bay for another day. He headed back up the stairs and dived into bed with the entries.

Cal Devenish had won a prestigious literary prize himself about five years previously. It was for his third novel, and the previous two – which had barely been in print – were yanked back into favour as well. The glow had been a long time fading, but now, along with the advance for a further novel, it had. Cal told himself that he was marking time, allowing himself the creative liberty of genuine abstraction. But on days like these, when he was confronted with other potential contenders' work, he was worse than rattled.

It didn't matter that about ten of the fifteen shortlisted stories were barely literate – at least their authors had managed to get the words down on paper. And anyway, reading bad writing was like playing against a bad opponent – your game suffered as well. Every duff sentence Cal read convinced him that he himself would never write another good one; every feeble plot he speedily unravelled hammered home the fact that he himself would never contrive another interesting one; and every wooden character's piece of leaden dialogue left him with the chilling intimation that he lacked any human sympathy himself.

The stories ran the whole gamut of predictable awfulness. There were chocolate-box romances, and dead-pet dramas; there were 'it was all a dream's, and Stephen King copycat nightmares. Naturally, there was also a whole subgenre of justification, stories about honest crims who would do a bank and give the proceeds to a charity; or else save kiddies from unspeakable nonces. The stories were so terrible overall that Cal decided to order them in terms of being least bad, because he had such difficulty in judging any of them to be good.

That's until he got to the last three in the batch – these definitely had something, although exactly what it was difficult to say. One was a kind of spoof space opera about an intergalactic empire called Printupia. The writer had attempted to compress five thousand years in the history of this enormous state into the six thousand words allowed, and the result was an astonishingly compacted, near meaningless prose. Cal wondered if it might be a satire on the ephemerality of contemporary culture; narrative itself characterised as a non-biodegradable piece of packaging, littering the verge of the cosmos.

The second story was a piece of well-sustained, naturalistic writing about two young black guys dealing crack in north-west London. The writer had done well with all the orthodox conventions of the short story, but then he'd got carried away and added magical realist elements that jibed. There was that, and there was the uneasiness of his spelling – he could never quite decide whether to come down on the side of phonetic transcription of non-standard English, or not. The result was far less accomplished than Cal hoped for when he began reading.

The third story was the strangest in the whole batch, the most unsettling. Ostensibly a description of a man's intense love for his dead wife's cat, 'Little Pussy' was written with a close absorption into the minutiae of a solitary man's life that reminded Cal of Patricia Highsmith's style. There were other Highsmithian elements: the sense the writer imparted that awful things *were* happening – both physically and psychically – a little bit outside the story's canvas. The story was told in the first person – but the narrator wasn't simply unreliable, he was altogether non-credible as a witness to his own life. Nothing dramatic happened in the story – the man adapted his routines to those of the feline, and so mitigated his mourning for his wife – but when Cal tossed the typescript to one side, he realised it was one of the cleverest and most subtle portrayals of the affectless, psychopathic mind that he had ever read.

At five that afternoon Cal called John Estes back. 'Mr Estes? Cal Devenish here.'

'Ah, Mr Devenish, any decision in the offing?'

'Yuh – I think so. There's a short shortlist I have in mind – the stories by Cracknell, O'Toole and Greenslade – but I haven't decided on an overall winner as yet.'

'That's not necessary – I only needed to know that the winner would be able to attend –'

'And he will?'

'Oh yes, no problem there.'

At two o'clock the following afternoon Cal Devenish, wearing an unaccustomed suit and carrying a superannuated briefcase, met the secretary to the visitors' board in the reception area of Wandsworth Prison. Estes was carrying a large bunch of keys; he was a small, dapper man who radiated considered concern. 'It's a pleasure to meet you,' Estes said proffering his manicured hand, 'I enormously enjoyed *Limp Harvest*.'

'Thank you, thank you,' Cal blustered – he hated references to his past success. 'You're too kind.'

'The inmates are also very much looking forward to talking with you –'

'How many of them will be here?'

'Ah, well, there's a thing.' Estes paused to unlock a door and they passed out of reception and into a high walled yard. 'By a great, good coincidence, the three inmates on your short shortlist are the only ones left here at Wandsworth – all the others had been transferred.'

'That's lucky.'

'Isn't it.' Estes broke off again to unlock a gate, and they passed into a second high-walled yard.

They were crunching across this expanse of gravel, under the slitted eyes of the cell windows in E Block, when Estes halted and turned to Cal. 'Mr Devenish,' he began hesitantly, 'I don't want to confuse in any way, or unsettle you, but I did wonder if you noticed anything special about the three stories on your short shortlist?'

Cal was nonplussed. 'I'm sorry?'

'If there was anything the authors seemed to have in common?'

'Well.' Cal mused for a few seconds, scrabbling to recall the stories he'd hurriedly flipped through in bed the previous day. 'There was an element of err . . . how can I put it . . . sort of *distance*, almost a remoteness in all of them –'

'I'm glad you noticed that,' Estes cut in, 'you see the thing is all three were written – purely coincidentally – by inmates who're under protection.'

'Protection?'

'Erm . . . yes, prisoners who're . . . erm . . . convicted sex offenders.'

'I see.' Cal began internally to rewrite his speech as they crunched on across the yard.

'I thought I err . . . ought to tell you, because the prize giving is being held on F Wing. It's the block over there, outside the main prison, that's why we have to go through all these yards . . .' Estes unlocked another gate with one of his lolly-sized keys. 'F Wing is the clearing house for all protected inmates in Britain –'

'Jesus!' Cal blurted out. 'You mean where we're headed is the biggest concentration of sex offenders in the country?'

'Five hundred and forty, to be precise,' Estes said with a limp smile, then he unlocked the door to the nonce wing.

Gerry Mahoney came by Danny's cell to pick him up and take him to the prize giving. He already had Cracknell and Greenslade in tow. All three prisoners had done their best to spruce themselves up for the occasion, and Greenslade had, optimistically, starched creases into his prison-issue denims. The Wing was uncharacteristically busy today, knots of prisoners hung over the railings on the upper landings, and there was a large number of suited men milling around by the POs' office.

'Wass goin' on?' Danny asked Mahoney.

'You're going on – those are all AGs come for the prize giving. You see, the actual cheque will be handed over by Judge Tomy, the Chief Inspector of Prisons, and all the staff here are expecting him to make a speech that isn't entirely focused on literature.' The creative-writing class walked to the end of the wing, then began climbing the spiral stairs to the Education Room.

Upstairs the desks and equipment had been tidied away and about forty chairs had been crushed into the room. By the time the four of them had taken their seats, near to the back, the rest were fully occupied. As well as the twenty-odd assistant governors, in regulation middle-management suitings, there were about fifteen uniformed POs and the Governor himself, who was accompanied by a white-haired, elderly man sporting a loud bow tie and a cashmere overcoat.

'Tomy,' Mahoney whispered to Danny 'don't be fooled by his appearance – he's one of the most outspoken critics of the Home Office there's ever been. You wait – he'll give this lot a lambasting.'

As if prompted by Mahoney, Judge Tomy now stood and took control of the proceedings. He welcomed them all to the Wing and then gave a fifteen-minute speech outlining every single thing that was wrong with the prison administration, from failure fully to end slopping out, to food lacking adequate nutrition. The Governor, the assistant governors and the prison officers all sat tight, sinister smiles on their thinned lips. They could do nothing – Tomy was the Inspector of Prisons, he was merely doing his job.

Cal Devenish, who was sitting beside Judge Tomy at the front of the room, was amazed by the elderly man's combative vigour. This was an Inspector who took his remit seriously. But Cal was far more concerned about his role in things. It was easy to spot the three men who he'd shortlisted for the Wolfenden Prize – they were the only prisoners in the room, crushed in between the rows of their jailers. The young black prisoner was obviously the writer of the story about the crack dealers. He looked intelligent, but his expression was on the aggressive side of fierce. Cal felt threatened whenever this gaze fell on him.

Next to the black guy sat an amiable-looking, white-haired man in his late fifties. Cal knew better than to be taken in by such superficial considerations, but it was really very hard to conceive of this man as being a *serious* sex offender. He might have been a flasher of some sort, Cal hypothesised, but not a truly revolting nonce. Anyway, by contrast, the man who was sitting next to him was so obviously the real McCoy that he made everyone else in the room look like Peter Pan by comparison. This individual's hideous countenance was the fleshly equivalent of a wall in a public urinal, the individual tiles grouted together with shit. He was terrifying. Cal pegged him as the science-fiction satirist.

Danny sat staring at Cal Devenish. So this was the man who was going to decide his fate? This lanky, bearded thing in a black suit, who so resembled a white equivalent of . . . the Fates. They were back. They lingered in the corners of the room. They hissed and cackled, updating Danny's doom on this of all days. Danny was paralysed. He looked at the Governor, willing him to look up and see this model prisoner, this aspirant writer so worthy of transfer. The Governor remained staring abstractedly at a broken lampshade which dangled above his head.

Cal Devenish got up to make his speech. He voiced some platitudinous – but for all that heartfelt – observations on the liberating, empowering capabilities of writing, especially for those who're in jail. Cal was going to analyse the three shortlisted stories in considerable detail, but the nonce revelations had put him off his stride. He confined himself to mentioning the strong points of all three, before concluding limply that 'Little Pussy' exhibited all the hallmarks of a compelling moral ironist. Cal had no hesitation therefore in awarding the Wolfenden Prize for Prison Writing to . . . Philip Greenslade.

Cal Devenish almost gagged when Philip Greenslade was within a few paces of him – the rot of the man's corrupt soul was that strong-smelling. Cal felt even sicker when he had to shake Greenslade's hand – it felt like the clamp of a laboratory retort stand, only thinly upholstered with flesh.

'Thank you so very much.' Greenslade's tone was wheedling, despite there being nothing to wheedle. 'I can't tell you how much I value your judgement . . .' He gripped Cal's hand a little tighter, and Cal thought he might scream. 'I so look forward to having a proper discussion with you about literature when all of this is over.'

Cal realised that he'd given the prize to the wrong man – there hadn't been a particle of ironic distance in 'Little Pussy': the author *was* a psychopath.

The Governor turned to his deputy who was sitting beside him. 'Is that the Greenslade who's always petitioning for a transfer to a cat. C? The sickening nonce who did that murder?'

'Yes, Governor, that's the man.'

'Well, since he's won this bloody prize, let's use it as an excuse to get shot of the tedious bugger. Prepare the papers for his transfer when we get back to the office.'

Danny was very nearly in tears – he simply couldn't believe it. How could this twat Devenish have chosen Greenslade's story over his own, it made no sense at all. The only way Danny could prevent himself from crying out was by staring straight ahead and gripping the back of the chair in front of him as tightly as he could.

Gerry Mahoney tried to bank down Danny's distress. 'I've no idea what got into Cal Devenish,' he said. 'I know him slightly and I've always respected his literary judgement. Mind you, if it's any consolation I've heard it rumoured that he has a bit of a drug problem. Perhaps that's what queered it – he couldn't cope with the realism in your story . . .'

But Danny wasn't in the mood for a post-mortem. He got up and began to shoulder his way to the front of the room. His cell was preferable to this shit hole full of screws. At the door, in his haste to get out, he collided with a tall suit, which turned to reveal that it was owned by the Governor. 'Sorry, sir,' Danny muttered.

'That's all right – ah! It's O'Toole, isn't it?'

'Yes, sir.'

'Well, well done, O'Toole, it seems you took my advice on committing yourself to a useful course of study. Mr Mahoney tells me you have a genuine talent – see that you cultivate it.'

'I will, sir.' The Governor turned to depart, but once he'd gone a couple of paces he turned back to face Danny.

'And O'Toole.'

'Yes, sir?'

'Better luck next year.'